A
Letter
To
Amy

By William G. Hutchinson

For Nora

And for my mother,

Two remarkable women for whose love

I will be eternally grateful.

All characters and situations in this narrative are fictional, and any similarities or resemblance to accounts or persons, living or dead, are coincidental.

PART
ONE

CHAPTER ONE

Lia Albermarle lifted herself from the recliner where she had spent another restless night. A crocheted afghan that had alternately warmed and choked her lay at her feet on the living room floor. She had been awake to hear the sleet frozen on the north wind as it dashed against the dining room window. It was sometime after that when she finally drifted off to sleep, dozing really, for bare half-hours at a time. The ice pellets slanting against the window pane must have given way to snow sometime during the night because the clattering eventually subsided. She went to the dining room window to see the extent of the storm. Deliberately looking away, she snapped open the drapes, not wanting to look until she could absorb the full scope of the storm. Today was her eightieth birthday, yet she never tired of the variety of nature's moods.

For a moment she stood drinking in the picture of her world of more than sixty years, now silent and wearing a frozen white veil. She was perplexed by the memories that had masqueraded as dreams during the past few nights, shedding the dust of more than six decades, like the old maple tree in the front yard would throw off its frosty burden by tomorrow or the next day. They were as clear in her mind as the fresh snow was white. But why? In the shadow cast over the window by the eave above, she could see her reflection in the glass. Why now? The face staring back barely resembled the young woman from sixty years ago. This face sagged, and the hair, thinner now, wasn't black, or even gray, but white, like the snow itself. These eyelids drooped over hazy pupils that were once so deep and brown 'they even made the deer envious,' her daddy used to say. So why had this young woman, brown eyes glowing, white teeth, whiter still against her dark skin, why had she suddenly appeared? Now, especially, when reality stared back at her in the dining room window. She shivered. Grandma had started talking about when she was young just before she died. Grandpa used to visit her in her dreams. He was always young and tall. "He was like a young oak tree," she'd say smiling, "dressed in the suit he wore the day we were married." Probably the suit he was buried in too, since he died five years later, leaving her with three children.

Whatever the reason that her former self had waltzed through the few hours of sleep she'd had over the last few nights wasn't what was really bothering her. It was that last night, somewhere between the sleet hammering against the windowpane and the hush created as ice pellets morphed into ten billion different snowflakes, that *he* sauntered over the horizon of her dreamscape. She hadn't seen his face so clearly for many years. But there he was standing right in front of her, or at least who *she* used to be, arms spread open, grinning as wide as the horizon itself. He didn't say a word – didn't need to – they were together again. And that was enough.

She smiled at the world outside. She was eighty years old today and Lord willing she might just live eighty more. She was smarter now and could…the telephone cut in on her musing.

"Auntie Lia? Can you hear me?"

"Yes, Dear."

"I'm on my cell phone and the battery is just about dead, so I have to make this quick. Did it snow down there last night?" There was mild panic in her voice.

"I'm looking out the window right now, and it looks like we got seven or eight inches. How about up there?"

"I don't know, they're saying we got about a foot or so. I went out to see if I could get the car out and everything's completely snowed in, and the power is off, too. That's why I'm calling. To tell you I can't make it down today. Will you be okay if I don't come?"

"Oh sure, Honey, don't you worry about me. I've got plenty of food and we haven't lost power, so the house is nice and cozy."

"I feel so bad about not being there for your birthday. I had planned to make meatloaf and baked potatoes and everything. Now I don't know when I'll be able to make it down. They're saying another big storm is on its way down from the Gulf of Alaska tonight, so we may get more snow from that than we got last night."

"All the more reason for you to stay in Tacoma then, and not even think about coming down here until this all clears up. Sooner or later it'll all melt, and the roads will be open again. Then you can come down and cook that meatloaf. Don't you worry about me, just stay inside where it's warm."

"Are you sure you'll be alright?"

"Positive. Now listen, you stay inside and try to keep warm until the power comes back on. You'd better save your battery in case of emergency. I'll hang up now."

"Okay, then. I'm sorry it worked out this way. Happy birthday, anyway. I'll call as soon as the power comes on."

Lia hung up the phone and went back to the window. Margaret Runville always was a sweet child. She was the only one left that Lia still had any contact with. Margaret was the only child of Lia's older sister Anne. Even though she was only fifty-one and had never married, she acted like an old hen fretting about her chicks. It was hard to imagine her as a successful attorney, the way she could carry on about a little bit of snow. Back when the Nisqually earthquake hit in February of 2001, Margaret was so upset that she thought about giving up her practice and moving back east where she still had people from her daddy's side. You'd have thought Mount Rainier had just blown its top. But she eventually settled down and life went on. She was always smart as the dickens, but real excitable. Anyway, the snow would eventually melt, and she would drive down and make her Auntie Lia a nice meatloaf with baked potatoes and Brussels sprouts and banana-cream pie. Margaret always was a sweet child.

She left the drapes open and went into the kitchen. A cup of spice tea is what a snowy morning in January called for. When the kettle had boiled and the teabag released its spicy goodness in tumbling currents visible through the glass mug, Lia went back to her recliner. She pulled the afghan up around her knees and set the cup down on the lamp table alongside. Somehow Weston Allen Johnson had slipped out of his grave and walked right into her dream, looking as shiny and beautiful as the day they said goodbye. Even after more than sixty years his hair was still the color of corn silk at the end of the season when you go to shuck the last of the sweet corn, not really yellow and not really brown. He was as young and tall as ever, not old and droopy like she was. His smile made her heart race whenever she saw him approaching. It still did. And here he had come back into her life in the middle of the night, unannounced and looking every bit as handsome as he did back in 1943.

What confused her was why? Why now – on her eightieth birthday? Of course she had thought about him night and day back then. He left from Fishermans' Terminal in June to fish off the north coast.

The wars in Europe and the South Pacific were both in full swing and still escalating, so it was inevitable that Wes would be called up. He had said that if he could get his sea-legs under him, when the draft notice came he'd enlist in the Navy instead of going to the Army. Sailors always ate better than soldiers.

The hot tea and warm embrace of the easy-chair loosed the

chains of concern for snowy streets and stranded commuters and all the misery that another day's news would bring. Putting the chair in the recline position she allowed herself to entertain the invitation that beckoned her to let the last sixty-three years fall away and again inhabit the thoughts and ambitions of seventeen year old Lia Albermarle. Closing her eyes, she gave in.

****

Lia knew he was watching her as she waited for the bus at First and Pike. In those days she helped her neighbor, Mrs. Dawkins, clean an office on Friday afternoons after school. He had walked past and given her a long inspection from the corner of his eye. She watched him until he went into a doorway farther down the block. When the bus came she didn't give him another thought, until at the next corner he got on. He pretended to look confused, like he didn't know where to sit, and finally chose a seat at the back of the bus next to her. 'Imagine that,' she remembered thinking, 'all of a sudden this bold white boy comes and sits down next to me.' They rode in silence for a few blocks.

"My name's Wes." She could feel him looking at her. "I'm a senior at Delfman High." She just looked out the window. "I was helping my friend get his uncle's boat ready for fishing." Obviously, he wasn't going to keep quiet.

"So where's your friend?" she said, still watching the traffic beyond the bus window.

"He's waiting for me back at the car."

"Why you on this bus, then?"

"'Cause I saw you," he hesitated, "and I knew I couldn't forgive myself if I went home without at least talking to you."

Maybe it was a line. Lots of boys tried to use lines on her. Well, he was the first *white* boy. But lots of boys used lines to pick-up girls.

"Isn't your friend gonna be mad at you for leavin' him sittin' in the car?"

"Oh, I don't think he'll be mad about sitting in the car." He grinned.

"No? Why you so sure 'bout that?"

"Because the car's locked and I have the key. He'll be mad at me 'cause I left him *standing* by the car. Especially if it rains." When she couldn't contain a smirk any longer, he continued, "Since I've put my friendship on the line, won't you at least tell me your name?"

In her mind she could see the look in her daddy's eyes and see him mouthing the words, 'What the...', as she said, "It's Lia."

He reached out a hand. "Actually, Lia, my name is Weston Allen Johnson, but my friends call me Wes."

She didn't shake his hand. "Pleased to meet you, Weston Allen Johnson."

By now the bus had gotten to Lia's stop. She stood up to get off, and catch her transfer. Frantic to make the moment last, he blurted, "So, Lia, is it possible that we could meet again?"

"I don't think that would be such a good idea." She smiled and scooted past him into the aisle.

Later, when she had time to think about it, she wished she'd had the courage to say 'maybe.' It wasn't just that he was charming, but he seemed sincere, like he really would have felt bad if he hadn't been able to talk to her. Most boys seemed to have only one thing on their minds and they made little pretense about it.

Two weeks went by and she again found herself waiting at the bus stop at First and Pike. She had thought about Wes several times over the last two weeks, but knew that in 1942 there was no future for a black girl and a white boy in Seattle.

She was tired, and climbing the two steps to board, her legs felt like concrete. The bus was crowded so she had to stand on her tiptoes to see if there were any open seats at the back. It was then that she heard her name and looked back to see a white face with dirty blond hair, bold in contrast to the black faces around him. He was smiling and calling her name. A white hand shot up and motioned for her to come sit down. It was Weston Allen Johnson, sitting in the back with all the colored riders.

"Lia, come on, I saved you a seat."

She approached cautiously. "What are you doin' here?"

"I wasn't sure what time you'd get on. I remembered that it was the number fifty-five bus, and that we met on a Friday afternoon, so I got on early. I took a chance that you'd get on sometime this afternoon." He was pleased that his strategy worked.

"How long have you been ridin' this old bus?"

"Today I've only been on here for an hour or so. Last week I rode around for about three hours before I figured out that you weren't coming."

He was right. She hadn't felt well last Friday afternoon and had gone home early from school. Mrs. Dawkins had to do the cleaning by herself.

"You been ridin' this bus for the last two Friday afternoons just so you could see me again?" Her eyes narrowed.

"I wouldn't exactly say that. I wanted to talk to you...get to know you...not just see you."

"I thought you said you were a senior this year. How come you don't have school?"

"All I have for the last three periods on Friday afternoons is study hall. I've already got enough credits to graduate. So, for the last two weeks I've suddenly gotten sick right after lunch. And here I am." He didn't sound proud of himself for lying in order to cut class. He made coming to see her sound like a moral imperative, the same as going to war to defeat the Nazis. What choice did he have? "But I would be willing to stay for my last three periods, if you would agree to meet me later in the day, or say, on Saturday or Sunday."

"So, *Weston Allen Johnson*, you don't have a girlfriend around wherever it is you live? Why you want to go to all this fuss just to see me?"

"It's Wes. And no I don't have a girlfriend. And why do I want to go to all this trouble to see you? I can't rightly answer that for myself. I just know that from the moment I saw you at the bus stop, I had to get to know you."

"*You had to get to know me?* Boy, are you crazy? What'd you think? That I was gonna be your girlfriend or somethin'? I don't know the first thing about you. Except that if my daddy was to see us together, he probably kill both of us."

"Why? Because I'm white? You can't see yourself being

friends with a white fella?" Wes was smiling again, this time to avoid letting her see him get upset, or at least that's what Lia thought.

"It don't matter what I see. Don't you know that? It's what the world sees. And the world can't see a white boy and a colored girl together without gettin' mad. *Real mad.* Look, I think you're nice an' all to go to the trouble to try and find me, but I don't live in your world and you don't live in mine. I didn't make it this way; it's just the way it is." Now *she* had to smile and look away. Why couldn't a white boy and a colored girl be friends? And they had been told the enemy was over there in Nazi Germany and way off in Imperial Japan. Maybe they didn't have to go that far to find an enemy just as divisive.

"So, then your answer is no, we can't be friends?"

Lia was sure that if she answered no, she would never see him again. And as much as she knew she should and be done with his sandy hair and boyish smile forever, a knot caught in her throat and made that impossible. It was 1942 and it was Seattle, Washington, USA. Why couldn't a young white man, who within a year of graduation might be buried under a few feet of Pacific island soil or beneath a white cross on a European hilltop, be friends with a black girl in the country that was supposed to be the model of freedom for an oppressed world?

"I'm not sayin' its right; I'm just sayin' that's the way it is." She gathered her jacket around her and got ready to get up. Wes didn't say anything. "*Okay,*" she sighed, "Why don't you meet me at the bus stop next Friday? Maybe we can sit on the bench and talk awhile. I don't know why, but I'm willin' to go that far, if you are."

He smiled. "I'm willing to start there." The bus rumbled up to

Lia's stop. Before she could get out into the aisle, Wes squeezed her hand. "I'll be here next week."

*****

When Lia approached the bus stop on the following Friday, Wes was already waiting there. The closer she got the more she could feel her heart race. It had been raining off and on most of the day, but just then there was a lull. She swallowed hard and stopped for a moment. Looking up into the gray overcast, she whispered, "Lord, don't let my daddy get wind of this."

"There you are." Wes got to his feet, smiling. "I was hoping you'd make it before it starts to pour again."

"I was just thinkin' the same thing. If the weather turns bad, I got to go."

"I got here a while ago so I looked around a little. Down in the middle of the block there's an Oriental market. We could go in there if it starts to rain. There's just one old guy behind the counter. I don't think he'd give us a second thought."

"Maybe that would be better. I can't stay very long anyway; Mama will be lookin' for me to catch the first bus. I guess I have a few minutes, though."

They walked down to the market that Wes had scouted out. He was right, there was an elderly Chinese man behind the counter working in a ledger. When they entered he looked up. "Need help?" he asked.

"No sir, we're waiting for the bus. It's about to start raining again." The old man smiled and went back to his books.

"Are you nervous? To be here with me, I mean."

14

For the first time Lia noticed that his eyes were the color of Puget Sound on a cloudy day. "I don't know why I'm nervous. It's not you...I guess I feel like I'm sneakin' around doin' somethin' wrong. And then I ask myself, 'What law am I breakin'?' Lia looked down at her feet. "I 'spose you'd have to live in my house to understand?"

"You mean your folks couldn't accept me 'cause I'm white? And even though they don't admit they hate white people, they're suspicious of every one they meet?"

"Somethin' like that, I guess."

"The reason I know that is because my father is exactly the same way. If he knew that I was here talking to you he'd...I'm not sure what he'd do."

"So why you here, then? Some kinda experiment for civics class? Why you so set on gettin' to know me?"

"I told you last week that I can't even answer that question for myself." He looked away. "I guess if I'm honest, part of it is curiosity. I mean I've never really talked to a colored girl before." He glanced back in time to see Lia roll her eyes. "But it's more than that. When I walked past you at the bus stop the first time, it was like everything else went blank and all I could see was you. I know you must have thought I was rude, but nothing like that had ever happened to me before. And when I told you that if I hadn't gotten on that bus to talk to you I wouldn't have forgiven myself – well, I meant that."

"So why doesn't a boy like you have a girlfriend? Don't you have any colored people in your neighborhood?"

"You got the wrong idea. I'm not looking for a purple, red, yellow or whatever color girlfriend. I saw you and thought you were the most beautiful girl I'd ever seen. I just wanted to talk to you. That's all. I thought maybe we might have more in common than we're supposed to. Or than our parents want us to. I'm not trying to prove anything. Like some experiment. I don't know, maybe I'm wrong. Maybe it's impossible for white and black people to get together. But I stand by what I said: Since the first time I saw you I thought you were the most beautiful girl in Seattle…or anywhere else for that matter. Whatever happens after this... I…"

"Weston Allen Johnson, shut-up." She reached up and touched her finger to his lips. "I gotta be on the next bus. But I like what you said. I guess I can try and find some time next week, if you still want to meet."

"Same time and place?"

"Okay," she said, then she was out the door and gone. He stood watching her until she was out of sight. Turning back he nodded to the old man and went out into the Seattle rain.

*****

Lia walked into the house and went directly to the kitchen where her mother was peeling potatoes. A kettle of water was already on the stove.

"What's for supper, Mama?" She snitched a piece of potato from the pile in front of her mother.

"Pork cutlets and mashed potatoes." She looked at the clock on the wall. "You're later than usual. Any problems?"

"No, the first bus was so crowded I decided to wait for another one."

"Well, now that you're here, put on an apron and help me with these potatoes. Your daddy will be home in no time and I want everything ready when he comes in."

Lia did as she was told. She slipped an apron over her head and set about peeling and cutting potatoes across from her mother. "Mama?"

"Yeah, baby?"

"Do you and Daddy really hate all white people?"

"What? What kind of a question is that? And where did you ever get that idea?"

"I don't know. It's just something that I've been thinkin' 'bout. Well? Do you?"

"Baby, I don't hate nobody." Her mother stopped and stared at her until she caught her eye. "Why? What happened to make you ask that? Did you have some trouble at school? Did somebody say somethin' to you?"

"No, nothin' like that. It just seems like you and Daddy hate all white folks. That's all." She put her head down, peeling furiously.

"Alright, Lia. Now I know these questions didn't just come out of thin air, so why don't you tell me what happened to make you ask 'em."

"Nothin' happened. It just seems like you two, or at least Daddy, is suspicious of all white people. I just want to know why."

"Honey, I can't answer for your father, but you have to understand that things were pretty tough for him growing up. His people came from St. Louis. He grew up when times was real hard.

I mean, things are only now startin' to pick up, what with the war and all. The last ten years been terrible hard, you know that. And you know your daddy's a hard workin', honest man. There've been lotsa times when he's stood in employment lines needin' work as bad as any man and been passed over just 'cause he's colored. That kinda thing don't just go away. A man as proud as your daddy don't get over that kinda thing easily."

"Do you think white people are bad, Mama? Do they all hate us because we're colored?"

"Lia, why don't you tell me what happened? Did someone call you a name or somethin'?"

Lia didn't want to tell the entire truth about what Wes had said, but since the floodgates of interrogation were already open, she decided to wade in a little deeper. "Nobody called me any names. It's just that...well, I was waiting for the bus today and there was this white boy waiting to get on, just like me. We started talkin' a little and he asked me if him talkin' to me made me nervous, 'cause he was white and all. I said no, it wasn't him, it was that I felt like I was doing something wrong." She looked up from her work. Her mother was still staring at her. "All I could think of is how Daddy mistrusts all white people and how angry he'd have been if he'd seen me talking to this white boy." Lia set her knife down and wiped her trembling hands on her apron. "See, he could tell that I was nervous and he said, 'Your folks wouldn't want you talking to me 'cause I'm white, right?' And then later he says that he knows how I feel 'cause his daddy feels the same way about us. Colored people I mean."

"What did you say when he said that?"

"I didn't know what to say. I guess I felt like it must have been written on my forehead or something. 'Cause it sure seems like that's the way Daddy feels."

"Baby, there is so much more you're going to experience as you get older. I don't know why the subject of race is so important...it just is."

"Did you ever have a white friend, Mama?"

"Once, when I was a young girl. There used to be a white family that lived near us. I used to play with their little girl. I think they were even poorer than we were."

"What was her name?"

"Agnes Louise Jensen. I don't know why I still remember that."

"Were you good friends?"

"I guess as close as young kids can be. Her daddy died, though. I think he had tuberculosis. Anyway, not long after the funeral Agnes's granddaddy came and moved her and her mama back to wherever it was they were from. I don't recall now. I never saw her again." Her mother suddenly started peeling potatoes again. "We'd better hurry up if we want to have supper ready for your father when he gets home." Lia didn't say anything more.

*****

At dinner it was just the three of them. Lia's daddy had come home in a good mood. "Starvin", he said. He worked as a splitter in a shake mill. The work was hard and dirty, but it paid piece work and Daddy was a hard worker. After spending most of the depression doing odd jobs and whatever he could to support the family, steady work as a shake splitter was a blessing. And there was talk of maybe getting on at the shipyard.

"So who wants to tell me what's goin' on here?" His fork was poised in front of his mouth, like he was holding the mashed potatoes hostage until somebody spoke up. Both Lia and her mother stared at their plates in silence. As far as Lia was concerned they might as well been waving big white placards with black letters saying: 'PROBLEM!'

Dinnertime at the Albermarle house was never quiet. Maybe these days it was quieter than in the past when all three girls were home and fighting about who didn't help enough or who got in trouble at school.

"Who's in trouble?" He looked from Lia to her mother and back to Lia again. "And why?" He swallowed the mashed potatoes. "Am I the only one still got their voice? Everybody else gone mute?"

Mama didn't look up. "Lia asked me something today that I couldn't answer."

Lia's father trained his glare on his daughter again, who still sat staring at her plate. "Well girl? Get it out here. What's the question's put such a muzzle on you an' your mama?"

Not looking up she said, "You're just gonna get mad if I ask it, Daddy, so it don't matter."

"Girl, it does matter. I may not say what you wanna hear, but now that the horse's out of the barn, it's too late to close the door."

"I asked Mama..." Her voice trembled. "I asked Mama why you hate all white people." She looked up to meet her father's eyes. "'Cause it just seems to me like you do."

Lia's daddy broke into a smile. He always smiled when something nudged him to the precipice of anger. It was like he was considering his response and the smile would disguise his course of action. So if he planned to strike out or to back off, it was all hidden behind the same even white teeth. Lia hoped it was the latter.

"Girl, where you get a question like that?"

"I don't know. It don't matter, Daddy."

"Well if it don't matter, why you ask it? 'Sides what d'you know about white people? You ever had to deal with the white man in his world? Everythin' been fixed to the white man's favor. Most shiftless, lazy white man always favored over a colored man. You ever had to face that? When you got babies at home just as hungry as the white man's babies?" The veins in his neck and forehead bulged out. His smile had vanished, hidden behind full brown lips pulled taut by clenched jaw muscles.

"No, Daddy."

He didn't hear her. "Look here, I was born in '95. My people was slaves not so many years 'fore I come along. People always talkin' 'bout progress, but I ain't seen nothin' change since I was a child. Seems like the white man always had his foot on our necks and always will, if he can. Only reason I got the work I got now is 'cause the war's took all the young men away. I'm doin' the work nobody else wants. Leastways them that can get better." He squirmed in his chair, as if the bile bubbling from deep inside him had to be accompanied by motion to make the words more potent. "Child, why in the world you ask me a question like that, anyhow? You been blind to the way white man treats us? You all sudden like got you a mess of white girlfriends wanna know why your colored Daddy 'don't like the white folks'?"

"No, Daddy, it's just that..." Her tongue felt like a stone in her mouth.

"It's just that what?" He leaned over his plate, exaggerating his need to get closer so as to hear better. Lia knew he was primed for a fight. She wanted to disappear and wake up somewhere else. Right now her daddy was an over-filled powder keg with a short fuse. Lia knew she was holding the match. "Answer me, girl! It's just that what?"

She didn't feel it at first. There was a moment of lightness, like she wasn't really sitting at the table, but floated above it. But like a breaking wave at high tide, nausea crashed down all over her. She was able to turn just enough so that her dinner missed the table and spewed out to the side. The last thing she saw was her daddy's face as she slid from her chair onto the floor.

*****

The room was almost dark when Lia awoke. A lamp on the bedside table glowed through a yellowed paper shade. Lia's daddy spoke quietly as he rearranged the cold compress on her forehead. As she emerged from the grayness, she realized that he wasn't talking to himself, but that he was praying. She knew that he was as upset with himself as he was with her.

"Baby? You okay now? Feelin' a little bit better?" He sat at the edge of the bed looking down at her.

Lia couldn't find her voice, so she just nodded.

"Baby, I'm real sorry about what happened at supper. I got no excuse for gettin' so mad. I don't 'spect you to understand how I feel. I been mad such a long time, sometime it feel like I can't control it no more...like I'm fit to explode."

She nodded again.

"What was it got you so fixed on talkin' 'bout white people?"

Fearing another episode like the one at supper, Lia gave a weak smile and said, "I don't know. I was just thinkin' 'bout things."

"Mama said you met a white boy at the bus stop downtown. Somethin' he said start you to askin' all these questions?"

"Sorta."

"What he say to you, got you so upset?"

Lia looked away as tears forced themselves down her cheeks. Her daddy reached a rough finger up and brushed them away. "Go on now, you don't have to be afraid to say what's on your mind. Did he say somethin' that upset you?"

She looked up at him. He didn't even look like himself in the darkness, more like a shadow figure that spoke with her daddy's voice. "It's nothing he said, Daddy, it's the way I felt when I was talkin' to 'im. I felt guilty. I felt like I was goin' behind you and Mama's backs doin' somethin' I shouldn't." Now she couldn't control the flow of tears. She wasn't sure why. It may have been the release of all the emotion from supper time or it may have been because she knew that there could never be anything between Wes and her. "It doesn't seem right to me to hate people just 'cause of their color. And I don't wanna feel like I'm doin' wrong just 'cause a white boy talks to me."

"Lia I don't 'spect that you can know the way I feel 'bout the white man, seein's how you never had to go through what I have. And it ain't really that a white man's white, I mean that his skin's white, it's what his whiteness means." He started to pace around the room. "All my life I been told I 'can't' by some white man, and if they wasn't tellin' me I can't, and then they was tellin' me I got to. I got to sit back there or I got to drink outta that fountain or I can't go to that part of town or I can't live up there yonder. And it ain't only me they tell that to, it was my daddy and his daddy and

Lord knows how many before them. A man oughtened to have that kinda say-so over another man just 'cause he white." He sat back down next to her. "I remember when I was just a kid we used to pick apples from trees that grew on a vacant lot. Maybe at some time or other there was a house on the land, but by then there wasn't nothin'. Anyways, one real hot summer day three or four of us boys figures we'll pick us some apples and go down by the creek an' eat 'em. On the property next door there was an old white man livin' in kind of a shack. We always called him the Russian 'cause he had a strange way a talkin'. So on this day that we decided to pick these apples that didn't belong to nobody, no how, the Russian sees us from his place next door and comes runnin' at us with a potato fork in his hand. I don't think none of us was more'n eight or nine years old, but here he come chargin' at us like we was enemy soldiers or somethin'. We seen him and we all ran different directions. I guess I must've run the wrong way 'cause he raises his arm and he throws that potato fork at me just like he was trying to scare off a stray dog. Next thing I know I feel somethin' knock me down and all of a sudden there's nothin' but pain goin' all through me. One of the tines stuck me right through the calf. Well, he runs up and stands right over me and I think for sure he's gonna kill me just like he would a stray been stealin' chickens. But he grabs the handle of that fork and puts a foot on my leg and jerks it right out. All he said to me was "Little nigga' bastards got no right to dem apples." Then he turned around and walked away. And know what I remember most? I remember that funny way he talked. As much as I remember the hurt in my leg, it was the way he talked that I remember most. 'Cause when I limped away all I could think about was he wasn't even American. He was from some other place. And he didn't own them apples anyway. They was planted long before he ever come to America and long before he come to St. Louis. But because he was *white* he stuck me with that potato fork and wasn't nobody could say nothin'." He put his foot up on the edge of the bed and rolled up his pant leg. On each side of his right calf was a scar that was wide at the center and tapered down at the ends. It was smooth and dark against the coffee color of her daddy's skin. "Look here, girl, I got me a whole lifetime of stories like that. Since the time I was just comin' up I been havin' to let the white man do whatever he want to me." He stood silent for a moment looking down where she lay. "Like I said, I been mad for a long time." Without another word he left the room.

Alone again, Lia rolled onto her side and stared into the shadows. She could hardly believe that her daddy could have ever let anyone treat him like that, even as a young child. That kind of hatred was beyond her comprehension. But her daddy's experience was very different from her own. Of course she was expected to sit at the back of the bus, and she'd heard white folks make rude remarks about colored people, but nobody had ever threatened her.

No wonder Daddy was so angry. Still, what did that have to do with Wes? But what was the point anyway? It wasn't like he was proposing marriage. But, to think of her daddy as a little boy, brutally attacked because he was colored… Maybe that was the problem, though. If every colored person thought every white person hated them, then it was inevitable that there could never be any change. Why was it necessary for the past to constantly be played over and over like the newsreels at the picture show?

The issue of race and anger and what might be possible between Wes and her raced through her mind until she couldn't keep it straight anymore. She could think about all that tomorrow; right now sleep offered a welcome escape.

CHAPTER TWO

I was walking down First Avenue in Seattle. I remember that the sun had come out and I felt good. It was during my senior year, and my friend Denny Wilson and I had skipped out after lunch to go up and help his uncle get his boat ready for fishing. We didn't really do much of anything, since neither of us knows anything about boats. We just helped him clean a little and scraped paint and such. It was really just an excuse to cut class on a Friday afternoon.

I guess I got bored 'cause I told Denny that I was gonna take a walk and that I'd meet him back at the car in an hour or so. I went up the hill from the Bay and walked down First Avenue. When I got to Pike Street I saw a girl sitting at the bus stop. Bang! All of a sudden it's like my vision gets all fuzzy and all I can see is this beautiful colored girl sitting on the bus bench. At first I thought it was one of the dizzy spells I get sometimes. I never have told anybody about them, especially my folks, 'cause when I graduate I intend to go into the service. If anybody was to find out, it might come up during my physical and I don't want anything to keep me out of the service. The way I see it, Hitler and Tojo got a lot of payback comin' and I'm one of the fellas that's gonna give it to 'em. Anyway, so I see this beautiful colored girl waiting for the bus. She was dressed in real plain clothes, like she was comin' from work or somethin', but she looks young, like she was no older than me.

When I saw her I couldn't peel my eyes away. She had dark brown skin that had a kind of glow to it. When I got close enough to really see her, I'm sure she must have thought I was weird 'cause I was staring. I looked into those eyes, so dark brown they were almost black and for a second felt like I could fall into them and drown. She looked back at me and kind of glared. I think it was 'cause she probably thought I was thinkin' something dirty. I know it was rude, but honestly, I couldn't help myself. She was absolutely the most beautiful girl I had ever seen and it didn't even matter that she was colored. But I sure never guessed that the difference in our color would become such a big problem, so big that it became more important than the truth about how and where I would die.

So, after I had already made a fool of myself by staring at her, I walked down the block and hid in the doorway of a store. I peeked around the corner and watched her until the bus came. I remember it was the number fifty-five. When she was getting on I ran down and waited at the next corner until the number fifty-five pulled up. Then I got on and paid my fare just like I was any other passenger getting on a Seattle bus on Friday afternoon. At first I had to look around to find her. The bus was pretty full, but there were still open seats in the back where all the colored riders sit. I pretended to kind of look around like I wasn't sure where I was going and then went and took the seat right next to her. Normally I wouldn't be that bold, but this girl really put a hook in my jaw and whether she knew it or not, just by being there she was reeling me in.

I knew right away that she got real uncomfortable when I plopped down in the seat next to her. She was by the window or otherwise I think she would have gotten up and moved to another seat. I'm pretty sure she was afraid of having to sort of climb over me that kept her there.

I wasn't sure what to say at first. I'm not the smooth, Valentino-type that can just start talking to any girl he meets. Anyway, she had her eyes glued to the traffic outside, so I wasn't sure if she was gonna talk to me no matter what I said. Finally I decided the simple approach made the most sense so I said, "My name's Wes."

She kept lookin' out the window like I must have been talkin' to someone else, so I said, "I'm a senior at Delfman High." Then I said somethin' about bein' down at the Bay to work on a boat with a friend.

She kinda let out a sigh, like she was all of a sudden exasperated with me, and without even looking my way says, "So, where's your friend?"

When I heard her voice and knew that she was talking to me, it was like I had died and gone to heaven. It was like hearing the angels sing.

I knew that she was real suspicious of me so I just tried to act natural, like I talk to colored girls all the time. I hadn't really intended to make a joke about leaving my friend, Denny, maybe standing by the car back down at the parking lot. But then she asked me if he wouldn't be mad at me for leaving him sitting in the car to come and talk to her, so I told her, 'no, he'll be mad 'cause I'd left him standing outside where it might rain.' When I saw that she couldn't help but smile at the thought of him standin' in the rain, I got real bold and asked for her name. She hesitated at first, like she wasn't sure if it was a good idea, but then she just spit it out – Lia. Her name was as beautiful as she was.

All of a sudden the bus pulls to a stop and she has to get off. I stood up to let her get out, but felt kinda desperate 'cause I hadn't had time to find out anything about her. I think I kind of stammered for a second and finally asked her if we could get together sometime. She half-smiled and said that she didn't think that would be a very good idea. Then she got off the bus. That was it.

I decided right then that I was coming back to old bus number fifty-five. In fact, I would be back there the very next Friday. Oh, sure, I knew what she was saying about it "not being a very good idea." My father hates colored people. I've heard that all my life. I also knew that it was crazy to think that the two of us could ever be more than casual acquaintances.

On the way home I told my friend Denny about this girl named Lia that I met on my walk. I said she was sitting at the bus stop and she was so beautiful that I had to get on the same bus just so that I could try and talk to her.

"Man-o-man," he says, "that's a great idea. Just act like you always ride the bus and see if you can get to know her. So...what happened?"

"Well, I sat down in the seat next to her," I tell him, "and we rode for a few blocks. I think she was shy 'cause she didn't even act like she knew I was there."

"Yeah *and*...?"

"And nothin'. I just sat for awhile and then said, 'I'm Wes. I was down at the Bay with a friend helping get a boat ready for fishing.'"

"Did she say anything when you said that?"

"Yeah, she says, 'So what're you doin' on this bus, then?' So, I told her the truth, that I had seen her at the bus stop and thought she was so beautiful that I had to get on so that I could talk to her. Then she wants to know about my friend...won't he be mad 'cause I left him sittin' in the car? And I tell her, 'No, he won't be mad 'cause of that, he'll be mad 'cause the car's locked and it might rain.'"

"Yeah, thanks a lot, buddy."

"But that got her to smile, so then I asked her what her name was and finally she said 'Lia.'"

"So…are you gonna get together? Does she have a phone?"

"That's the problem. I asked her if maybe we could meet somewhere again, and all she says is, 'I don't think that would be a good idea.' And then she gets off the bus."

"No-oh! You mean you went to all that trouble and you didn't get her phone number?"

Denny acted like he was really upset, like he wouldn't have let her get off the bus until he had a number written on the palm of his hand. The truth is the guy is so shy that the only dates he's had are ones that I've set up for him when we double. Denny would have never gotten past the 'staring at her' stage.

"Yup. I tried, but she acted like I had the plague or somethin'."

Denny glanced over at me. He had this strange look in his eyes. "Did you say somethin' that made her think you were weird?"

"I don't think so. I told you what I said."

"Maybe she's real religious or somethin'. Maybe she's like Jewish, or Catholic, or somethin' like that. Maybe she figured out that you're a Presbyterian." He laughed.

I wasn't sure how much to tell him. Don't get me wrong, Denny Wilson is my best friend. I love him just like a brother. But Denny can hold onto an opinion even if it doesn't make any sense. I was pretty sure he would think more along the lines of my father.

"I don't think it was that. I think there was some other reason." I looked over at Denny and smiled. He knew that there was something I was leaving out.

"Okay. What gives? You're not tellin' me everything. What

happened? Did you come on too strong or what? Why'd she give you the heave-ho before she even got to know ya?"

I just kept looking straight ahead, driving down the road. "Maybe it's 'cause she's colored." Out of the corner of my eye I could see Denny shaking his head.

"Man, I knew there was somethin' fishy about this whole story. Was there really even a girl *at* the bus stop? Or did you just make that up? Am I supposed to buy this bit about you falling for a colored girl and riding the bus just so you can talk to her? I'd like to hear ya tell your old man that story."

I didn't say anything. We rode along in silence for awhile. Finally, Denny couldn't hold it in anymore. "Are you tellin' me the truth or are you just messin' with me?"

"Why would I tell you a story like that? I mean really, why would I make that up?"

"So you actually got on a bus just to try and meet a colored girl?" He wagged his head like a fighter trying to shake off a jab that had gotten through. "Wes, what's wrong with you? You gotta know there's no way in hell that can work. Tell me you know that."

I just kept driving. Like I said I loved Denny like a brother, but that doesn't mean I wouldn't have popped him in the kisser if he'd pushed me too far. We rode the rest of the way without mentioning Lia again. When I pulled up in front of his house he got out and before closing the door leaned in and said, "I think that colored girl did you a big favor. She must have known the score when it comes to whites and niggers – they don't mix," he smiled, "and if you don't believe me, I *dare ya* to ask your old man."

Denny was definitely right about my father. I never was sure why he hated colored people the way he did but he never tried to hide it. Maybe in some strange way that was part of the attraction to Lia. Don't get me wrong, she is beautiful, and if there's such a thing as love at first sight, I'm in up to my chin. But somewhere inside of me there was something that wanted to teach my old man a lesson.

Like I said, I can't say for sure what happened that made him hate colored people so much. I don't know much about his life as a kid. He lived in North Carolina until he was twelve, and then his family moved west when things got too hard back there. They tried California for a few years, but I guess that didn't work out, so Grandpa moved the family up to Seattle around 1915. My dad was sixteen, and had to start work as soon as they got here. I think he always resented that he had to quit school and start working to help support the family. Everything about those days has sort of been buried and off limits for as long as I can remember. Although Dad did accidentally let on that something happened in North Carolina which made it necessary for them to leave. I don't know exactly what, but I know that after Grandma died, I never heard him speak to Grandpa again.

One night when I was about eight I overheard my dad talking to my uncle. I had gotten up to use the bathroom and they were downstairs in the dining room. I could tell they'd had quite a bit to drink because they were talking real loud. I crept down to the landing on the stairs and listened for awhile. Mom was pregnant with Fergie so she'd gone to bed early. Dad and Uncle Danny were talking about my grandmother's death.

"The old goat killed her. It's no different than if he'd put a gun to her head and pulled the trigger." My father was angry. He was also drunk. From a young age I recognized that the combination of the two almost always meant trouble.

"Al, I don't know if you can say that. You know Mama was

always real fragile...in the head, I mean. I don't know if it was really something he did or it was something she imagined he did." My uncle was trying to keep things calm. Grandpa and Uncle Danny always got along better than the other boys.

"Danny, how can you be so dense? And why do you always cover for him? You're not too young to remember why we left Carolina. If we hadn't gotten outta there when we did, Mama probably would have done this twenty-five years ago. Or maybe she would have killed *him* instead, which would have been better by far, and that nigger bitch, too." Just then my mother got up to use the bathroom because I heard the doorknob to my parents bedroom turn and had to scamper back to my bed so she wouldn't catch me eavesdropping.

The snippet of conversation I'd overheard that night rang in my head as I drove home after dropping Denny off. Now it was beginning to make more sense to me. If Grandpa had been involved with another woman and Grandma found out, that could explain why they had to move from North Carolina. Grandma was probably the kind of woman who could never accept a life sentence of whispered gossip about her cheating husband. *Especially* with a colored woman. Dad somehow knew what had gone on and held Grandpa and his colored lover responsible for the forced relocation and gradual disintegration of the family.

When I got home the place was deserted. I guess Mom and my little brother must have been out shopping or running errands, because only Smitty, our old mutt, met me at the door. I went upstairs and lay down on my bed. Fergie and I shared a room, so it was nice to be able to just lay there in the quiet without the little pest around to annoy me.

I let the encounter with Lia run through my mind. I don't know what the real attraction was. I know at first it was strictly visual.

But then I got on the bus and sat next to her. It's definitely one thing to see somebody from a distance and admire or be attracted to their beauty. But when I actually got next to her and saw her up close – the luster of her skin and the depth of those smoky eyes, the soft roundness of her lips, when I could hear her breathing and feel the life in her, it was like when you catch a bird and hold it cupped in your hands. No matter how gentle you are and how much you try not to squeeze, and no matter how innocent your intentions you can still feel its heart beating and the nervous energy it radiates just because you've gotten too close. That's how I felt sitting next to her. She was like a little bird trapped in the seat next to me. All I wanted to do was be able to connect with this exotic creature. I wanted to understand her world and admire her beauty and I wanted her to see something familiar and attractive in me. *She just wanted to fly away.* "I don't think that would be a good idea." That was all she said. But it didn't really matter because I already knew that I was going to be on the number fifty-five next Friday afternoon. If that didn't work, then I'd keep going back until I did see her again.

I must have dozed off, because sometime later I felt little hands shaking me awake. Fergie was standing next to my bed with his hand on my shoulder. "Mom said it's time to get up and come down for supper." He began pirouetting around like a ballet dancer and smiling.

"What's so funny, runt?"

"Nothin'. 'Cept that mom knows you cut class today. She ran into Denny's mom at the store, and I guess his mom found out that you guys went to Seattle 'stead of bein' in class."

I got a sinking feeling in my stomach. My parents are real hung up on me getting my high school diploma. Especially my dad. He always says that if he hadn't had to quit school, *he'd* be foreman at the paper mill and Elmer Rivers would have to listen to *him* rag instead of the other way around. I knew what was coming at supper—a big helping of 'I wish I'd had the opportunities you've had...'

"Is Dad home?" I asked.

"Workin' late." He had stopped spinning and was staggering back and forth trying not to run into anything until his equilibrium returned. When the dizziness subsided, he started the routine all over again. He had just stopped again as I closed the door behind me.

Downstairs Mom already had the table set and was putting a plate of pork chops next to a bowl heaped with mashed potatoes. She didn't look at me as I came in. "Did you have a good day at school?"

I knew what was coming. "Fergie already told me that you ran into Mrs. Wilson at the store."

Now she stopped and gave me 'the look'. "Weston Allen Johnson what were you and Dennis Wilson thinking? Are you trying to get kicked out of school before you even graduate?"

"Mom, I don't have anything but study hall on..." She cut me off.

"You know your father would have given almost anything to have been able to stay in school and get his diploma. Wessy," she was using the same plaintive voice she'd been using since before I was Fergie's age, "I just don't want you to mess up your life. You're just about to take such a big step toward success."

Poor Mom. If she could have only known what was to become of me in a short time, I think she would have simply hugged me and not said a word. Like me, though, she would have to wait.

We were just about finished with dinner when my father came in. I had hoped that I could finish and go up to my room before he got home. I knew that if anything was said about my absence from school, we'd have to start 'the inquisition' all over again.

"So how was school today?"

"It was okay, except at lunch Timmy Morgan threw-up out on the playground. But other than that it was okay." Fergie was wearing the same smile from his ballet act earlier. "I kinda think Wes is in trouble, though."

That was all Dad needed. He stopped eating and glared at me. Mom was doing her best to look busy gathering up the dirty plates and leftovers.

"Why would Wes be in trouble? And how would you know anything about it?"

Fergie began to squirm in his chair. My father didn't like troublemakers, nor did he care for tattletales. Fergie was in a panic to redeem himself. "'Cause me and Mom ran into Mrs. Wilson at the store and she'd found out that Denny and Wes had ditched school to go help his uncle with his boat." He took a quick breath. "Can I be excused now?"

"Yes, you may." It was Mom this time. "You can help me get these dirty dishes to the kitchen and then help me wash and dry them."

"Aww, Mom, do I have to do the dishes?" He glanced at my Father and quickly dropped the protest. "Okay. I guess I can help. *If you really want me to.*"

When they had cleared the table and retired to the kitchen, my dad and I sat in silence for a few moments.

"So what's this about you ditching class to work on a boat?"

"Dad, it was no big deal. We left after lunch to go help Denny's uncle get his boat ready. That's all. Besides, all I missed was study hall."

"It may seem like no big deal to you, but I doubt that Principal Clarke would agree. And I know I certainly don't. Son, you better get it through that thick skull of yours that you need an education if you're going to get anywhere in today's world. I suppose you want to end up like me…working like a nigger in a stinking paper mill."

I started to get up. I knew what was coming for the thousandth time and I didn't want to hear it again. My father wasn't ready to release me, though.

"Wes, sit down. I'm not finished talking to you." His face was getting redder by the moment. "Boy, I wish for one week you could do what I do and know what I know. You wouldn't be so quick to throw away the opportunities that *my hard work* has provided for you. Why, you might actually be just a little bit grateful."

"I'm not trying to seem ungrateful. I know you work hard. But all I missed was study hall. That's it."

I don't remember exactly what he said after that. My father had never forgotten any of the opportunities life had forced him to pass up, and when he was angry he bound all his disappointments together like the strands of a whip. Whoever was closest felt the sting of his unfulfilled ambitions.

*****

It was two weeks before I saw Lia again. Actually, I did go back to the bus stop the very next Friday, but didn't see her. I figured that maybe I was just too early, so I rode the bus for at least two hours, making the same loop around downtown over and over. The driver finally asked me if I was lost. I lied and told him that my family had just moved to Seattle and I was trying to familiarize myself with the area. He looked at me like I was from Mars. "I see," was all he said.

On the Friday after that, though, I was already on the bus and sitting near the back where all the colored riders sit. I guess I'd been riding for about an hour when the bus pulled up to the stop at First and Pike. I could see her from the window as we rolled toward the curb so, of course, I got excited. Lia got on looking kinda frazzled. The bus was really crowded so she had to stand on her tippy-toes to try and find a seat. That's when I stood up and called her name. At the same time I waved to signal her. Man was she surprised. I don't think she could believe it was me. Anyway, she made her way back to where I was sitting, but real cautious-like.

"What are you doin' here?"

When I told her that I had gotten on the bus just so that I could see her again, she acted like she was angry. She asked me about school. I don't think she believed I was really a senior. Then she wanted to know why I didn't have a girlfriend, and why I'd spent the last two Friday afternoons riding the bus just to see her again. When I told her that I had wanted to get to know her ever since the moment I saw her sitting at the bus stop two weeks before, she kind of hit the roof.

"What'd you think? That I was gonna be your girlfriend?" She said that if her daddy saw us together he'd probably kill both of us. Well, I knew exactly what she was talking about, but I wasn't talking to her daddy. I wanted to know what *she* thought. That's when I asked her if it was because she couldn't see past the color of my skin.

"It don't matter what I see, it's what the world sees. And the world can't see a white boy and a colored girl together without getting real mad."

Like I said, I didn't care about anything except what *she saw* and what *she thought*. So I asked her if there was no way we could be friends, then or ever. That seemed to catch her off guard. She stopped for a few seconds, like she had to think about what she was saying, instead of what she thought she *should* say. She admitted she didn't know how to answer, and that she wasn't saying the way things were was right. I guess she must have known I was serious because she suggested maybe we could meet at the bus stop the next Friday and just talk for awhile. She couldn't commit herself to any more than that. That was good enough for me.

*****

We met again the next Friday. I got there a little while before she did. As I sat at the bus stop waiting for her, I wasn't sure if she was going to show up. It looked like it was just about to let loose with more rain when I saw her walking toward me. She stopped and looked up for a minute. I had gone and looked around a little before she got there. I found a small Oriental market partway down the block. There was just one old man working behind the counter, so I suggested we go down there just in case it started to rain. Lia seemed relieved by the idea. I think being seen talking to me was a bigger concern than getting wet standing at the bus stop.

When we went into the store the old man didn't hardly give us a second look. We stood by the front window so we could keep an eye on the bus stop. I knew she was uncomfortable talking to me face to face. So I said, 'Are you nervous to be here with me?' She said she felt like she was doing something she shouldn't, like she was sneaking around behind her folk's backs. She couldn't really say why, that I'd have to know what it was like to live in her house. I told her I knew exactly what she meant because my father felt the same way about colored people. That seemed to set her off, 'cause all of a sudden she demands to know what I doin' there with her then. Was this some sort of experiment for civics class, or something like that?

I admitted to her that at first some part of me was just plain curious. Telling her that didn't go over very well. So, I decided to tell her the truth. That from the first moment I saw her I thought she was the most beautiful girl I had ever seen. I *had* to get on that bus to try and talk to her. I wasn't out to prove anything and maybe I was too stupid to realize that it really *wasn't* possible for us to be friends. But no matter what, I still thought she was the most beautiful girl in Seattle and that was that. She must have heard something she liked or just got tired of listening to me, because suddenly she reached up and touched my lips with a beautiful brown fingertip.

"Weston Allen Johnson, shut up." She was actually pleased with my little speech. So we made plans to meet at the same time and place on the following Friday. That was it. I watched her walk away. We were still the same people. She was black and I was white. But we'd taken the first step to just being Lia and Wes. Neither of us could know what was in store for us, but there was one thing that I was pretty sure of – I was in love.

*****

We continued to meet on Friday afternoons for several weeks. It was strange how much we had in common. We even had similar plans for the future. I wanted a family and so did she. I was pretty certain that I was going to be called up soon after graduation, so all of my plans would have to wait until after the war was over. I figured I'd try and sign on with a fishing boat out of Fishermans Terminal and work until my notice came. I wanted to see if I could get my 'sea legs' so that I could enlist in the Navy. The thought of digging foxholes and eating canned rations didn't appeal to me. Besides, Japan had attacked our Pacific fleet while most of our boys were asleep on Sunday morning. They slaughtered them before they even knew what was happening. No, I was pretty sure I wanted to join the Navy.

It was after we had met every Friday for four or five weeks that I suggested we try to meet somewhere else. The stolen minutes together once a week weren't enough for either of us. Since voluntary gas rationing was strictly practiced around our house, I had to be careful about how much I drove the car. Grandpa had gotten so he couldn't see very well anymore, so he gave me his old Ford for my seventeenth birthday. I don't think my dad really approved, but since he wasn't speaking to Grandpa he didn't say anything. I had to work during the summer to earn money to keep it running. And I had to pay for my own gas. Fortunately Grandpa had put new tires on it the year before, so it was in pretty good shape.

Lia was the one who came up with a suggestion that seemed like it might work. At the YMCA on Madison Street they held dances and social nights to entertain the colored troops home from the war. Lia's parents never questioned her participation on a Friday or Saturday night, just as long as she was home by eleven o'clock. Her idea was that she would tell her parents that she was going to a dance at the YMCA. I would drive down and pick her up a block away. There was a park not too far away, in a mostly Oriental neighborhood, where we could go and sit in the car. That way we would have a couple hours to talk. I'd make sure she was back by ten or so, just so she could make an appearance at the dance. As long as nobody got too nosy or noticed that she wasn't there the entire time, we could enjoy some time together without having to talk inside the store.

I was nervous the first time I picked her up. The dance at the YMCA was set to start at eight o'clock on a Friday night. My friend Denny and I were supposed to be going to a game between Delfman and cross-town rival Central High. I even got him to call during dinner just to reinforce what the plan was with my parents listening. Denny still wasn't in favor of Lia and me being together, but he was my friend and I knew I could count on his help.

I went by Denny's house around seven o'clock. Normally I would have just pulled up in front and honked the horn, but that night I wanted his parents to see me. I was trying to cover my tracks as best I could, so the more witnesses to the 'game decoy', the better. I even went into the game with Denny, but as soon as it started I slipped out and headed to the place where I had agreed to pick Lia up.

I'm not sure why I was so nervous as I turned onto East Madison. When I got down to Twenty-Third I turned into a hardware store parking lot and parked alongside the building in the shadows. I doused the headlights and slumped down in my seat. There were quite a few people walking past on their way to the YMCA. Lots of young colored men in Army uniforms and once in a while a couple of sailors passed by laughing and talking with one another. Sitting in the darkness I wondered how many of these young men, hardly any older than me, might be going to their last dance or seeing an old friend for the final time. Funny thing was, regardless of the uncertainty, there was a feeling of excitement in the air. It was no different for Lia and me. Even though our fathers would be against the idea of us having a relationship, maybe violently against it, both of us felt a sense of anticipation at what the future held.

I closed my eyes against the giddiness making my heart flutter. For a moment our parents weren't an obstacle, society's opinion didn't matter and even the thought of going to war couldn't diminish the glow behind my closed eyelids.

I couldn't have been sitting like that for more than a minute or two when Lia tapped on the passenger side window. I reached over and unlatched the door for her. Like the little bird from the bus she seemed to float in and light on the seat next to me as gracefully as a robin lands on a power line. The silence of the moment was broken by the rustling of her dress; the atmosphere charged with the fragrance of perfumed soap. I looked over at her. Maybe it was the mood brought to life by the darkness, maybe it was the magic created by taking a risk...whatever it was, we looked at each other for a moment and without a word leaned closer until our lips met. I wrapped my arms around her, and pulled her close to me.

"I've wanted to do that since the first time I sat next to you on the bus."

"I've wanted it to be possible, but wouldn't let myself believe it could." She leaned in and put her head on my shoulder. For a few moments there in the dark nothing existed beyond the confines of the car. *Finally, we had found each other.*

"We should get out of here before somebody sees the car parked next to the building. Might look a little suspicious. So where's this place you said you know of where we won't raise any eyebrows?" I asked.

"It's a little park not far from here. It's mostly Oriental people that live around there. They mind their own business. I think we can park by the duck pond and sit in the car without anybody noticing."

We drove to the park in near silence. Lia gave directions and I did as I was instructed. In a few minutes we were sitting in a gravel parking area with only a distant streetlight interrupting the darkness.

"What did you tell your folks you were doing tonight?"

"I got my buddy Denny to cover for me with a story about the football game between Delfman and Central. I picked him up at his place and even went and watched the game for a few minutes, just to be seen. Then I left and headed over here to meet you."

"Wes," Lia's voice was insistent, "are we crazy? I mean, why we gotta sneak around like this just to be together for a few minutes? Do you honestly think it's possible that this messed up world could ever get used to seein' us together?"

"I don't know, but right now I don't know what else we can do."

"Me either, 'cept maybe tell the truth that the two of us probably can't ever be together."

"No. I'm not willing to accept that. I'm just getting to know you, and the more I know, the more I wanna be with you. We can't let everybody else tell us what's best for us. Besides, I expect within a few months of graduation I'll be called up. If the country expects me to go and fight the war, how can it tell me who I can or can't fall in love with?"

"Are you falling in love, Wes?" She was sitting close to me. Her words were so hushed I think she breathed them, or maybe I heard her thoughts.

"I don't know. I'm not sure I'd know if I was. All I know is there's something about you that makes me happy when I'm with you and makes me ache inside when I'm not."

Lia's eyes glistened. "That's why I can't accept things the way our daddies want them either."

We sat talking as the Seattle rain washed over us, scrubbing away the differences that our fathers stubbornly clung to.

We stayed as late as we could, neither wanting the time to end. But I knew Lia had to get back to the YMCA to keep up appearances, and I had to get back to Denny and the other guys from school. Driving home I couldn't have cared less about Delfman and Central and the rivalries that spring from boys playing games. Suddenly sports and all the associated high school drama seemed childish and tedious. And my parents' concerns about me jeopardizing my future created a contradiction that rose up like Mount Rainier in my path, especially since I was beginning to see *Lia* as my future. Knowing that our families could never accept us together put everything in an impossible light. Our fathers loomed as the biggest threat to our life together so, by comparison school and whether I graduated or not seemed insignificant. Still it wasn't time to bring everything out into the open yet. Barring some unforeseen circumstances to prevent it, I was going to be called upon to fight the war. Until that chapter of my life was resolved, Lia and I couldn't begin to write the story of us together, regardless of how our fathers' ardent hatred might try to prevent it.

*****

Lia and I continued to meet as often as we could. All through the fall and winter of 1942 and into 1943 we used the same plan. Denny was always a reluctant participant in the deception we created to make our meetings possible. He never outright disagreed when I asked for his help, but I could sense that our friendship was beginning to show the strain. At the heart of Denny's difficulty with Lia and me was an attitude not much different than my father's. He simply didn't believe whites and blacks should be together. It was because of this racial bias that Denny became an accomplice in the lie manufactured by my father to explain my disappearance. It was a plan expressly designed to break Lia's heart.

CHAPTER THREE

On a soggy Friday night in March of 1943, Lia and I met as usual in the parking lot of the hardware store. There had been a nearly continuous drizzle for most of the month. That meant we rarely saw another person from our spot in the park. The seclusion proved both good and bad. While it provided uninterrupted hours during which our hearts were forged together, it also allowed us to push the limits of our physical exploration far beyond what was considered appropriate. We had crossed a line and we knew it. And there was no way we could ever return to things as they were before.

Driving back so that Lia could make her official appearance at the YMCA, she suddenly said, "Wes, what would happen if I got pregnant?"

Her question shattered the silence like a hammer, making my heart thump inside me. "I'm not sure. Why? Do you think you are?"

"No, I don't think so. I guess I've just been thinkin' about what would happen if I was. That's all."

I could feel her looking at me. I wanted to assure her that as far as I was concerned there was no turning back. I had decided that I wanted to spend the rest of my life with her, no matter how young we were, nor what anyone else said. If we had to move to a desert island so that we could be together, then I'd start studying charts tomorrow.

"Lia, I don't have answers for questions that haven't had to be asked yet. The only thing I know for sure is that I'm in love with you." I squeezed her hand. "No matter what else, I'm in love with you."

We pulled alongside the hardware store and she got out. She brushed the wrinkles from her dress, adjusted her coat and disappeared around the corner of the building. I gave her a couple of minutes to walk down to the YMCA and then slowly made my way out and down the street.

As I got closer, I could see young colored people leaving and entering the building. Because of the drizzle, most people just put their heads down and hurried into the night. I tried to catch a glimpse of Lia when two women caught my attention just outside the door. Silhouetted against the front of the building, they appeared to be arguing. One woman was pulling on the sleeve of the other and making exaggerated gestures with her other hand. I slowed and rolled down my window. They were yelling, but I couldn't see them clearly in the shadows. Suddenly, one of them stopped struggling and called my name. *It was Lia*. She jerked her arm free of the other woman's grasp and ran into the street toward me. I braked and pulled to the curb. An instant later Lia was at the open window. Even in the rain I could see that her eyes were puffy and her cheeks wet with tears.

"Lia! What's happening? Who's that woman?" I didn't have to wait long for the answer.

"I'm her mother. That's who '*that woman*' is. And don't think I don't know what's been goin' on between you two, either."

"Mama stop, please. I'm sorry I been sneakin' around, but what else could I do? You and Daddy could never understand. Mama, I love him…and he loves me."

"Lia, you don't know nothin' about love. Girl, you're hardly more'n seventeen years old. This boy got you all filled up with notions about love. All he got on his mind is *one thing*."

I'd had heard all I could. "Mrs. Albermarle, that's not true. I do love Lia. And she just told you she loves me. We're sorry if that doesn't fit with your idea of how things should be, but that's the way it is. I mean no disrespect, Ma'am, but Lia and I want to be together. No matter what our parents think."

Her mother was silent. I watched a half-smile form on her lips. For just a second I thought maybe she would relent; maybe she'd been convinced by my sincerity. I was wrong.

"So, you're the boy from the bus stop. The one whose folks hate coloreds." She didn't wait for me to answer. "I bet your Mama and Daddy don't know nothin' about your little colored girlfriend. Do they?" She glared at me, forcing her words through clenched teeth. *"Well, do they?"*

I was caught off-guard. I hadn't realized that Lia had told them about our meetings at the bus stop. It was clear I had two choices: To attempt to deceive her or to tell the truth about who I was. To lie about my parents would have been to lie about who *I* was. More than that it would have been a betrayal about how I really felt about Lia. "No. They don't know about us. I haven't told them for the same reason Lia hasn't told you."

"Well, you don't have to worry yourself 'bout that, young man, 'cause you ain't gonna see my daughter no more." She grabbed Lia by the arm again. This time Lia made no attempt to struggle. She stood in the rain like a drenched rag doll staring down at her feet. "If you know what's good for you you'll forget about this here girl. If her daddy finds out about this, God help you both."

I watched helplessly as she dragged Lia away into the darkness. When I could barely make out the last of their misty shapes disappearing into the night, I yelled behind them as loud as I could, "LIA! I LOVE YOU!!"

*****

My parents were already in bed by the time I got home. I tiptoed to my room and closed the door. Fergie was asleep in his bed, so I quietly undressed and lay under the covers, staring at the ceiling in the darkness. I felt both desperate and helpless at the same time. I needed to talk to Lia, but had no idea how to contact her. I knew she didn't know my phone number and I didn't even know if her folks had a phone. Isolated and miserable, I did the only thing I could. I pulled the covers over my head and prayed that I would see her again.

I spent Saturday and Sunday locked in my room. Mom was convinced that I had the flu, so she brought aspirin and chicken soup up to me. On Monday morning I dragged myself out of bed and made it to school. I avoided Denny all morning, not wanting to let on about Friday night. Just before the lunch bell rang, I got called to the office. When I got there I was told I had an emergency call from my grandmother. I picked up the phone, knowing it couldn't be either of my grandmothers, unless they were calling from the cemetery.

"Hello?"

"Wes, it's me. Baby, don't say anything. Just listen. I'll be on the number fifty-five on Friday afternoon after I help Mrs. Dawkins. It should be between four and five. Meet me on the bus. Okay? I love you." She hung up.

"Grandma? Remember I told you I can't leave school until two forty-five. I'll come over then. Okay? Bye." I turned to the secretary, "She wants me to come over and mow her lawn. Says it's getting way too high with all the rain." I smiled. "She's just confused and lonely. I'll stop by after school and make sure she's alright."

The secretary gave me an admiring smile and nodded. "I hope

my grandson will do the same for me some day."

*****

Just as she promised, Lia climbed aboard the bus at four-thirty on Friday afternoon. I had been riding for about a half hour. When I saw her climb the two steps and look for me toward the back, my heart jumped. I felt like God had answered my prayer as she walked down the aisle to where I sat.

She slid into the seat next to me and put her hand in mine. "At the end of next week Mama is sending me to live in Olympia with my Grandmother."

"But what about school? It's not out for another two and a half months."

"She said it don't matter. I'm goin' and that's it."

"Did she tell your father what happened?"

"No. She knows that'd make it bad for everybody. She made up a story 'bout how Grandma's not feelin' good, and how she needs me to come down and help her out around the house. S'posed to only be for the summer."

"What did she say after you two walked away on Friday night?"

"She said that I wasn't to ever see you again. That you would only use me and then throw me away when you were done. She said if I still was to see you that I'd get my heart broken. Stuff like that."

"Lia, you can't believe that. I would never hurt you. More than anything I want us to be together. I'm not sure how, but I'll think of something. I just need some time to think. Okay? Please. We'll have to go along with things right now, but I'll come up with a plan. I promise."

"Look, Wes, my grandma doesn't have a phone. So after next week you'll have to write to me. I been thinkin' and I figure we can use made-up names just in case we're not the ones that get to the mail first. They'll just think it was a mistake. I know Mama will tell grandma the whole story about us. I don't know if she'll be watchin' me real close or not, and I'm pretty sure she'll send me to get the mail at the post office, so that should work out okay. But just in case, we should try an' play it safe."

"What name should I use on the letters when I write?"

"I been thinkin' about that. Use your middle name, Allen, for my last name. And you know how you sometime tease me about my real name bein' Amelia and not really Lia, like everybody else calls me? When you write, use the name Amy since you're the only one's ever called me that. Did you get all that? How you gonna write to me?"

"Amy Allen at ... I don't know the address. What is it?"

"It's Post Office Box 524, Olympia, Wash. Can you remember that?"

"May 24th. Olympia, Washington. I got it. May twenty-forth is my mom's birthday. That's how I'll remember it. How will you write to me?"

"I'll address the letters to Mr. Ford, just like your car. Maybe you should use your grandfather's address to avoid trouble at your folks' house. Send me the address the first time you write." Lia managed a little smile. I could tell that her weekend had been as rough as mine. I wanted to hold her and kiss her and promise that

I'd never leave her, that we'd get past this rough spot and someday tell our kids about it. I didn't get the chance. At the next stop she got up and whispered, "I've got to go. I love you."

So, that's how Lia and I continued our relationship. At first it seemed strange to be writing to Miss Amy Allen at PO Box 524, Olympia, Wash., but eventually it came to seem normal. I actually enjoyed writing letters because I could think over what I wanted to say, or start over if I said something stupid. But we always kept up the charade all the way through the letter. I never opened the letter with Dear Lia, or Dearest Lia, or My Darling Lia, I always started 'Dear Amy.' So if my parents or her grandmother should get curious and open one of our letters there would be no incriminating evidence, just ordinary letters accidentally misaddressed. Sometimes I would write something personal very lightly in pencil just at the inside crease of the envelope flap.

The letters were our only lifeline while we were both biding our time, waiting for school to end, and for me, the war to begin. We had no specific plans other than that we had decided to spend our lives together. How and when we could begin was yet to be determined.

CHAPTER FOUR

Lia and I wrote to each other at least twice a week. As she had thought, her grandmother almost always sent her to the post office to get the mail. And I used my grandfather's address without any problems. I told him that it was a game I was playing with a girl from Olympia and gave him a wink. He never asked any questions, but more importantly, he never mentioned the letters to my parents.

Finally, school ended with no further drama. I finished the year without getting expelled for missing those Friday afternoons I'd spent with Lia. Even Denny settled back into the routine we used to have, gradually asking fewer and fewer questions about 'the colored girl that's got you plumb crazy.' I never did tell him that she had moved to Olympia because her mother found out about us.

Graduation was on a stormy Friday night during the third week of May, 1943. Dad was proud and Mom cried. Grandpa shook my hand after the commencement and squeezed a ten dollar bill into my palm. He just smiled and winked. I believe I could have told him the whole story of Lia and me and he would have slapped me on the shoulder and said, "Do what your heart tells you, Son." But I never said a word.

As planned, I was able to get a job as a hand on a fishing boat. There was such a short supply of able-bodied men because of the war, the Skipper of the *Jean White* was really happy to get me. He knew that I expected to get my call-up notice within a few months but said that was alright with him. I also told him that I was hoping to get a feel for the water, so that I'd have a better sense of whether to enlist in the navy instead of the army. He guaranteed I'd have my taste of sea-duty before I ever had to put my signature on a naval enlistment document.

*****

The first week of June was so brilliant Monet himself couldn't have captured it adequately. We were supposed to ship out on a Sunday morning at five o'clock. I had been helping get the boat ready and provisioned during the three days prior. The Skipper wanted us all on board on the Saturday night before just in case something changed. Of course Mom and Dad and Fergie wanted to come down and see me off. And as much as I wanted them to feel good about what I was setting out to do, Lia was all I could think about. It had been almost three months since I had seen her and as each day passed I felt like something inside me was evaporating, leaving me a little emptier than the day before. Now I was going to be gone at least ten or fifteen days. Only during that time I wouldn't even have her letters to keep our lifeline open. I tried to tell myself that the separation was good. Who knew where I might be in a year. We told each other we were practicing for the time when our letters really would be our only connection over the lonely months and distance separating us.

We finished our chores around seven-thirty on Saturday night. Skipper decided to take us all out to a steak dinner instead of having to dirty up the galley. He also said that with a couple weeks of galley fare to look forward to, he needed a good steak to start the trip right.

By nine-thirty we were all back on the boat and settling down to sleep. Since I was the newest member of the crew I had to sleep on the pilot house floor. There were only three bunks in the forward compartment, so the Skipper and the two regular hands got seniority. Skipper said it didn't mean anything since once we were underway someone would always have to stand watch so there'd always be enough bunks.

At first I didn't have any trouble drifting off and even in the cramped quarters got real comfortable. I awoke around midnight though, and found it impossible to go back to sleep. Maybe it was the excitement of finally getting out on my own or maybe it was that I beginning to get a sense of how endless life's possibilities could be. I lay in the pilothouse listening to the boat groan and rub against the dock as she subtlety rose on the incoming tide. Suddenly, I was so excited I had to write Lia a letter. I got a sheet of paper and pen out of my duffel bag and sat hunched beneath the little oil lamp the Skipper kept burning in the pilot house. I couldn't keep what I was feeling to myself and had to share it with the girl I loved, even if I couldn't call her by her real name.

It was around two o'clock when I felt my eyelids getting heavy again. I had finished the letter and put a stamp on it. I was hoping the Skipper would let me run to find a postbox before we set off in the morning. If not I would have to wait until we got into Westport to off-load our catch before there would be an opportunity to mail it.

Thoughts of Lia and me cascaded in waves through my mind. At last sleep overtook me.

*****

Skipper had us up at three-thirty. The remaining gear had to be stowed and everything made ready to get underway. I had told my parents we would be leaving around five o'clock, as soon as the tide changed. The Skipper wouldn't want to waste any extra fuel fighting an incoming tide so that meant we'd be leaving as soon as he saw the water go slack.

I didn't dare ask permission to go look for a postbox, although I really wanted to get the letter in the mail so I could share my excitement with Lia. I decided I'd better hold onto it until we got into Westport.

Mom and Dad and a yawning Fergie showed up at four-thirty. I was back on the stern trying to look busy when I saw them coming down the dock. The sun was just beginning to reach golden fingertips over the eastern horizon as they walked toward the boat. Backlit by the dawn they appeared to be floating along, their feet not even touching the planks beneath them.

I heard Mom first. "Oh, look, there's Wes at the back of the boat." She quickened her pace and waved. "Wes, honey, here we are. I hope we're not too late."

The Skipper came out of the pilot house just as they were hurrying down toward the boat. "This your family?"

"Yup. It was mainly my mom's idea to come down and see me off. You know, her firstborn's going out on his own, and all that."

The Skipper smiled. "Well now, that's real nice. Why don't you take 'em below real quick like and let 'em see where you're gonna be sleepin'."

"Sure it's okay? I don't want to hold us up on account of my family."

"Son, I don't want your mama worryin' about you for the next two weeks 'cause she don't think you're gonna eat proper and sleep in a real bunk. Get it?"

"Sure thing, Skipper." They were right next to the boat by now, so I motioned them to come aboard. Fergie jumped up and over onto the deck, while Dad helped Mom over the rail.

"The Skipper said I could take you below so you could see the whole boat."

"Wow!" Fergie stood wide-eyed for an instant before bounding into the pilot house. Dad stepped over and shook the Skipper's hand. I heard him introduce himself and then start with the usual,

"I'm glad to see Wes getting some experience. It'll help make a man out of him." At the same time Mom yelled at Fergie.

"Fergus Lee Johnson! You get back here this instant!" Mom took up a position aft of the pilot house door. She was still pointing down at the deck when Fergie popped his head out to try and read how serious she was.

"Aw, Mom. Wes'll make sure I don't touch anything."

"It's okay, Mom, he won't hurt anything. We only have a couple minutes, so I'll make this real quick. The other fellas are still getting things ready, so I'll just take him down to the foc'sle so he can see what's down there. He can tell you all about it until I get back."

"Alright, dear. Fergie, you do exactly as your brother says." She gave him the 'or else I'll make your life miserable' look. It seemed strange to have my mom talk to me like an adult. That was something I'd have to tell Lia about in my next letter.

Fergie and I went into the pilot house. He had to run his fingers over the wheel and inspect the helm station. He jumped down the two steps to the forward compartment and carefully inspected the head. He opened each drawer beneath the forward hanging locker. It was just the two of us down below. We sat on the starboard bunk for a minute not really talking about anything in particular. I had never considered that I might miss the little pest, but as we talked for those few moments I realized that Fergie was as much a part of my life as Mom and Dad.

By the time we got back up on deck, my parents were already down on the dock saying goodbye to the Skipper. The other deckhands were standing by the lines. I hoisted Fergie up and deposited him over the rail onto the dock. We all hugged and then they were on their way. We cast off and headed into the brilliant

June morning. I caught a final glimpse of Mom, Dad and my kid brother climbing the gangway toward the parking lot. Taking a deep breath, I inhaled the promise of all my tomorrows.

We steamed straight north through Puget Sound. Places I'd never seen before rose and then fell away behind our stern. Everywhere I looked from the Seattle waterfront all the way to Whidbey Island and into the Strait of Juan de Fuca, the landscape was a mixture of liquid blue fringed by green-black fir trees spiking into the sky. I would have to write Lia about the beauty of the state we called home.

Everything about the trip agreed with me except the constant motion. Skipper thought it was sea-sickness, but I knew that the motion aggravated my dizzy spells. I also knew I couldn't say anything, for fear that the Skipper might think I was too much of a liability to have aboard.

When I'd finished my chores in those first couple of days that it took us to get out into the Pacific, I'd go up on the bow and stand with my eyes closed. It didn't seem to matter if my eyes were closed or open, sometimes the dizziness came with such force that I had to hang onto the rail or just sit down wherever I happened to be. One time the Skipper noticed that I seemed disoriented and asked me if I was okay. I laughed it off and said I was fine. "I was just thinking about my girlfriend, that's all. I guess of everything, she's what I miss most."

The Skipper laughed out loud. "Well that's just great. Listen here boys, we got us a brand new 'mud-puppy' what's in love. Listen, Son, don't none of us wanna hear you sobbin' in your bunk while we're tryin' to get some shut-eye. So if you don't mind, try and do yer cryin' while you're standin' watch alone. Okay?"

I laughed it off with the rest of the crew. It was a relief that the

Skipper didn't read anything else into my spells. From then on anytime someone noticed me faltering they'd give me a nudge and say something like, "Okay, Loverboy, let's pick it up a little... she'll *probably* still be there when you get back."

*****

It had been five days since we left Seattle. We were about thirty miles off the north coast. The weather had been fantastic. Skipper said he couldn't remember a June when the winds had been so calm and the sun so warm. He said he could remember years when the seas were so rough, it was like living in two worlds – the one at the top of the waves and the one in the troughs. It was either the stinging spray lashed against your face by a homicidal wind or the eerie feel of a graveyard.

Besides the weather, we'd had good luck with the fishing, so our fish hold was steadily filling up. If the weather held and the fish kept finding us, Skipper said we might be headed back by the eighth day.

We all had to be out on deck during the daylight hours to tend the gear and put the fish in the hold. By the end of a long day everyone was tired and hungry. We took turns cooking and cleaning up. The food was never fancy, but it was always plentiful and hot, or at least mostly warm.

It was after everyone had eaten and the galley dishes washed that the men began to settle in for the night. The Skipper had set up watches in four-hour intervals. There wasn't much light down in the foc'sle after the sun went down, so that area was off-limits for anything but sleeping after dark. Sometimes the guys off-watch would play cards in the pilot house or out on deck. I pretty much kept to myself and thought about Lia and the life we were going to build together.

Everyone had his assigned watch, and after a few days we all settled into the routine of life aboard. My watch was from two o'clock in the morning until six o'clock. That meant I had to stay awake and keep an eye on things while we were hove-to. I'd go out on deck every few minutes to make sure everything was secure and that our navigation lights were burning bright and clear. Often I'd see other boats off in the distance visible only as small red, green or white lights bobbing on a world of perpetual motion.

For the first couple of nights the Skipper surprised me with a visit at three or four in the morning. He asked me what I'd seen and if everything was all right. I reported the lights from other fishing boats and anything else distinguishable against the shifting horizon. He never said much, just grunted and rubbed his head. I guess he must have been convinced that I could handle the responsibility, or finally just got too tired to keep checking on me, because the visits stopped.

At daybreak on our seventh day out, a menacing gray wall appeared on the southwestern horizon. Nobody took particular notice until around noon when the wind started to pick up. The increased wind created steep waves that made our tiny wooden world roll and tip like a bathtub toy. The Skipper had us secure everything especially well. When the rain squalls began to lash the boat we buttoned our rain gear and kept working. The severe rolling really aggravated my dizziness. I must have gone pale because one of the guys suggested I go below and get in a bunk until I got feeling better.

"Everybody gets seasick if the weather gets rough enough. You should get below and see if you can shut your eyes. This storm'll blow through in a while and then the sun'll come back out. Just you watch."

I looked at the Skipper. He had been listening to the

monologue, and as I caught his eye he gave a nod of agreement. I guess they were right. There was no sense for me to be jostling about with my head lolling side-to-side and my eyes rolled back. So I went down to the forward compartment and eased myself into the lower bunk.

When I awoke it was almost five o'clock. The weather had calmed a little and the guys were still out on deck working. I got out of the bunk and tried to stand up. For just a moment my legs felt like they would sustain my weight, but suddenly collapsed beneath me. In a moment my whole world was immersed in thick shadow. In the next instant I felt my forehead bounce against the planking on the cabin sole.

I lay there for several minutes trying to will my body to respond to the commands my brain was sending to it. Although I was conscious my limbs seemed disconnected from my mind. It was as if someone had thrown a switch cutting off the circuit that kept all my systems operating and synchronous. I felt like a prisoner sentenced to an indefinite term in a cell cleverly disguised as my own body.

Fortunately, as suddenly as the switch was turned off, it came back on. When I tried to lift my arm it responded, as did my legs. I sat up, letting my brain clear, and eventually got to my feet. Although I was still dizzy, everything seemed to be working again. I went into the head and latched the door behind me. A red lump was forming where I had hit my forehead. I stared at my reflection in the mirror. The face looking back seemed strange. It looked like me, but just minutes earlier had lay paralyzed in the forward compartment. I didn't know if I could trust it anymore.

I replayed the episode in my mind and knew something was seriously wrong. This had to be way more than sea-sickness. I stayed a moment longer and then spoke aloud to the image in the mirror, "Just hang on until you get back to Seattle."

When I got out on deck, the sun was peeking out from behind mountainous white and gray clouds. The most recent line of squalls had blown through bringing a provisional calm to the sea. Although the swells were still high and close together, the wind wasn't turning the wave-tops into daggers of salt spray. I had to brace myself against the pilot house as the boat rolled in response to a swell speeding beneath her keel. She rolled back the other way as we dropped steeply into the following trough.

The Skipper gave me a little nod. "Feelin' any better, Son? Looked like you were sound asleep down there."

"I feel a little better." I was lying and hoped the Skipper couldn't see right through me. "Where do you want me?"

"It's still a might rough out here. Tell you what...why don't you see if you can throw some grub together for the rest of us. The way she's rollin' we're not havin' much luck nohow."

"I'll get right on it. Ham sandwiches and some soup okay?"

"Son, after a day like today, 'most anything's gonna taste like Mama's Sunday dinner."

I went back into the pilothouse and started working on the sandwiches. Against the back wall there was a small galley with a gimbaled two burner stove and a cutting board. Underneath was an ice-box and storage for some canned goods. All the other food-stuffs were stored in crates under the two lower bunks.

As I began to slice some cheese and onion to go with the ham, a wave of dizziness passed over me mirroring the motion of the ocean swell passing just a few feet beneath me. I braced myself and waited for equilibrium to return and then quickly sliced some bread and ham. I put a pot of coffee on the stove and emptied three cans of soup into a pan next to it. In fifteen minutes everything was warmed and ready to eat. By the time the men had finished with the food the coffee would be ready. I made sure that everything was cleared away and secure in the galley and went back out on deck to tell the Skipper.

"All ready?" The Skipper didn't look at me any longer than it took to get my answer. "Okay, men, let's make sure everything is dogged down and the gear made fast, and we'll take a break. Young Mr. Johnson has been nice enough to fix our supper."

The other men saw to last minute tasks and headed past me into the pilothouse.

The Skipper stood just aft of the door. "Wes? You gonna join us?"

"I think I'll stay out on deck for awhile. The air feels good on my face. I'll try and eat a little later."

"Suit yourself," he said and pulled the door closed behind him.

I stood for several minutes with my back and the palms of my hands pressed against the aft wall of the pilothouse. Looking over the stern I could see fat, express-train swells hurtle toward us, and each time the *Jean White* lifted her behind just in time to let them pass harmlessly away.

I thought about my next move. Tomorrow was our eighth day out. The way the Skipper had it figured we shouldn't have to be out more than ten days or so. All I had to do was convince him and the other two hands that I was fit to do my job for a few more days. I'd decided that I was better suited to marching on dry land than bounding up and down on an unpredictable sea. "I'll join the Army," I said to the next swell as it rolled up on the stern.

*****

After the men had eaten and the galley was cleaned up and made secure, everyone went back to their tasks. I could hear the Skipper talking to the other two men. He wasn't trying to exclude me, but his tone wasn't meant to include me either.

"With any luck, we should be able to head back in another day or two. I think we'll off-load our catch at *'Sea Treasure'* and re-provision in Westport."

So the Skipper wasn't figuring to return to Seattle as originally planned. That meant I had a decision to make about whether I was going to be honest with him about my dizziness, or try to bluff my way through another week or two of fishing. I needed some time to think this through. The bump on my forehead made a compelling argument for getting off the boat in Westport. I could probably get a bus back to Seattle or hitch a ride if I had to. There was one additional benefit to going home by bus – Olympia was almost exactly midway between Westport and Seattle. If I worked the timing out just right I might be able to get off in Olympia. If I got really lucky I might be able to hang around near the post office and catch Lia going for the mail. But I wasn't looking forward to telling the Skipper that I was a wash-out after my first trip. I knew he was counting on me to fill a gap until I was called up.

I tried to convince myself to do my best to finish the trip with the boat. Although I longed to see Lia, I felt obligated to the Skipper and the other guys. As I mulled it over I tried to play down the episode in the forward compartment. Maybe it was only the extreme motion of the boat that aggravated the dizziness. If I could hang on at least until we got back to Seattle, I could make a fair assessment of how I felt about sea-duty. At least if I rode it out until we got back I would have fulfilled my commitment to the men. Leaving them in Westport would create an unnecessary burden on everyone. After such a rough day, the one thing I was certain that I *would* do is stand my watch. All three of the others were sure to be dead tired.

*****

Reed Hanley had worked with the Skipper for more than twenty years. He helped him decide on some of the details of the *Jean White* back when she was still on the drawing board at Sorel Boatworks. He was a man acquainted with hard work and the various moods of the Pacific Ocean. But today, despite a nearly sixty-year love affair with this greatest of all oceans, she had beaten him into near delirium. It was for that reason he stood holding onto the bunk with one hand and shaking me vigorously with the other.

"Kid, wake up. It's your watch," he whispered. The tone of his voice communicated more than his words. He was exhausted. If I had chosen to ignore his summons and lingered just five more minutes, I believe he would have simply crawled into the bunk and sprawled his gangly mass right on top of me. He craved sleep and a lumpy mattress wouldn't have bothered him even a little.

I, on the other hand, had been awake for quite awhile. I was arguing with myself about the wisdom of standing watch. I had considered trying to beg-off, but the message in Reed's words convinced me that there was more at stake than my personal comfort.

I swung my legs over the edge of the bunk and stood up. Before I could grab my boots and step back, Reed had already launched himself onto the mattress I had been occupying. He moaned and rolled over. I'm sure he was asleep before I tiptoed up into the pilot house. I slipped my feet into my boots and then leaned down toward the forward compartment. Only the sound of hardworking men relishing the comfort of deep sleep met my ear.

Out on deck the world was anything but tranquil. Although the wind had calmed down, the sea was alive with motion. The size of the swells was harder to distinguish under an opaque sky. The moon and stars were completely obscured, so that even the horizon was impossible to make out. In this dark world sky and sea were mirror images of the same oblivion.

The air outside helped to clear my head. My dizziness had diminished, leaving me feeling refreshed and more confident. As I looked into the darkness surrounding the boat, it occurred to me that maybe the landscape in motion produced the dizziness as much as the motion of the boat. My plan for the following day would be to try and keep my vision focused on an immobile object whenever possible. If I could look down at the planks on the deck unless I had to direct my attention elsewhere, it might help with the dizziness. I began to feel optimistic about trying out my experiment.

The first hour of my watch passed quickly. I made sure the navigation lights were bright and clear and checked all the gear on deck to make sure that everything was secure. It was around 3:15 that I heard something thud amidships against the boat. I sprinted to the gunwale and peered over the rail into liquid darkness. At first I couldn't tell what had hit the boat, but as my eyes adjusted I could make out the branches of a partially submerged tree. My heart began to race. I knew that hitting deadheads in the water could spell real trouble for a boat like the *Jean White*. My first thought was to run below and wake the crew. But then I remembered the peacefulness of the forward compartment when I had leaned in to listen hardly an hour before. No, I needed to investigate a little more before I alerted the Skipper and crew. I knew the chief concern would be that branches thrashing below the waterline not be allowed to damage the prop or shaft. I ran into the pilothouse to grab the emergency flashlight that the Skipper kept at the chart table. In a moment I was back at the stern to see if the menace had made its way aft and under the boat. I trained the beam directly over the stern and down into the water. Sure enough the tree had been pushed partially under the hull as she rode up on swell. All the while the *Jean White* kept rising and falling with each succeeding wave. I grabbed hold of the stern rail and leaned out as far as I could. Beneath me slick branches jutted out in every direction. With the beam from the flashlight I followed the line of the trunk away from the boat to the right. It appeared that the latest wave-action had carried the water-logged tree trunk into a position perpendicular to the hull. I was hopeful that the next one would break it completely free and send it bounding off until it washed up on a deserted stretch of beach.

Waiting for the next swell seemed to take an eternity. I silently prayed that God would reach down and snatch the giant from beneath our little boat. I didn't want to hesitate and endanger the boat and crew, but at the same time didn't want to unnecessarily rip the men from their cocoons. Finally the boat rose up in response to the rolling swell. I felt another brief thud and then *Jean White* seemed to lighten slightly on her feet. I was pretty sure we had broken free of the deadhead, but bent deeply over the stern to verify my suspicion. I leaned down as close to the water as I could, peering intently until my eyes began to bulge. The branches were nowhere to be seen, just the sloshing of cold, black seawater against the hull.

It was too late when realized I had kept my head down a moment longer than I should have. I also knew there was nothing I could do about it. I hung doubled over the stern, my face just inches from the water as the passing swell pushed us up like an elevator car. In an instant the switch had been turned off again and I was paralyzed by another wave of dizziness. I remember seeing the flashlight tumble from my outstretched hand into the water. It flipped and rolled, pointing its yellow eye up at me until finally the depths swallowed it. I tried to will my other hand to hold firmly to the stern rail, but leaning over so far had put my center of gravity too low. No matter how loudly my mind screamed for help, my body gradually relinquished its grasp on the last solid surface I would ever touch. The *Jean White* rose to the top of the swell and then began her swift descent into the following trough. As we slid to the bottom my feet lost contact with the deck and my hand twisted free of its grip on the rail. The temperature of the water didn't even register in my mind as the boat raced past me, drawn up the face of the next wave.

I was aware that I was drowning and yet I was bathed in an unexplainable calm. I had imagined mind-numbing panic in a situation such as this; sure that I would feel the ocean currents sucking me down into the blackness. Instead the water seemed much calmer than when I was aboard the boat. It was more like a lake than the ocean.

I thought about how Mom would be devastated by the loss of her little boy and wondered if Dad would feel any recrimination for his endless lectures. I thought of Fergie having our room all to himself and wished I'd tried to be closer to him. Suddenly I remembered the night Lia's mother came to the YMCA and the conversation we'd had driving back to the hardware store parking lot. I had told Lia that the only thing I knew for sure was that I was in love with her. I was glad that I had told her that. Those were the last words I repeated in my mind as the water closed around me.

CHAPTER FIVE

Albert Johnson yawned and looked at his watch. It was ten forty-five on Monday night and he was tired. Tomorrow meant another day laboring in the stench and noise inside Becket Paper Mill.

"Smitty! Outside! C'mon, you stupid mutt. Get out there. And make it quick."

The old dog shuffled past him through the open screen door. While he waited, Albert Johnson turned off the lights in the kitchen and dining room and stood waiting in the glow from the upstairs landing. The house was quiet now. His wife had gone to bed to read, and Fergie had finally submitted to threats of physical violence to get him off to bed.

Albert rubbed his forehead and yawned again. Another day had come and gone and all he had to show for it was an aching back and the promise that tomorrow would grind by with the same tedium as today. He sighed. "Smitty! Get in here. Now!"

With the dog in he turned to trudge up his bedroom and lose himself in the final refuge left to him – sleep.

Halfway up the stairs the phone rang. Under his breath, he cursed. This better not be that idiot Elmer Rivers telling him that he needed to be in at five-o'clock instead of seven. He turned and went down to the living room.

"Elmer, this better be good, considering everybody else is already asleep."

The voice at the other end hesitated. "I'm trying to reach the Johnson family. Who am I talkin' to?"

Albert didn't recognize the voice, but knew it wasn't Elmer Rivers. "Uh, I thought you were someone else. This is the Albert Johnson. Who is it you want to talk to?"

"Are you Wes's father?"

"Yes, I am. Why? Who's calling?"

"Mr. Johnson, this is Eric Morton, I'm the Skipper of the *Jean White*. We met at the dock last week."

"I remember you. What's the problem? Has Wes gotten into trouble?"

"Mr. Johnson, I'm real sorry to have to tell you this over the phone, but I'm pretty sure your boy, I mean, Wes…well, I think he's dead."

Albert Johnson shook his head. He wasn't sure if he was really on the phone or if in his exhausted stupor he had fallen asleep and was dreaming this conversation.

"What do you mean you're *pretty sure*? How can you not be absolutely sure if somebody's dead or not? That just seems like a damned stupid thing to say." There was no response. "Is he or isn't he dead?"

"Mr. Johnson, what I mean to say is that Wes is missing. He wasn't anywhere to be found on board the boat this morning when I went up to relieve him from his watch. We searched the boat right away, but he was gone. All I can figure is that something must have happened out on deck and he fell overboard."

"Where are you now? I mean, where are you calling from? You're not still on the boat, are you?"

"No, sir. We're in Westport. After we found Wes missing, we searched the area for a couple of hours and then headed straight here to report him to the Coast Guard. I'm at the Coastie Station right now. It's dark now, but they're gonna do a search at first light." He hesitated. "Mr. Johnson, I don't wanna get your hopes up. When these boys go out tomorrow, it'll be for recovery, not rescue. Like I said, I'm real sorry."

"What do I tell my wife? Maybe he's dead. Maybe he's not? When will you get back to Seattle? We need more than this."

"As soon as I get cleared from the Coast Guard, I'll catch the first bus for Seattle. The men are gonna off-load our catch and stay with the boat here in Westport. I'll meet with you folks just as soon as I can and answer any questions as best as I can."

"So, you'll be back by when? Wednesday? Thursday?"

"Probably Wednsday. It all depends on the bus service. I'll call just as soon as I get in and get cleaned up. We can meet somewhere or I'll come to your house." There was silence at the other end. "Mr. Johnson, I been fishin' for more'n thirty-five years. I've never lost anyone until today. I feel terrible about this. I can't tell you how sorry I am."

"So I'll hear from you as soon as you get in, right?" Albert Johnson had already taken leave of his conversation with Eric Morton. His mind was desperately searching for the words to tell Wes's mother that her son was never coming home again. He hung up and sat down in the darkness.

*****

Raylene Johnson clutched a cotton handkerchief as she stared out her second story bedroom window. Down below a modest back yard in need of mowing reached a million green fingers up toward the June sun. She had hardly spoken over the past day and a half since her husband had informed her of Wes's disappearance. As ever, Albert had fought with the words until in exasperation he just spit out the bitter news like a mouthful of bile.

"Missing? What's it mean? Oh dear God! What I'm saying is Wes is dead, Raylene. He somehow must have gone overboard and nobody knew about it. They just found him missing in the morning after his watch. *They looked for him.* They didn't find anything. Why? How? Raylene, don't ask me those questions."

For thirty-six hours Raylene Johnson had been living with those few dreadful sentences hacking through her consciousness like a shard of broken glass. Each time she replayed a slight variation of the same scene in her imagination. Each time she saw her little boy, the one everyone knew by his charm and smile, pleading for help while a ravenous ocean sucked him into it's black depths. Each time she could hear him scream: *"MOM! MAMA! DON'T LET THIS HAPPEN! HELP ME! MOM! PLEASE! HELP ME!"* He was always searching with desperate eyes, looking for *her.* The look on his face in every scenario was a mixture of terror and disappointment. He called for her help and she never came. Then sinister waves would cover his head and she'd catch one last glimpse of his brown hair tossing in the current before he disappeared forever.

She was still staring out the window when her husband called up from downstairs. "Captain Morton is just coming up the front walk. Raylene! Did you hear me?"

She dabbed at her eyes and stood up. Walking over to the mirror above the vanity she paused to look at herself. Her hair lay flat and tangled, pressed to one side. Puffy circles created their own shadows under her eyes. She was still in the bathrobe and nightgown she'd been wearing for the past day and a half. So what? she thought to herself. She walked out and down the stairs.

Eric Morton stood just inside the front door nervously twisting a cap in his hands. She could see that he was nearly bald save for a few strands of blond hair combed across the top. From the staircase he didn't look like the imposing Skipper that Wes had told them about. Right now he looked like a trembling schoolboy called to account for his misdeeds. Normally Raylene Johnson prided herself on her willingness to forgive. She believed grace should always triumph over strict justice. Today however, she wasn't sure there was grace enough to pacify the hatred welling up inside her.

She heard Albert say, "Come in Mr. Morton." His voice sounded perfectly normal. For a moment she hated him for that. "Have a seat." He pointed to a chair in the living room.

Eric Morton walked over and sat down as he was told. Raylene followed him with her eyes but said nothing. Her husband followed him and was just about to sit down on the sofa when he looked up at his wife. "Honey, you remember Mr. Morton. Why don't you come down and sit here with us so we can hear what he has to tell us about Wes and how he…what happened on the boat." He reached a hand toward his wife who remained motionless on the stairs. Silently she descended the last few steps and sat down next to her husband.

Eric Morton fumbled for words. He couldn't bring himself to look directly at Raylene Johnson and at the same time could feel her eyes boring into him.

"First of all, let me tell you both how very sorry I am for what happened. I…"

"No," she said. "No. Where's Fergie? Albert, go get him and bring him down here. I want him to hear what happened to his brother. *You see, Captain Morton, you didn't just lose our son, you lost Fergie's older brother."*

"Raylene, stop. There is no point in dragging Fergie into this. He's already gone through enough. He's been up in their...*his room*...ever since we found out. Raylene, don't do this."

Raylene Johnson didn't divert her stare from Eric Morton even momentarily. "FERGIE! GET DOWN HERE THIS INSTANT!"

"I'm sorry, Mr. Morton, I didn't know she would be like this. Raylene please, leave the boy out of this."

At the top of the stairs a door opened and closed. Without another sound, Fergie appeared on the stairs. Pale and listless, he stood looking down at the adults. Like his mother, puffy circles formed smudges under his eyes. He descended slowly, one hand on the banister, the other hanging motionless. As he got close enough for his mother to touch, she reached out and drew him into herself. Burying her face in his chest, she sobbed deeply. Rather than protest, he raised a hand and stroked her tangled hair. Neither of the men spoke.

"Fergie," she whispered between sobs, "is Weston's little brother, Mr. Morton. They shared a room. Can you understand that? Whatever you have to say to us, you have to say to all of us."

Albert Johnson stared at his feet.

"I understand, Mrs. Johnson and I apologize. I want all three of you to know how sorry I am for the loss of Wes. We all liked him aboard the boat. He was a hard worker and a fast learner."

"Mr. Morton, what we want to know is how this could happen. And *what* happened. We need for you to explain why Wes was alone and nobody helped him when he fell overboard." Albert Johnson looked quickly from Captain Morton to his wife. "We have to somehow figure out how to make sense of this. We'll go crazy otherwise."

"I understand. Okay. The way we do things aboard the boat is like this: We all work out on deck while it's light and then we heave to. Somebody always has to be on watch though, so I assign each man a four hour watch. Wes's watch was from two until six in the morning. He was the newest hand so he had to stand the crummiest watch. That's the way it's always been."

"So it was when he was on watch alone, sometime between two and six in the morning that he disappeared?"

"Yes, sir, that's right. I was the one to relieve him at six. Usually I'd get everybody up and going at that time, but let the last man on watch have an hour or two to catch a little rest. Wes never complained about standing watch. The first few nights I went up to check on him at three or four, but everything was always ship-shape. Once I figured he could handle things I quit checking on him."

"Had he been acting strange or anything? Say anything to make you think he wasn't alright?"

"Not really. At first he got a little sea-sick. Everybody does, though. Then he settled into the routine. Oh, I guess he seemed kinda empty-headed those first few days. You know, like he couldn't keep his mind on things. We figured out that it was 'cause he was missin' his girl so much. He'd kinda walk around starry-eyed. But that's just a young fella' in love, I s'pose." The Skipper attempted a smile. "He said that he really missed her."

Albert Johnson glared at his wife. This is exactly the kind of thing she would hide from him. He didn't even know that Wes was interested in a girl, much less be so gaa-gaa that he couldn't think straight.

"Raylene? Did you know anything about Wes having a serious girlfriend?" He could tell from the stunned look on her face that she didn't know any more than he did. Looking back at the Skipper, he asked, "Did he ever say what this girl's name was? Did he tell you anything about her at all?"

"No. He never got into details with any of us." Eric Morton sat uncomfortably, waiting for more questions from the Johnsons. "One other thing that might have had an effect on him was the weather our last day out. Up until then, we'd been havin' the best weather I've seen in June. But then around noon on Sunday the wind started to blow. We ran into some real heavy squalls and the water got pretty rough. For most of the afternoon it felt like we were on a rolley-coaster. I think it made Wes feel pretty bad. I sent him down to ride it out in a bunk, 'stead of havin' him bouncin' around with the rest of us out on deck. I think he slept a good bit of the afternoon. After that he was on galley duty and later got some more sleep while the rest of us stood our watches. He relieved Reed Hanley at two. Reed said he got right up and didn't say anything. He didn't figure there was any reason to worry. Said the wind had calmed down by then, but the water was still a might rough. Didn't figure there was any reason to think the boy couldn't handle it."

"Mr. Morton, what do you think happened to our son?" asked Raylene Johnson.

"I don't rightly know, Ma'am. I guess he could have fallen overboard, although I can't imagine how; or he could have been knocked overboard by a wave. Although a wave big enough to carry him away would have left some evidence, I imagine. Probably would have busted some tackle loose or the like."

"You don't think anyone would have noticed if the boat had been hit by a wave big enough to kill my son?" Her eyes narrowed and her voice took on a sarcastic edge.

"I think it's likely one of us would have been jarred awake. But after so many hours of fightin' huge waves and fishin' gear, a man's ready to collapse. I'm not sure any of us would've felt a wave unless it knocked the boat down on her side. A fella gets so tired, none of us may have noticed. Like I said Ma'am, I don't think it was a wave. I think somethin' must've happened and he fell overboard."

The Johnsons had little else to say. Eric Morton did his best to answer their remaining questions. After a time of squirming uncomfortably, he got to his feet and excused himself.

"Again, I am real sorry for your loss. If there was any way that I could change things I would pay any price to go back and do things over. I'll be calling the Coast Guard later today to see what the search turned up. I'll call as soon as I hear anything. I wish there was something more I could say." He looked from face to face, hoping for some small sign of understanding or forgiveness. There was none. He crumpled his cap in his hand and let himself out.

*****

"Gladys? This is Albert Johnson. Oh, well, that's very kind of you, Gladys. I guess we're getting by. This is just something you can't plan for. We're just trying to make sense of the whole thing. Listen, the reason I'm calling is actually to talk to Denny. Is he home? No? No, it's nothing pressing exactly; I'd like to ask him a couple of questions about how Wes had been acting lately. Will you have him call me? Thank-you, Gladys. Okay, I'll tell her. Goodbye."

*****

Denny Wilson sat fidgeting on the couch. Albert and Raylene Johnson sat across from him, doing their best to put him at ease.

"Thanks for coming over, Denny. I know you and Wes were good friends. He always spoke of you like a brother."

Denny Wilson swallowed hard. "We were like brothers. I mean, I felt the same way about Wes."

"Denny, we wanted to talk to you because we think maybe you could help us put together some pieces to the puzzle surrounding Wes's disappearance."

"Anything I can do, Mr. Johnson, I'll tell you anything I can."

"Good, Denny. That's fine." Albert Johnson nodded. "You see, the Skipper of the boat that Wes disappeared from said that he'd been acting strange. You know, like he'd walk around kinda starry-eyed, you know, preoccupied."

Dennis Wilson's expression didn't change.

"The Skipper said his excuse was that he missed his girlfriend so much, it was hard to keep his mind on his work." Albert Johnson got up and went to the window. "Denny, does that make any sense to you?" He walked back and sat down again. "See, 'cause we didn't even know Wes had a girlfriend."

Denny Wilson looked at his hands folded in his lap.

"Denny?" Albert Johnson leaned forward. "What can you tell us about this girl?"

The young man couldn't control the tears any longer. The dam broke, wringing sob after sob from him. Albert Johnson moved over next to where he sat, and looking desperately to his wife, reluctantly put an arm around him. "It's alright, son, let it go. Let it go. Just let it all come out."

"I don't know if she's the one for sure." He wiped his nose and eyes on his t-shirt. "I didn't think he was seein' her anymore, 'cause he hadn't said anything for quite a while. I told him it couldn't work between them. Honest, I told him. And every time I covered for him so that he could see her without you folks findin' out, I felt real bad. But what could I do? Wes and I were like brothers, just like you said, Mr. Johnson, so what was I supposed to do?" His eyes pleaded for understanding.

Raylene spoke up. Her voice was soft and motherly. "Whatever you did for Wes, dear, I'm sure it was because you were always his best friend. We understand that. But, Dennis, Weston is gone now. You are in no way betraying your friendship by helping us to understand how he was feeling when he…when he disappeared. Do you understand that, Dennis? Wes would want you to help us to find some peace in all of this. Don't you think?"

"Yes, Ma'am."

"So, now," she continued, "tell us what you know about this girl. Where did he meet her? How long had he been seeing her?" Albert Johnson moved back to the chair next to his wife. "Do you know her name or where she lives?"

Dennis Wilson took a deep breath and wiped his eyes. His voice broke, so he swallowed and began again. "Mrs. Johnson, do you remember that day last fall when Wes and I cut study hall so we could help my uncle with his boat?"

"I remember."

"Well, after a while Wes got bored, so he walked up to First Avenue just for the heck of it. He said he was walking down the street at First and Pike and saw this really beautiful girl at the bus stop. Anyway, he got on the same bus at the next corner just to try and meet her."

"That's how he met her?" Albert Johnson smiled. "So what? Was she older than Wes or something? Why all the secrecy? He didn't think we'd approve?"

"No. It wasn't that. See, I told him right from the beginning that there was no way it could work. No way possible. I even told him that if he didn't believe me that he ought to ask you Mr. Johnson. That you'd tell him straight up. No way."

"Dennis, dear, you're not making any sense. We understand that Wes met this girl on the bus and wanted to continue to see her, apparently without our permission, but what you haven't said is *why*. What would Wes's father have told him 'straight up'?"

Dennis Wilson began to slowly shake his head. "I told him. I told him to ask you Mr. Johnson, that you'd tell him…"

"Tell him what, Dennis?"

He laughed. It was a desperate, frantic, when all else is lost, kind of laugh. *"That whites and niggers don't mix. That's what. She was colored. That's what. She's a colored girl."*

No one said a word. Raylene Johnson dabbed at her eyes with her cotton handkerchief. Her husband was struck with an uncharacteristic silence. Finally, like an animal stunned by oncoming headlights, he bolted up the stairs. The bedroom door slammed shut behind him.

Raylene Johnson looked up. "Thank you, Dennis. I think you'd better go home now."

*****

She looked at the clock. It was almost three-thirty in the morning. Raylene Johnson lay in the dark bedroom wondering if it was at precisely this moment just a couple of days before that her baby had taken his last breath. Perhaps it was her that he was thinking of. Perhaps not. She rolled over to exorcise the demon and realized that her husband wasn't in bed with her. Slipping on a bathrobe, she followed the glow rising up from downstairs.

On tiptoes she crept down toward the light in the living room. He sat staring at the ceiling, a glass of whiskey balanced on his knee.

"Albert? Are you alright?"

"No. No, I'm far from alright."

"Do you want to talk? Or would you rather I left you alone?"

"Do what you want, Raylene. I don't care anymore." He took a sip from his glass. "I just can't figure out how this all could have gone so wrong. I mean Wes was always a *good* kid. I know he had his own ideas, but how did things go so wrong?"

"Are you talking about falling overboard and drowning? That going wrong?"

"Hell no! That was a freak accident. I'm talking about my son falling in love with a nigger. That's what went wrong." He shook his head. "Didn't I teach him right? Didn't he know how I feel about that? Why would he go behind me like that? Purposely stab me in the back?"

"Albert, I don't think Wes intended to stab..."

"Well, I been thinkin' about it," he cut her off, "and when his little nigger girlfriend doesn't hear from him she'll come sniffin' around. And I'm gonna' be ready for her. There won't be any runnin' away. Hell, no. I'm gonna' give her just what she's got comin'."

"Albert, please don't do anything to make things worse. Please. Fergie and I have had all we can take."

"Don't worry, Raylene. I'm not gonna do anything illegal. Do you think I'm stupid? Things aren't like they used to be. No. I've got a plan for when she comes snoopin'. She's gonna get more that she ever bargained for."

Upstairs in the dark Fergie sat shivering despite the summer heat.

PART TWO

CHAPTER SIX

Through the sound of his own screams he watched them dragging her away. Amy resisted, but was overpowered. From where he lay on floor her abductors appeared to be only empty robes, void of flesh and bone. He struggled to his feet, but a blow sent him tumbling backward where a boot pinned his face against the concrete. From the corner of his eye he could see the head of a sledge hammer dangling near the floor. It disappeared, but from the shadow on the wall he traced its ascent in a high arcing motion. For a millisecond the room was still; even Amy seemed to hold her breath. Then there was only pain.

He jarred awake and stared into the darkness. They had come for her again, leaving only the throbbing in his ankle as evidence. With his other foot he touched the cast on his right leg. Without turning on the light he reached for a pain pill.

*****

Robert Dawes looked out over Puget Sound. Away on the horizon earth and sky dissolved into monochromatic haze as rain began to fall. He shivered and zipped his coat.

Between him and his appointment with Jackson's Boatyard lay fifteen miles of frigid saltwater. He hadn't planned to schedule hull work for the middle of January, but with a broken ankle wasn't able to do much anyway. Besides, his trawler had popped a seam or something, because she had close to a foot of water sloshing around in her bilge. As it was he had to run the pumps every few minutes just to keep up with the leak.

The rain fell harder as he nudged the throttle forward. He flipped on the wipers and poured a cup of coffee. It was time for more pain medication.

The tachometer jumped to 950 rpms. Five knots was just fine on a day like this. There was no sense pushing the old girl. As long as the leak didn't get any worse, they'd be alright. Beyond making his appointment at Jackson's, Robert didn't have anywhere else to go.

He forced himself onto the helm station chair and swung his right leg up onto the chart table. Elevating it helped to keep the pain from throbbing to the rhythm of the engine.

*****

It was late afternoon when he arrived at the boatyard. Lonnie Brooks was headed down the gangway to the work dock just as Robert limped from the wheelhouse to ready his dock lines. The rain had let up, leaving a gray canopy over the water.

"Just stand off for a few minutes, Mr. Dawes, and I'll get the lift positioned and we'll haul her out straight away."

Robert waved to signal that he understood. He was grateful that Lonnie could get him onto the lift right away. The burning in his ankle was escalating. All he wanted to do was to take more pain medication and lie down with his foot elevated. Since *NoraLynn* was where he presently called home, he didn't even plan to disembark while they had her up on stands. Lonnie could use a ladder to come aboard. They would need her up in the yard for at least three or four days. Robert was going to use the time to work on the forward compartment. That, and rest.

*****

Early the next morning a voice roused him from a new dream. Instead of battling the shadow figures, this time he was standing knee-deep in breakers the color of the sky. A breeze was blowing just hard enough to evaporate the perspiration on his forehead.

Amy was there too, sitting on a crescent of white sand with dense jungle foliage as the backdrop. Thick strands of hair hung down to her shoulders. The strain of the months leading up to her death were washed away like a receding wave. She was smiling and talking to him, but he couldn't hear her. What was she saying? Finally the sound penetrated the fog between sleep and consciousness, but it was a man's voice.

"Hey, Mr. Dawes, are you awake up there?" Lonnie Brooks stood down below in the yard. He didn't wait for an answer. "I'm gonna have the boys push out the rolling stairs for you. I noticed yesterday that your leg seems real tender. Don't seem like the ladder will do you much good."

Without getting up Robert yelled back, "Okay, thanks Lonnie. I'll come down afterwhile."

Robert lay for a few moments letting his eyes adjust to the darkness of the forward compartment. In the case of *NoraLynn* it was a space just big enough for two bunks on one side, one above the other, with a single bunk opposite. There was also a hanging locker with three drawers below at the point farthest forward where the bunks formed a 'v'.

A mixture of thoughts coursed through his mind as he stared at the ceiling overhead. It was strange to dream about Amy being healthy again. Lately all his dreams had been about the months she'd spent battling cancer or about the hooded figures that invaded his sleep and came to take her away. Both were too real.

Uninvited, scenes from her death snapped into focus in his mind's eye. She was shrinking away and there was nothing he could do for her. For the first time since he had broken his ankle he was glad for the pain. It broke the spell. Amy was dead and he hadn't been able to save her. Today was today, even though the edges of the day she died still ran like watercolor, changing the hue of every day since.

Amy had died in June; within six weeks he rented out their house and moved aboard the boat. He fled to the comfort of the second woman in his life – the *NoraLynn*. Besides, the old girl needed him, too. He reached for another pain pill.

*****

After breakfast Robert filled his thermos from the coffee pot and thought over the things he needed to do. He knew Lonnie would be back soon to discuss his plans for working on the boat; he'd probably send Rusty up to check out the bilge for signs of trouble.

Poor Rusty, he had to do all the bilge crawling. He stood just over five feet tall in cowboy boots. Red hair, like steel wool after a winter out in the rain, was short and neatly combed. For a man who appeared to be in his late sixties, he looked to be in terrific shape. His forearms could have been whittled from white ash, and his step was still lively. It was precisely that youthfulness and compact stature that sentenced him to life as bilge inspector. Lonnie though, stood better than six feet tall with a midsection that left tight spaces out of the question. There may have been battleships into whose underbellies Lonnie Brooks couldn't squeeze.

The good news was that *NoraLynn's* bilge was large considering her length of thirty-six feet. She had been built as a fishing trawler in 1934 at Sorel Boat Works on Vashon Island. Christened the *Jean White*, her name was changed to *NoraLynn* after she was converted to a pleasure craft. For more than a half-century she had cruised the fishing grounds from the Columbia River bar to the Strait of Juan de Fuca and all of Puget Sound.

The *Jean White* was sold at auction in 1992 to settle moorage debts. Captain Jeffrey Rand rescued her after she had languished for several years tethered to an obscure dock on the Duwamish Waterway.

Captain Rand put her up in a local yard and went to work replacing her rotting decks and pilothouse. Her hull was restored to new condition using select yellow cedar shipped down from Alaska. Aft of the pilot house he laid out a salon with a galley and dinette. All this was framed with windows for natural light. But what really gave the living area charm was a small Franklin stove with glass doors. The tiny afterdeck was where Captain Rand installed the hatch through which Rusty would have to make his way to inspect the bilge.

Robert finished his coffee and hobbled up into the pilothouse. He braced himself and let the throbbing in his ankle subside before continuing down to the forward compartment. Below was the head with just enough room for the toilet and a tiny sink. A hand-held shower drained into a holding tank, as did the galley sink and toilet. Across the companionway was another locker for foul-weather gear and miscellaneous junk.

Despite her nearly total refit over the past years, the one area that had been left original was the forward compartment. The starboard and port bunks were original, although at some time they had been reinforced with wooden platforms. Originally designed as open wooden frames with interwoven canvas straps to support the mattresses, plywood platforms were later placed over the frames to support the mattresses.

It was the lower bunk that Robert planned to remove to install the new chest of drawers. He had salvaged six drawers from a thrift-store dresser. Each one was oak and featured a pull in the shape of an anchor. Perfect. Fashioning a suitable chest in the space shouldn't be too difficult.

He was still considering the details when Lonnie called up to him again, "Mr. Dawes, are you feeling up to comin' down to the shop? I thought maybe you and I could go over the plan before we get started and let Rusty climb up there and scout the bilge."

Robert smiled. Poor Rusty.

"I was just thinking about doing that exact thing, Lonnie. You beat me to it. Let me grab my crutches and a jacket and I'll come down"

Robert got ready and slid the pilothouse door open. Rusty was already outside on the stairs, waiting to come aboard.

"Oh, hey Rusty, you guys are up and at it already, huh?"

"You bet, Mr. Dawes. At our age if we don't get things done early they aren't likely to get done at all." He smiled. "Guess I'm the lucky fella that gets to crawl down into the bilge today. Where's the hatch cover?"

"You'll see it just outside the salon door. It's hinged, but there's a bungee hanging from the rail to hook it to. Don't want you to get trapped, Rusty. With the way she's been leaking there might be quite bit of water down there."

"Probably not the worst I seen. Let me hold your crutches while you get over the rail."

When Robert got situated at the top of the rolling stairs, he stopped, "Oh hey Rusty, if it gets too nasty and you need to take a break, there's a full thermos of coffee sitting by the galley sink. There's clean cups underneath."

"Thanks. I may take you up on that."

The shop, as it was referred to at Jackson's Boatyard, was really a metal building with three bays. Each bay had roll-up doors at either end. All the fiberglass work and painting was done inside two of the bays. The third was divided into the wood shop and the machine shop. In a corner of the machine shop was Lonnie's office.

Lonnie smiled as Robert came in. "There you are Mr. Dawes. Hope I didn't wake you too early this morning."

"Not at all," lied Robert, "I had just been thinking about getting up."

"Good. We kinda like to get an early start around here. Say, how's that leg doin' this morning? By the way you're gettin' around it looks a might painful."

"Yeah, I fell and broke two bones in my ankle last week and can't seem to keep from jarring it. I'm taking pain meds but they don't seem to be helping much."

Lonnie shook his head. "Takes time for breaks of that nature to mend. I've busted a bone or two myself. C'mon in and sit down. This shouldn't take long. Can I get you some coffee? I'm about to pour myself another cup."

Robert followed the older man into an office slightly larger than the desk it was built around. Papers and catalogs were piled over nearly the entire surface. A T.V. tray in one corner held a coffee maker and a stack of Styrofoam cups. Robert eased himself onto a steel folding chair just inside the door while Lonnie hummed as he fiddled with the coffee pot.

"Thanks Lonnie, but I've had my limit already this morning."

Robert remembered seeing Lonnie for the first time. They had met at Amy's funeral. He didn't even know who he was as Lonnie approached him at the reception. Lonnie's gray hair had been tamed as well as possible, considering that he wasn't wearing his baseball cap. From the look of discomfort registered on his face he might have been wearing a straitjacket and not the plain black suit that probably left the closet exclusively for weddings and funerals. But Robert sensed his sincerity when Lonnie extended his hand to express his condolences.

"I'm Lonnie Brooks. I knew your father-in-law. I was real sorry to hear about your wife. As a little girl Amy used to come up to the boatyard from time to time with her dad." He paused, "Your mother-in-law never liked me much though."

Lonnie's honesty had brought a smile during a time when tears appeared like uninvited guests.

"She never liked me much either."

Since then Robert had taken *NoraLynn* up to the yard one other time. A couple of months after Amy's funeral the boat had developed a problem with water in the fuel.

Today they discussed plans for repairing the leak. Lonnie was sure that it was a fastening that had come loose, and that it would be a simple fix. He showed Robert samples of new paint formulas and suggested that while she was up in the yard it might be a good time to freshen up the bottom. The zincs were at the point of needing replacement too, so they might as well do it all now since she was out of the water.

Robert agreed. He'd do whatever was necessary. Besides, he didn't care about the cost. All his bills were paid, his needs were minimal and the mortgage was covered by the renter. The hermit's life was neither fun nor romantic, but it was frugal. Anyway, Amy had always insisted they have life insurance. So now he had $500,000 sitting in certificates of deposit that couldn't have mattered less to him. He would trade every dollar for just a few more days with her. That option, however, was never offered.

"Okay, Lonnie, sounds good. You guys do what you think she needs." Robert stood up, supporting himself with one crutch. "I'm going to start a little project of my own up in the forward compartment."

"Oh? What do you have in mind?"

"I've decided what I really need is more stowage for my personal stuff. Right now I'm basically living out of a duffel bag so I bought an old bureau and salvaged the drawers. I was thinking I would tear out the lower bunk on the port side and frame up a chest of drawers in the space."

"Well sure, that could be done easily enough." He thought for a moment. "You know, I bet we've got any material and tools you may be lacking. When you want to get started give a holler and Rusty can come up and see what else you might need. Rusty is a master carpenter. And that's a fact." Lonnie grinned. "Yessir, a project is just like medicine. It'll get your mind off that leg of yours."

*****

Robert hurried through the drizzle that had begun again. When he got to the top step and was about to ease himself aboard, he caught sight of Rusty.

Seated at the dinette, a cup of coffee in front of him and a hand pressed against his forehead, Rusty was staring out the aft windows, apparently lost in a daydream. Away to the horizon Puget Sound sprawled like an old photograph; a mixture of grays and darker grays.

"Hey Rusty," he called out. "Suppose I can get you to give me a hand? These stairs have gotten real slick."

Robert didn't really need help but he didn't want to intrude on the old man's thoughts without warning.

Rusty looked up. "Hold steady, Mr. Dawes, I'll be right there." In a moment he was out the pilot house door, offering Robert a hand over the rail.

"Hope I didn't interrupt anything, Rusty. It looked like you were trying to decide if I was serving you Folger's Crystals™ or not."

Rusty smiled. "No, I was just thinking about the old days and boats like this one. You might already know, but this old gal has seen more of Puget Sound and the north coast than most of 'em. There aren't too many like her anymore...just like there aren't too many of us old coots left that used to work them." He sighed. "Guess I'm just gettin' old."

"So, did you find anything sinister down in bilge? You don't look too wet, so I'm assuming the leak must be fairly low. Or had most of the water leaked out?"

"That's exactly what happened. There's a spot where a plank's pulled away just enough to let her start to leak. Should be easy to fix, though." Rusty thought for a moment. "Did Lonnie talk to you about the new bottom paint we're carrying?"

"Yes, he did. We're going to give it a try and I guess put on new zincs, too."

"That ought to put her in pretty fair shape." Rusty motioned toward the open pilot house door. "You'd better get inside, Mr. Dawes. Don't want to add pneumonia to your list of ailments."

Robert hesitated. "Hey, while I got you here for a minute Rusty, let me get your opinion on a little project I'm starting while you guys work on the hull."

Robert hobbled into the pilothouse with Rusty following. He eased himself onto the helm station chair.

"Aaah, that's a little better." He reached into his jacket pocket and grabbed his prescription bottle.

Rusty went into the galley and returned with a glass of water. "Here, you'll probably want this."

"Thanks. I'm not used to dealing with this much pain. Sometimes it just creeps up on me and then suddenly feels like somebody set my boot on fire."

"So I'm assuming your project isn't going to require too much physical effort, right?"

"I don't think so. I want to tear out the lower bunk to port down below and build in a chest of drawers. I need more space for my personal gear." Robert laughed. "You know Lonnie insists that you are really an amazing carpenter."

"I bet he does." He stepped down into the forward compartment. "Are you planning to leave the top bunk then?"

"Yeah. I thought I could just tear out the lower platform and use the vertical supports to frame-up the space. Then I'll build a kind of cabinet base and attach it to the rails. I brought some ready-made drawers with me that ought to work pretty well." Robert stayed seated, waiting for the pain medication to kick in.

"I saw the drawers stacked in the salon. With the drawers ready-made it shouldn't take more than a couple of sheets of plywood. That way you can sand it and give it a nice finished surface to stain. Use the right stain and it should look like it's been there the whole time."

"That's exactly what I was hoping for. Lonnie said you guys probably have some material in the woodshop that I could use."

"Truth is we have lots of material that'll never get used. Most people want marine-grade for their projects. Normally I'd agree, but in this case ACX should work just fine. It's not nearly as expensive, either." He ran a finger over the small oil lamp hanging above the chart table. "After lunch come on down to the shop and we'll pick out what you need. The tear-out will be the messiest part. After I get the guys working on refastening that seam, I'll come up and see if I can give you a hand. Once the obstructions are out of the way, you can make your measurements and we'll get everything cut."

"Sounds good. The only thing I'm not sure I can do is get down on the cabin sole to remove the platform, but if you can help me with that I should be able to do most of the rest of it myself."

"I'm sure you will. Well then, I'd better get the guys after that seam repair so that we can get on with the scraping and sanding. The rain is supposed to clear up tomorrow for a couple of days. It would be nice to take advantage of the dry weather and do all of the hull work outside in the yard."

"Okay." Robert got his crutches under him. "I'll see you later, Rusty. I appreciate the help."

"No problem." Rusty slid the door shut.

Robert eased himself down the steps to the forward

compartment. The pill was starting to work, leaving him lightheaded. He sat down on his bunk and imagined the lower bunk on the opposite side gone with a stained bureau in its place. He would use a medium oak stain. It would match the drawer fronts perfectly and the whole thing would add a "salty" feel to the V-berth area. Right now, however, he needed to lie down and get his foot elevated. He lay back and closed his eyes. He wished Amy could lie down next to him.

*****

When Robert awoke it was early afternoon. For the time being the medication was keeping the pain in his ankle to a mild hum. The few hours of rest had refreshed not only his body but his mind, too. He felt like himself again, even though he had slept through lunch. He went to the galley and made a peanut-butter and banana sandwich, topping it with a drizzle of wild honey from Feder's Farms of Mt. Vernon.

Feder's Wild Honey was always a favorite of Amy's, almost up until the time of her death. She joked that had she been able to have children, she would have sent Robert up to the Skagit Valley at midnight to buy Feder's Honey instead of ice cream and dill pickles.

Robert knew that although she made light of never having been able to conceive, Amy had really wanted a family. Her parents had been killed by a drunk driver fourteen years earlier, and by then it was evident to both of them that their union was not destined to produce children. He had convinced himself that Amy had made peace with being childless. After her parents died, however, a wistfulness came over her. Maybe it was the realization that Robert was all she had left, or maybe it was that she sensed that she was nearing the final years of her life. She died at forty-five, two weeks after their twenty-third wedding anniversary.

Robert poured a cup of coffee and looked down into the yard. Two men were working on the fastenings. Occasionally the sound of hammering traveled up to where he sat. They were busy doing their own work and had no idea that he sat up in the galley above them pleased to observe these brief moments. Coming here was a good idea. It was obvious the boat needed the attention, but it was also therapeutic for him. Lonnie was right – the only thing that healed broken bones was time. Broken hearts, too.

Noticing that the rain had stopped, Robert put on a jacket and headed for the stairs. He had a project to get started and didn't want to waste another moment.

*****

"Well, there you are, Mr. Dawes. Did you come down to look over some plywood so that you can get started with that project?"

"I did, Lonnie. Is Rusty around? I was hoping he might show me what he would suggest. I had him look at the space earlier."

"He should be right back. He had to run home for a minute. He said he forgot something when he left the house this morning."

"Lonnie, why do you always call me Mr. Dawes? My first name is Robert."

"Dunno. I guess it's the way my daddy brought me up. He always said that in business calling a customer Mr. Smith or Mr. Dawes was a sign of respect. Like you appreciated their business. I don't imagine it's something I'll ever get out of the habit of doing. No offense, you understand."

"No, no, none taken. It's hard to get used to someone older than me addressing me as Mr. Dawes. I guess I should just shut up and accept it as a sign of respect like you said."

"Funny thing, I remember your father-in-law saying almost the exact same words to me. He couldn't understand why I called him Mr. Allen. Wanted me to call him...uh…"

"Walter."

"Walter, that's right. I'm gettin' so I can't remember a blasted thing."

"I wouldn't worry too much Lonnie. You and Rusty still seem to be on top of your game. When I get to be your age I hope to be able to do half as well."

"Careful what you wish for, Mr. Dawes. Rusty and I ought to have both retired a long time ago…that is if either of us had a brain in our heads." He let out a long sigh. "But here we are, still gettin' our heads wet and our b'hinds nearly frozen off, chasing around other folks' boats just like we enjoyed it." He laughed out loud. "Come to think of it, we must, 'cause we never seem to leave. There's Rusty now."

Rusty got out of his truck and came around to where they were standing.

"You two look like you're up to no good." He looked at Robert. "You really ought to watch the company you keep, Mr. Dawes. What's the Bible say? 'Bad company corrupts good character' or something to that effect."

"Rusty, after all these years you surely can't blame your questionable character on me. Isn't that right, Mr. Dawes?"

"Hey guys. I just came down to check out some plywood."

"Okay, Mr. Dawes, let's go take a look at the woodpile and see if we can't find you something useful for your project."

*****

By the time Robert got back aboard *NoraLynn*, the two workers were busy scraping the hull. It was after three o'clock and a fresh westerly breeze had cleared out the clouds, leaving only blue sky. The weatherman had gotten it right this time. Even better was that the clear weather was twelve hours ahead of schedule.

Rusty had said that he would return shortly with a power saw. Once the lower bunk was removed Robert could measure the space and draw a diagram of how to cut the plywood sections. He scuttled into the galley. His ankle was throbbing again, so he washed down a pill with coffee.

Thinking ahead, he got a notebook and pencil and began a diagram of the bureau. He already knew the drawers would fit into the front opening; the question that remained was the spacing. He had in mind how he wanted it to look when it was finished, but would need to check his figures after the bunk was removed.

He was still working on the drawing when Rusty came aboard, carrying a plastic box and a power cord. Robert waved him in.

"Okay, here we go," Rusty said, sliding the pilothouse door shut. He laid the box and cord on the galley table. "I wasn't sure if there was an outlet near enough to the bunks to reach with just the cord on the saw, so I brought one along."

"Good idea," said Robert, "I have one somewhere, but I'd have to find it."

"Well, good then. I'll just plug this in here in the galley and get started. This shouldn't take but a few minutes." He looked at Robert's diagram. "I see you've pretty much got it planned out. As soon as I get the tear-out done you can take your measurements. There may even be enough time this afternoon to get the plywood ripped so that you can draw your cutouts for the drawers." He left Robert at the dinette and headed for the forward compartment.

Not wanting to be in the way, Robert planned to watch from the companionway outside the head. Before he could get moving, Rusty called back, "Any more of that coffee?"

"Absolutely, I'll make a fresh pot. Take about five minutes."

He could already hear the screech of the reciprocating saw when he filled a cup for Rusty. By the time he got down to the foc'sle Rusty was cutting through the last joint holding the bunk in place. The end that had already been cut free sagged toward the cabin sole. Rusty finished cutting and wrenched the platform free.

"Stand clear, there, Mr. Dawes and I'll take this thing right into the salon where we can look it over. I think you're right, this will make a real good top for the chest of drawers."

Pulling it close to his body he squeezed through the companionway and up the steps into the pilothouse. Robert leaned back into the doorway to the head. As Rusty passed, he could see the original canvas straps still stapled in place underneath the plywood platform. Rusty continued into the salon and placed the bunk on the floor with the webbing facing up. He stood up and put both hands on his lower back.

Robert had followed him and stood out of the way back by the dinette.

"Are you okay, Rusty?"

"Oh yeah, you know, things just don't work like they did thirty years ago."

"I've been feeling a lot like that lately." Robert moved closer to get a better look at the webbing. "I guess I'll want to tear all that old canvas out so that it can't interfere with the top drawers, don't you think?"

Rusty knelt down next to the bunk. "I imagine it'll come right out. This stuff must be seventy years old. It's probably nearly rotted through."

He reached down and grabbed hold of the canvas strips at the edge closest to him. The cloth easily tore away from the side rail. Moving over to the next strap, he repeated the motion. He had torn away several pieces when something appeared from between overlapping strips of cloth. From where Robert was standing he could see it tucked into the center of the weaving. When the material separated, the exposed edge of an envelope became visible.

"Hold on, Rusty. There's something sticking out from between the straps in the middle. It looks like an envelope. See if you can grab it from where you are."

Rusty leaned over and lifted the straps at the center. As they separated, Robert could now clearly see an envelope tucked out of sight in the pocket formed by the intersection of two straps. "Right there!"

Rusty moved to the side to see what Robert was pointing to. "I see it." He picked it up and turned it over. There was no return address, just the name of its intended recipient.

"I can't make it out without my glasses, Mr. Dawes. You'd better have a look."

Robert tilted the envelope to better capture the light slanting in through the salon windows. His breath caught in his throat and he felt flushed. Releasing the crutch from under his right arm, he let it fall back against the bulkhead and slumped into the dinette.

"Are you all right, Mr. Dawes?" Rusty got to his feet, "What's it say?"

"It's addressed to Miss Amy Allen," he whispered. "Amy Allen was my wife's maiden name. This is weird. I mean, this envelope is so old. I don't know, it's just weird."

He couldn't tear his eyes away from the name on the envelope. And as much as he wanted to, he couldn't stop tears from welling up either.

"What's the address?"

Robert read aloud:

> *Miss Amy Allen*
> *Post Box 524*
> *Olympia, Wash.*

It was obviously some other Amy Allen. His Amy had grown up in Bellingham. Her parents had bought the house where she grew up before she was born. After they married, Robert and Amy bought an old farmhouse on Whidbey Island with a down payment his grandfather gave them as a wedding gift. Besides those two houses, she had never lived anywhere else.

It was simple as he thought about it. Amy Allen was probably a very common name. Clearly, this letter was written years ago. There was no postmark and it was still sealed. Evidently being wedged between the layers of canvas had protected it from the years of marine air. It looked as if it had been pressed between the pages of a book.

Robert felt his face burn. He brushed away hot tears and smiled.

"Whoa, sorry, I guess I kinda got ahead of myself there. You must think I've lost my mind, reacting like that to something as innocent as my wife's name on an old letter."

Rusty shook his head. "The thing that's most obvious to me, Mr. Dawes, is that you loved your wife very much. From what I've seen, I'd say she was a very lucky woman."

Robert stared at the envelope, gently touching the dried ink.

Rusty was quiet for a few minutes. Finally he said, "Hey whatever happened to that coffee you were going to make. I could really use a cup."

"Oh, right, the coffee. Actually, I poured it and it's sitting right there by the coffee maker. I was just headed down to tell you it was ready when you finished cutting the bunk free. Guess I got sidetracked."

Rusty took a sip. He took his cup with him and returned to tearing the canvas webbing away from the bunk rails. Occasionally he looked up to see if Robert's expression had changed. Finally, he posed the question that he'd been wanting to ask since they discovered the letter.

"So Mr. Dawes, are you going to open it?"

Robert thought for a moment. "I don't think so. I mean, well, it was written to someone else, even if it was a long time ago."

"At this point I doubt there's anyone around to care. Probably just personal news from some fisherman. That's how most folks used to communicate – by letters. Guess I'm just the curious sort." He continued to work on the bunk. "Can you see how much the stamp cost? Finding out when it was issued would probably give you an idea about when it was written."

The sun was beginning to sink closer to the western horizon, so the light bending through the salon windows was now reddish and hazy, not bright white like a while ago. Robert reached above the table and switched on the lamp. Turning the envelope at an angle again, he let the light play over the front. Against a purple field a white eagle stood out. Across its chest flowed a white banner emblazoned with a slogan, but he couldn't make out the words. What he could see was the cost of the stamp. "It's the number 3 with the old cents symbol that you hardly ever see anymore," said Robert. "And it's got an eagle with a banner across it's chest, but I can't read what's written on it."

Rusty was thinking. "I don't remember much about the war years, I was just a little guy back then. But it sounds like something that was probably issued during World War II. You know, it's possible that the postmaster here on the island could look that stamp up for you. I don't know what difference it would make, but it would be interesting to get an idea of how long that envelope has been tucked away."

Robert had regained his composure. What Rusty said made sense. It would be interesting to at least find out approximately when the letter was written. If she wasn't living, maybe Miss Amy Allen had grandchildren or someone to whom a letter like this might mean something.

By now Rusty had finished tearing all the webbing away from the side rails. He wadded it up into a ball.

"Trash?" he asked, looking around the galley.

"Just lay it there for now," said Robert. "I've got some other stuff I need to get down to your trash container."

"Okay, I guess that's about all the damage I can do right at the moment. If you want to finish measuring and then come on down to the wood shop, I think there's still time to rip the plywood."

"I appreciate the help, Rusty. The truth is I'm kinda out of the mood right now. I think I'll heat up some soup and make a sandwich and call it a day. I'll get up early tomorrow and get right on this thing. Okay?"

"Sure thing. That's fine with me." Rusty unplugged the power cord and headed back toward the forward compartment. "I'll just gather up my tools and be on my way."

As he wound up the cord he called back to Robert, "There's a bit of a mess down here. Think you can get it cleaned up or do you want me to bring the shop-vac up?"

"I'll get it swept up after I eat something. Don't worry about it."

Robert made sure Rusty got all his gear and thanked him again. It was good to be alone. He put a can of soup on the stove to warm and looked at the envelope again. It seemed so strange to read Amy's maiden name after trying to accustom himself to life without her. He wondered what Amy would be thinking if the roles were reversed. What if *he* had died? What if she had discovered an envelope, a really old envelope, with the name Mr. Robert Dawes at PO Box 524 in Olympia, Wash written on it? *What would Amy do*? Robert smiled to himself. He had a pretty good idea. She would immediately think it was a sign from God. She would assign some spiritual significance to the fact that the name was the same as her deceased husband. She would likely ask God to reveal to her the next step she should take. And she would push Him one step further, too. Revelation of the next move wasn't good enough for Amy. She would ask Him to show her "in a way that I understand can only be from You." Crazy, that was one of the things he missed most about her. She was a believer. Even though he had sometimes mocked her faith, Amy's assurance that life wasn't merely random chance had somehow been a source of comfort to him. Even when she lay dying, she was sure that though she was beyond the help of modern medicine, she could still be healed. If not, the pity belonged with those who must remain behind. She was going to be transported to a place of eternal joy where "He has wiped away every tear."

A line from a poem he had read came to mind: "I hope she finds an emerald garden where the honeysuckle perfumes the dewdrops."

"I hope you've found it, baby," he said aloud. "Show me what I should do now." He added "In a way that I understand can only be from you."

CHAPTER SEVEN

Robert unwrapped the plastic bag from around his cast and hobbled out of the shower. He would shave tomorrow – probably. Nobody expected a vagabond to be clean-shaven anyway. Right now he had more important things to do. He was anxious to get down to the woodshop so that Rusty could help him finish the bureau. He also needed a ride to the island post office to see if the postmaster could help him trace the stamp's year of issue.

It was strange to feel excited and optimistic. Although he hadn't received any confirmation from beyond as to what he should do next, there was an excitement building in him. Maybe he had already been given the answer in the discovery of the envelope itself. That had occurred to him in the early morning hours as he lay in his bunk. He reasoned that if he hadn't broken his ankle and then discovered the leak in *NoraLynn's* hull, he would have had no reason to come to the boatyard. If he hadn't planned to use his down time to tear out the bunk and replace it with the bureau, he might never have discovered the envelope. So those events by themselves could be sufficient evidence to believe that there may be some special reason for discovering the letter. There was one other thing: His brother, Mark, lived in Olympia. Robert had been feeling guilty about never returning his brother's phone calls, not even at Christmas. So if it turned out that the letter was just "personal news from some fisherman" as Rusty had suggested, it may at least provide the motivation he needed to get down to Olympia and reconnect with Mark and his family. So maybe Providence was involved after all.

Morning broke out in a shade of blue usually reserved for August, although a brisk westerly kept the temperature chilly. Robert noticed that Puget Sound was dotted with whitecaps. All it took was a really windy day to make one appreciate the unwavering character of solid ground.

Rusty stood in the doorway, watching him approach. "Morning, Mr. Dawes," he called out over the wind. "Well, you were true to your word; here you are bright and early. Did your day finish any better than it started?"

"You know, it really did. Once I ate something and thought things over a little more, I got sort of excited about finding the letter. You're probably right, it may just be the mundane stuff that a fisherman would write to his mother, but it's exciting because it's been lying there for who knows how long?" He fumbled for the drawing in his jacket pocket. "Which brings up another point, Rusty. Do you suppose sometime today you could give me a ride to the post office to see if we can figure out the year the stamp was issued?"

"Absolutely. Why don't we get goin' on your project first, and then along around lunchtime we'll run into town and see what we can find out."

"Great! I'll tell you what, let's see if Lonnie wants to join us, and I'll buy you both lunch. I could use some real food after my sorry attempts at cooking."

"One thing I can guarantee, Mr. Dawes, is that Lonnie Brooks never turns down a free meal."

"Excellent, then let's get going on this. I'm looking forward to getting this thing built."

*****

It was around mid-morning when they finished cutting and staining the sides and back of the bureau. Rusty had convinced Robert that it would be much easier to pick out the shade he wanted and get the major surfaces stained before putting it all together.

He had the men who were scraping *NoraLynn's* hull stop for a few minutes to carry the bureau pieces up and stand them in the forward compartment. Rusty made sure Robert had everything he needed and then went back to work. While Robert waited for the stain to dry, he considered how he might go about calling his brother Mark.

Robert was twelve years older than Mark, so their relationship had never been really close. Robert was out of college and married by the time Mark got to high school.

So what would he say? Could he just call him and say that he had discovered an old letter stuck away on his boat and thought he might come to Olympia to try and deliver it? Oh by the way, sorry that I've been so reclusive. Sorry I haven't returned even one of your calls and then had the phone disconnected. Sorry that I've acted like you and your wife and three kids don't exist. It's just that … It sounded like insincere nonsense. Come to think of it Robert wasn't even sure if he had ever mentioned the boat, much less the small detail that it was now home.

Mark and Laura had only been married for six years, but in that time the stork had visited three times. He was a driver for a large express mail service, so he made a decent wage and had good benefits, but there was nothing left over. What that added up to in a practical sense was that their two bedroom house needed an addition that they were always planning to build, but living too close to the edge to pay for. So, Mark and Laura had a bedroom and all three of the girls shared the other bedroom.

Robert went to the galley drawer where he kept his cell phone. He turned it on and discovered that there was no signal. So much for calling Mark. He thought about going down to Lonnie's office to ask if he could use the phone. No, he'd wait until they all went to lunch and look for a pay phone. He didn't want Lonnie to overhear him stammering out an apology.

*****

Around noon Rusty came by. "Mr. Dawes, are you ready to go?"

"Right with you, Rusty. I'm starving. How about we go to lunch first and then swing by the post office?"

"Fine with me. Lonnie is gonna drive his own truck so that he can get back to the yard as soon as we eat. You and I can go in mine. We'll run by the post office afterward and by the time we get back that stain should be dry enough for you to start putting things together."

"Sounds great. I really appreciate all the help you two are giving me." Rusty stood on the stairs and held Robert's crutches as he eased over the railing.

"You know I believe your ankle must be feeling a little better," said Rusty. "You seem to be getting around better than before."

"Yeah, I don't know. Maybe it's starting to heal or maybe I've been so caught up in this whole thing with the letter that I haven't thought about it much today. Maybe the distraction is better than the medicine."

*****

Jackson's Boatyard sits at the north end of Noble Island. One mile to the south is the village of Barton. Jacob Barton pioneered Noble Island in 1858, at first clearing land for apple trees. When he realized that the plentiful rainfall came from a nearly continual overcast, he gave up the orchard business and started selling oysters. But Noble Island also became a stopping point for the salmon fleet of years past. On the island boats could re-provision and get emergency repairs done. Those days had long since ended by the time Lonnie bought Jackson's Boatyard. Now a mere four hundred residents called the island home year-round. A couple hundred more came for the summer boating and camping season; but in January Noble Island looked almost as desolate as when Jacob Barton first came ashore. To get there you could come by private boat or take the morning and evening ferry. If you missed the evening run, it might mean a chilly night in your car.

Rusty pulled up in front of Andy's Diner. Andy's was a steep roofed, clapboard building that looked like it dated back to the time of Jacob Barton. Originally built as a hardware store in the twenties, it had been home to such enterprises as the island grocery, and for a short time during the forties it served as the public school. For the past ten years, it had been the food establishment of Mr. Andy Conner. Andy was the owner, cook, waiter, dishwasher and janitor. Although the service was slow, and the sanitary conditions questionable, Andy knew how to cook. There was always a bottomless coffee pot standing by, too. Self-service, of course.

Lonnie was already seated at one of three back-to-back booths along the front window. Beyond them two tables occupied the center section of the diner and near the kitchen was a counter with four stools.

As Robert and Rusty came in an old-timer at the counter turned around to see what was happening.

"Say, young fella', if you been hangin' around old Rusty there and have only got a busted foot to show for it, you haven't fared too bad." He grinned through gray whiskers and missing teeth.

"That's what I hear. I guess Rusty's just taking it easy on me 'cause he knows I'm new."

"Now Rufus, don't go scarin' the man. He's still got his boat up on stands up at the yard. I don't want him thinkin' it's gonna get worse than it already has." Lonnie smiled. "Old Rufus has been around here longer than any of us. They say his folks came to the island before the turn of the century. His papa was a friend of Old Man Barton. He knows everybody and everybody knows him."

"He seems good-natured enough," said Robert.

"Say, what's this Rusty tells me about a letter you found tucked in some dusty old bunk straps on your boat?"

"Weird, isn't it, after all the years and places that boat has been, that nobody ever found it?"

Lonnie looked out the window at the trees across the street. The wind whipped the branches of a giant fir tree as if it was a six-foot Christmas tree being shaken by a ten-year-old anxious for the holiday to arrive.

"Well, you know, that was a work boat for years and years. That's what the men did mostly – work. I doubt there was a lot of time spent writing letters and such. When you weren't out on deck workin' or in the galley cookin' you were probably in your bunk tryin' to get some shuteye. Did you bring it with you?"

Robert pulled out the letter while Lonnie put on his reading glasses.

"Hmmm. It says three cents. I'm almost sure it's from one of the war years. Must have seemed pretty strange seeing your wife's maiden name written on a letter going back that many years," Lonnie looked up.

"Yes, it was. It took me a minute or two to realize that Amy Allen is probably a fairly common name and that this is just a bizarre coincidence. Poor Rusty, I think he was afraid I was having a meltdown."

"Naw, nothin' like that." Rusty said, pretending he was reading one of Andy's homemade menus.

"Are you going to open it, Mr. Dawes?" asked Lonnie.

"I don't think so. At least not right away. I'm considering going down to Olympia to try and find Miss Amy Allen. If she's no longer living, then maybe there's some family member who might like to have it; kind of a window on what was happening in her life back then. I guess if I run into a dead end in Olympia and there's just no way to contact the Allen family, I might open it – just out of curiosity."

Lonnie was thinking. He looked back at the fir tree across the street. "Mr. Dawes, I might have a proposition for you. That is if you're genuinely thinking about going down to Olympia."

Rusty looked up from the menu.

"What kind of proposition?"

"Well, I've got a small diesel engine sitting in the machine shop that's just been rebuilt and is all set to be reinstalled. We pulled it out last fall from a Catalina 30 that belongs to a fella from over in Friday Harbor. Seems though, that he got transferred down to Olympia shortly after we yarded out the motor. He's a live-aboard like you so he rigged an outboard on a kicker bracket and motored it down there. My problem is that the Catalina is sitting in a marina a hundred miles away and the motor is stuck on this little chunk of real estate way up here."

"So you want me to deliver the motor to Olympia?"

"That's what I'm thinkin'. It would be easy to sling it up onto the afterdeck of your boat and lash it down so it couldn't move. It's already fastened to a pallet, so it'd be real secure. Then when you get to Olympia, all you have to do is tie up to South Sound Boatworks dock and they'll hoist it off. The Catalina owner's all set up with them to do the install, so that's it. Your job would be done."

"You know, I wasn't one-hundred percent sure that I was going to pursue this thing with the letter. I mean it's probably a long-shot that anybody is still in the area who even knew Amy Allen. But... and this may sound weird to both of you, I've been waiting for some sort of sign, like a confirmation, that I should take the time and trouble to go down there. I think you just gave it to me Lonnie."

"I don't think that's weird at all," said Lonnie. "I believe there are answers to questions way beyond our simple ability to understand. Sometimes we just have to trust that there's a reason for the way of things. Besides, I know for sure that this would be a real help to me."

He looked at Rusty who stared out the window.

Lonnie added, "By the way, I wouldn't expect you to do this for free either. I don't have the exact figures, but I'm pretty sure your yard bill for the refastening, scrape and paint, and any extras, will come to around four thousand dollars, maybe just a hair more. What I'll do is knock five-hundred dollars off your total bill when it's all been tallied as payment for delivering the motor. It's worth it to me not to have to crate it up and try to get a trucker to take the ferry out here to pick it up."

"Don't forget the plywood and shop time for the chest I'm

building."

"Tell you what...we'll just throw that in. What do you say? Do we have a deal?"

Robert extended his hand to where Lonnie met him halfway with a firm handshake. "I'm starving. I'm always especially hungry when someone else is picking up the check."

"Better hold on to your wallet, Mr. Dawes," said Rusty, "this may get costlier than you originally thought."

"Bring it on!"

Lonnie signaled toward the kitchen, "Okay Andy, I think we're ready to order when you get a minute. Got a mainlander here can't wait to spend his money at your establishment."

*****

"Wow, I'm really surprised. Andy makes a great burger and fries. From the looks of the place, I was afraid even my cooking may have been better. I might have to come back here again before I take off."

Rusty nodded. "I know. Andy's is the best kept secret in the Pacific Northwest. Probably a good thing. If all those Seattle people found out, we might have their traffic problems up here."

They drove the short distance to the village post office. Robert had said that he could make it on his crutches, but Rusty insisted. When they pulled into the parking lot Robert noticed a payphone outside. After they were finished with the postmaster, he would ask Rusty to wait while he phoned Mark.

The Noble Island Post Office couldn't have been more than ten or fifteen years old. It was a one story frame building, with cedar siding and a green metal roof. Inside it smelled of paint and copier paper. An L-shaped area housing the mailboxes was set back from the front door. To the right was another set of doors which could be locked so that patrons could still retrieve their mail even after the office was closed. In the area beyond those doors was a counter with two work stations and an antique door, probably salvaged from an earlier version of the United States Post Office, Noble Island, WA 98909. On the window was painted: POSTMASTER.

Rusty knew exactly where he was headed because he didn't even glance toward the woman standing behind the counter. Robert offered a diffident smile as he passed. By the time Robert caught up with him, Rusty was rapping on the glass. A slight, bald man looked up and motioned Rusty in. Robert followed close behind.

"Wayne," Rusty began, "this here is Mr. Dawes. He's a customer of ours out at the yard. We were workin' on his old trawler the other day, and darned if we didn't run across a letter stuck under a bunk. Anyway he's wonderin' if maybe you can help figure out what year the stamp might have been issued."

"How do you do, Mr. Dawes?" The Postmaster stood, offering his hand. "I'm Wayne Porter."

Robert couldn't immediately tell if this man and Rusty were friends. Maybe it was the way Rusty had barged in and started talking. Mr. Porter appeared to be more refined than Rusty, so Robert was trying his best to be a model of good breeding.

"It's very kind of you to let us interrupt your afternoon like this, Mr. Porter. I'm sure you're very busy. If it wasn't for the fact that I have to leave soon, we wouldn't have dropped in without making an appointment."

"I appreciate your consideration, Mr. Dawes, but I can spare a few minutes. I'm always interested in solving mysteries involving stamps. Philatelics is a hobby of mine as well as an avocation."

Robert glanced at Rusty in time to see him roll his eyes.

"Now then, you say you found a letter. May I see it please?"

Robert handed the envelope to the Postmaster. As he sat back down behind his desk, Wayne Porter said, "Please gentlemen, have a seat." He opened a desk drawer and pulled out an eye loupe. After examining the stamp he whispered "Win the War."

"I'm sorry, I didn't catch what you said," said Robert.

"Oh, I was just reading the slogan written on the banner across the eagle's chest. It says 'Win the War.'

"So I was right, it came out during World War II." Rusty sat back in his chair, obviously pleased with himself.

"Actually, this stamp came out in late 1942 and was used in great quantity all through '43 and into '44. So, to answer your question, Mr. Dawes, this letter was written as early as 1942 and potentially as late as 1944 or later, assuming someone may have hung onto the stamps. That, however, is improbable since correspondence by letter was something that almost everyone practiced." Now it was Mr. Porter who sat back in his chair, looking very pleased with himself.

Robert was about to get to his feet and thank the Postmaster for his help when Mr. Porter continued. "Mr. Dawes, I should remind you that this letter is the personal property of..." he glanced down at the envelope, "...of Miss Amy Allen of Olympia. I hope it isn't your intention to open it."

"No sir, just the opposite. I realize now that we're talking about a letter that's more than sixty years old. I doubt that the building that housed post office box 524 during World War II is still even there. What I plan to do is to go down to Olympia and find Miss Allen if she's still alive. If not, I'll try and find her next of kin. I feel strongly about doing this – for personal reasons. So to answer *your* question, I plan to try and get that letter into the hands of its rightful owner or her nearest relative."

Wayne Porter didn't say anything immediately. He looked past Robert, as though he could see the words projected into the air. Finally he said, "I think that's a fine idea. I wish you all the best in your search."

He stood up and shook Robert's hand. "Good luck, Mr. Dawes."

Rusty was out of his chair and opening the door before Robert could get turned around. Robert acknowledged Mr. Porter's kindness once more and hurried to catch up with Rusty. When he got outside, Rusty already had the truck started. Robert decided to wait on the phone call to Mark. Besides, this was a good excuse to put it off.

Back inside the truck he glanced over at Rusty. It was clear that he was upset. In his mind Robert quickly reviewed the visit to the Postmaster's office. He was pretty sure it wasn't anything he had done.

"So Rusty, I'm getting the feeling that you and Mr. Porter aren't exactly friends. Am I wrong?"

"That's one way of putting it. The guy's a pompous jerk. He always has been."

"Okay, I get it. You guys have some history between you then. Wow, I'm sorry. I didn't mean to put you in an uncomfortable situation."

"Since we were kids growing up in Seattle, I've never liked the guy. He's a few years younger than me, but even as kids he thought he was smarter than everybody else. *'Philatelics is a hobby as well as an avocation,'*" Rusty mocked Mr. Porter's voice. "I used to hang around with his older sister. He was always a pesty little whiner. Hasn't changed much either."

"You both grew up in Seattle and both ended up on this tiny speck of land in the North Sound. Man, talk about coincidence. This little old letter with my wife's name on it is nothing compared to you two ending up all the way up here."

He looked over at Rusty again. It was clear that he wasn't interested in a comparison of the statistical probabilities involving himself and Wayne Porter vs. Robert finding an envelope with the name Amy Allen on it. He shut up. They rode in silence the rest of the way back to the boatyard.

When they pulled up in front of the shop, Lonnie came out to greet them. "Any luck at the post office?"

Rusty didn't answer; he just hurried past Lonnie into the shop. Lonnie raised an eyebrow and turned back to Robert.

"Let me guess," he smiled, "I bet he had a run in with Mr. Wayne Porter. Am I right?"

"I wouldn't call it a run-in, but Rusty has a special dislike for Mr. Porter. He said it goes back to when they were kids. Seems like a long time to dislike somebody though."

"Did he tell you how he knew Porter all these years?"

"Yeah, he said they grew up together in Seattle and that he and

Mr. Porter's older sister had been friends."

Lonnie pushed the cap back on his head. "That's true. What Rusty didn't mention is that Wayne Porter's sister was his wife *after* they grew up." Lonnie was smiling, but it wasn't an amused smile, it was the nervous kind your mouth makes when you've said too much. "She died. I guess after that Rusty and Wayne Porter never saw eye-to-eye."

Robert didn't know what to say. He hadn't intended to pry and was surprised at Lonnie's willingness to divulge such personal information. The fact that Rusty had been married was no big deal; nor even that he was feuding with a former brother-in-law. It was that Rusty's wife had died, maybe even been lost to cancer like Amy, that deepened the niche in Robert's heart for the old man.

"By the way, the fellas are going to finish painting tomorrow by the end of the day, so the next morning we should be able to have that motor ready to hoist on and secure. I imagine we can get you back in the water and on your way by the next morning, although I'd like to see you give that paint at least forty-eight hours to cure before you get it wet."

"Okay, great," said Robert. "I just need to finish up the bureau and get my gear stowed before I leave. I've got a doctor appointment in Oak Harbor at the end of the week, so that'll give me plenty of time to get back for that."

Lonnie turned to go back into the shop. He hesitated a moment and then looked back at Robert. "Mr. Dawes, don't pay no attention to what I said. It's really nobody's business but Rusty's. Sometimes I just talk too much." Repositioning his baseball cap, he went inside.

*****

Back on board *NoraLynn*, Robert sat down at the dinette and pulled out the letter. The stain had dried on the plywood and he knew he should get busy down below, but he felt compelled to look at the letter again. He ran his fingers over the stamp and dried ink trying to imagine the hand that had sealed and addressed it so many years ago. How could that person have guessed in such a turbulent time in history what the future might hold? At that point the news from Europe and the South Pacific must have seemed frightening – menacing was probably a better description. He could concede that Rusty was probably right about it being just personal stuff from some fisherman and yet Robert couldn't explain his fascination with it; and the excitement that rose in him at the thought of laying it in the hands of Miss Amy Allen. He knew he might be setting himself up for disappointment. Realistically, it was improbable that she was still alive, and even less likely that she would still call herself Miss Amy Allen. Somehow that didn't matter just now. For the first time since his Amy had died, Robert felt that he had a reason to get up and get on with things, to move on with his life. And if this really was a sign from Amy, he'd do his best not to disappoint her.

*****

Robert finished putting the last screws in the front side of the bureau. He still had to set the top on and fasten it down, but decided first to bring the drawers down so that he could make sure they all fit correctly. It would be a shame to get the whole thing put together and find that there was a glitch that required disassembly.

First things first. He hobbled out to the galley and refilled his coffee cup. He drank the coffee then picked up a drawer and made his way back to the V-berth taking tiny steps while trying to hold on to the drawer and his crutches at the same time. When he got down the steps from the pilothouse he decided to try the same drawer in all six openings rather than make the punishing trip six times. Satisfied that all the drawers would fit, he pondered how he might bring the plywood top down from the salon. Just carrying one drawer up the steps to the pilothouse and down to the forward compartment had been difficult, so trying to wrestle a six-foot piece of plywood into the area was impossible. This would require assistance.

Robert slid open the starboard pilothouse door and stepped outside. The sun still shone brightly from low on the horizon but because the wind hadn't let up the air was chilly. He looked around for someone to ask for help. What he needed wouldn't take long, and didn't require superhuman strength, just a degree of mobility superior to his own. He looked over toward the shop and saw Rusty heading toward where two other men were setting boat stands under a sailboat that Lonnie had just hauled up on the travel-lift.

Robert hesitated. He didn't want to bother anyone, especially when they were getting a big boat up on stands. He watched until the routine had spun out like a choreographed stage performance. After the straps were cast off and the travel-lift repositioned at the end of the dock, Robert called to Rusty from the deck of *NoraLynn*.

"Hey, Rusty, sorry to bug you again, but do you think you could come up and give me a hand with the top when you get a minute. Doesn't have to be right now. Just whenever you get a minute before you leave."

"Sure. Not a problem. Let me get the guys straight on what we need to get started on this old ketch first thing in the morning and then I'll be right up."

Robert went back to work transporting the drawers. He was on the fourth trip back from the salon when his crutch caught on the step down from the pilothouse. Trying to regain his balance instead of letting the drawer fall to the cabin sole, he put his weight on his broken ankle. A lightning bolt seared through his leg. For a moment his heart seemed to shudder in his chest, leaving him breathless and dizzy. Desperate to keep from fainting and falling headlong into the forward compartment, he let the drawer slip from his hand and grabbed the bulkhead. He eased himself down onto the lower step with his legs crumpled beneath him. He needed a pain pill right away, but moving was out of the question. Rusty had said he would be along soon. That was good enough.

He wasn't sure how long he sat there; time didn't register as he sat huddled on the step. The pain bellowing from his ankle had all his attention. When Rusty slid the pilothouse door open the chill wind brushed across his face cooling the beads of perspiration. It felt good.

"Leave it open for a few minutes, Rusty," he called out. "I took a little tumble down here and that air feels good."

"Ah geez, Mr. Dawes, you didn't go and re-injure your ankle, did ya?" Rusty crouched down next him. "Do you want to lie down or go sit in the salon? What can I do to help?"

"I think I should probably get over to my bunk. Maybe you could help me to my feet and then bring me my pain pills. They're next to the galley sink."

"You bet." Rusty helped Robert to his feet.

"I guess I got a little overconfident about how much I could do on my own. I was carrying those drawers out from the salon and caught the tip of my crutch on the step. Like an idiot I tried to catch my balance instead of letting go of the drawer. I actually think I saw stars when I put my full weight on my ankle. Anyway, I guess that was a not-so-subtle reminder to let things heal before I get too rambunctious."

Rusty helped him into the forward compartment and got him seated on the edge of his bunk.

"I'll grab that pain killer and a glass of water and be right back."

In a moment Rusty was back with the pills and a glass of water. Robert said, "Thanks, I don't know if you noticed, but that coffee in the galley is fresh. Help yourself if you want some."

"Truth is I'm about coffeed-out. Used to be by this time of day I'd have started some pretty serious drinking."

"But not anymore?"

"Nope. I gave it up completely some years back. I'm not proud of some of the things I've done while I was too smashed to think straight."

Rusty looked over where Robert had been working. He picked up one of the drawers and slid it into place. "I haven't gotten drunk since the night my wife died." He didn't look back at Robert. "That fella at the post office, Wayne Porter? Well my wife, Marie, was his older sister. We don't get along so well, as you noticed, and the man *is* a pain in the backside, but the main reason for our differences is that he blames me for Marie's death." Rusty picked up all of the drawers that Robert had managed to bring down from the salon, fitting them into the openings in the front panel of the bureau. Each time he slid one in he would crouch down and feel the way it moved, gauging through his fingertips how precise the fit was. Almost as an afterthought, Rusty added, "And I guess maybe he's right."

Robert didn't answer. He wasn't sure why Rusty suddenly

seemed so willing to talk about personal demons. He was sure he had some point in bringing up the incident of his wife's death, but at the moment he didn't know exactly what it was.

"How long has she been gone?"

Rusty stood up from where he had been kneeling. He turned and said, "She died eleven years ago last Wednesday. It was on our thirty-fourth wedding anniversary."

"You mean she died on your anniversary?" Amy's death had been a shock even after knowing the certainty of the diagnosis, but to lose your wife on your wedding anniversary, that was too much.

"To say that she 'died' sort of makes it sound alright, you know, like with your wife bein' sick and all. Marie didn't die, she was killed." Rusty turned and went up the steps to the pilothouse. "I believe I will have some of that coffee, Mr. Dawes. Do you want some?"

"No thanks, Rusty, you go ahead. I'm just starting to feel like myself again. Either the pain pill is working or my ankle really is beginning to heal."

Rusty returned carrying a mug of coffee. "You know, while I'm up here I might as well get the top on and screwed down for you. I'd hate to see you hurt yourself again trying to get that thing into position." He set his cup down and went back to get the plywood top for the bureau.

When Rusty came back carrying the plywood sheet, he had taken off his jacket and was now wearing a T-shirt tucked neatly into his jeans. Robert slid down toward the end of his bunk when he came in with the panel. He lifted both legs up onto the bed, positioning himself so that he could face Rusty and still remain out of the way. As he watched the older man pick up the plywood and position it, he was again amazed at Rusty's physique. A short-sleeved t-shirt revealed freckled arms bursting with muscle. In contrast, standing out against the milky complexion of his upper arm, was the blue tint of a tattoo. It was a drawing of an anchor with a fouled line wrapped around it. Arched over the top were three letters in fancy script: GUS.

"So Rusty, is Gus your real name?" He wanted to steer the conversation back around to the death of Rusty's wife but didn't want to appear to pry.

Rusty looked up from what he was doing and then glanced at his bare arm. "Oh, you saw that. Yeah, that's my name but I never cared for it much."

"Have you been called Rusty from the time you were a kid?"

"No, I picked that up while I was in the service. I was helmsman on a destroyer and the captain started calling me Rusty. He said it fit me. I been calling myself Rusty ever since."

"Everybody used to call me Robby. Once I got to college though, I felt like I should be Robert. That's what I've been ever since – except to you and Lonnie. I guess I'm stuck with Mr. Dawes around here."

"Ah, I do that 'cause Lonnie always does. Don't really matter what we call each other does it? I guess it's how we treat one another that speaks the loudest."

Rusty was right about that. There was a melancholy tone in his voice. For a moment Robert felt self-conscious again about how he had reacted to the letter when he first saw Amy's name. He was sure he must have acted like the poor victim, once again reminded of the crime. Whatever the story behind Rusty's wife's death was, it seemed certain to involve circumstances far more bitter than

Robert's experience.

Rusty eyed the plywood top after it was set in place. It appeared that something wasn't satisfactory. He stepped back and looked from the front; and then from either end viewing down the front edge. He stepped back again to get a different angle.

"Something doesn't look right here. I don't know if we didn't get those sides cut just right, or if the top is a little warped or what. The whole top just looks a little out of whack. Like it's high on one side."

He stepped back to the front of the bureau and slammed a fist down at each corner. Bending his knees he checked every angle at eye-level. He repeated the hammering again, and stepped back again to see if it had made a difference. He still looked puzzled.

"What seems to be the problem?"

"Well it looks to me like the right side is slightly higher than the left. I'm sure we cut all the material exactly. I'm wondering if maybe the cabin sole hasn't sunk just a little on this side." He pointed down to the floorboards at the left side of the bureau.

He crouched down again and ran his fingers over the floorboards. "You don't happen to have a tape measure handy, do you?"

"Sure. Look just behind you there, across from the head, in the top drawer beneath the hanging locker."

Rusty got the tape and began to measure. Starting at the left front corner he went around the entire bureau enclosure, measuring up from the floorboards to the plywood top. Each time he called out the measurement and Robert repeated it back to him.

"Well that's the problem," he said. "The floor is almost an inch lower aft than it is forward. And it's even lower at the front side than in the back. That's really not surprising considering the age of this old girl." He stepped back and looked it over again. "If you want I can unfasten the sides and then shim the low area before I refasten it. That way the top would be level and everything would slide like it should."

"I don't know, Rusty. That sounds like a lot of extra work for such a small correction. Do you think it's really necessary?"

"Well, right now all the drawers seem to slide okay, but once you get her out on the water again and she starts to roll and flex, you might find that an inch or so is enough to make the drawers bind."

"You know what? It's okay. I think I can correct that myself. I'll have to wait till my ankle settles down a little, but I'm pretty sure I can fix it."

"I don't want to tell you your business, Mr. Dawes, but if it was mine, I stop right now and square it up as best you can. She's up on the hard, not rockin' around like when she's in the water. If you do it now, you won't have to do it later when it won't be so easy." Rusty looked at him with a fatherly smile. "Tell you what, I'll get started taking it apart and we'll just see how it goes. I don't have anywhere I have to be, so doing something productive here is at least as good as doing nothing at home."

"Are you sure I'm not taking you away from something else?"

"Positive," said Rusty as he got busy disassembling the bureau. "I might need another cup of that coffee, though. I really don't need another cup, but after so many years of hard drinking it's the actual drinking that I miss about as much as the booze itself. Lord knows I don't miss the hangovers."

Robert swung his legs over the edge of the bunk and struggled to his feet. The pill had taken the edge off the pain and he felt like he could get around again.

"Let me get by you, Rusty, and I'll go make some more. I was thinking I might throw together some scrambled eggs and canned ham for dinner. I've got some great dill-rye bread that I picked up before I came out to the island. It makes excellent toast. Are you interested?"

"Heck yes! 'Breakfast for dinner' – that's what Marie used to call it. She'd surprise me with bacon and eggs and fried potatoes now and then. She always said it was because she couldn't think of anything else. Really, I think she knew that I liked it."

"Okay then, I'll get up there and get started. I'll give you a holler when it's ready."

*****

"I think you'll find that shimming up the aft end of your bureau to compensate for the sagging floor was a good decision." Rusty pushed his plate forward and finished his coffee. "I also think you weren't exactly telling the truth when you said your cooking was so bad you needed to get out for a proper meal. Why, that was as good as any 'breakfast for dinner' that Marie used to make."

"Rusty," Robert was measuring his words, "I don't mean to pry, but you've said a couple things that confuse me."

Rusty didn't reply. He looked at Robert with clear blue eyes. It was a look that let him know that he wasn't entering a forbidden zone.

"You said that your wife didn't die, but that she was killed. *And* you said Mr. Porter holds you responsible for her death and that maybe he was right. If it's not too personal, what happened?"

Rusty looked away, his gaze absorbing the mixture of hue and texture that painted the landscape beyond the galley windows. Outside the remaining rays of daylight were exhaling their last ragged gasps of red and amber away to the south and west. The wind had abated, leaving the giant fir trees drooping lazily in the twilight.

"I told you she died on our wedding anniversary eleven years ago. Well, Marie was one to always do something special for our anniversary. Sometimes we'd take the ferry over to one of the bigger islands so we could have a nice dinner and spend the night in a motel. Ordinarily, though, she would make a real special meal and she'd buy a nice bottle of wine. I'd come home and Nat King Cole would be singing on the stereo and she'd make me dance real slow with her. I guess she had a romantic streak that always swam near the surface around our anniversary."

Rusty had said most of this while still looking out the window. It was as if he was replaying a familiar video in the darkened theater inside his head. He already knew all the dialogue by heart. Finally, he turned to face Robert. "Remember I told you that I was in the habit of starting to drink right about quittin' time? Well, that's what I did the night of my anniversary eleven years ago. A couple of us decided to have a beer or two right after work. That was alright, I guess, no harm done. But then we broke out the vodka and started to get seriously drunk. Now I knew all along what day it was. I knew it was my anniversary. I knew that Marie was cooking a special dinner for the two of us. I knew that she had put on a nice clean dress and done her hair in the afternoon. I knew she was waiting for me to come home and get showered and shaved and change clothes. We were gonna dance to Nat King Cole and eat the special dinner she'd made. We'd toast to another thirty-some years together and then in the end we'd probably go to bed and make love."

"But you were out getting drunk with the fellas from work."

"That's right. I was only thinking about myself and getting drunk."

"What happened?"

"January was real cold and nasty that year. Soon as the sun went down it seemed like the air and everything it touched turned to ice. Along toward eight or so we were still sittin' around drinkin' and tellin' jokes like a bunch of school boys. Marie had expected me home by six-thirty or seven at the latest. I guess she got worried that I had slid off the road on the way home. I'm sure that's what she must have been thinkin' 'cause when she set out from the house it must have been to look for me. Anyway, I got so that I couldn't even read the time on my watch but one of the boys said it was getting toward eight. That's when it hit me that I'd left her sittin' all alone at home on our anniversary. Well, I hightailed it outta' there as fast as I could. The road was real icy, but you know, it seems like you can't kill a drunk. I got about a half-mile from the house when I saw the flares set out by the road and the sheriff's deputy down in the trees with his flashlight. Marie's car had hit a patch of ice and skidded off the road and down the bank. She plowed straight into one of these monster fir trees. Medical examiner said she died instantly."

"And that's why Mr. Porter blames you."

"He's got a point, don't ya think?" Rusty rubbed his forehead with a freckled hand. "If I'd gone straight home that night Marie would probably still be alive today."

Robert had asked and now he knew. He wished he'd never allowed his curiosity to seek out the details. There was nothing left to say. Reassuring words couldn't put the pieces back together again and nothing could reconcile Rusty to the outcome of his choice eleven years before.

"So I quit drinkin' that night. I've never gone back to it and may God strike me down if I ever do. I've even taken to reading the scripture a little. I find some comfort there from time to time. Truth is I'm just waiting out my time here, hoping that I'll see Marie again, even if it's just long enough to throw myself at her feet and tell her how sorry I am that I was so selfish that night. Beg her to forgive me. Think that's possible, Mr. Dawes?"

Robert didn't know why, but heard himself answer, "I'm certain of it, Rusty."

The old man smiled gratefully. "You know sometimes something so simple comes along. We know exactly what we should do and yet, for whatever reason, we don't do it, and it ends up costing us an awful price. It changes our lives forever."

"I think I know what you mean, Rusty. And I wish I had some swell words to ease your pain. I don't know much about God but I know my wife would tell you to have faith. There's a place where 'He has wiped away every tear.' I hope you get to see Marie there again some day."

"Me too," he whispered.

CHAPTER EIGHT

The wind began to gust again around midnight. Robert lay in his bunk listening to the air push fir boughs back and forth like huge Oriental fans. Light from the digital clock washed over his comforter with a faint glow. He checked the time again. It was two o'clock and he hadn't as much as closed his eyes since the wind woke him. It was odd to be lying there with nothing but the sound of the wind outside and the glow of the clock for light. He had a sense of being caught between two dimensions. He was completely awake and yet he felt suspended between the time and space occupied by Rusty and Lonnie, and Mark and the kids, and that place Amy called reality, or eternity.

He half-closed his eyes with the wind in full voice in the treetops. It was as if he could talk to Amy and know that she could hear him. At first he didn't say anything, afraid to spoil the moment. At last he whispered, "Amy, if you can hear me I want you to know that I'm trying to get back on track. I haven't known what to do since you had to leave. I haven't been able to force myself to see any purpose in things. Mostly all I've managed to do is sit around and feel like I've been robbed – like you were stolen from me. I get angry when I see people together who seem like they don't even care about each other and I know that I'd trade anything to have you back. But I know that you would want me to move on. I can almost hear you telling me that this isn't what God has for me. Right now I'd like to hear what God *does* have for me. And then I hear a story like Rusty's and I think that my life has been pretty easy by comparison. I don't know anymore. I hope I'm doing the right thing with this letter. I don't think it was an accident that we found it after all these years. Besides, it'll force me to get things straightened out with Mark. I don't have any excuse; it's just that living without you has left such a giant hole in my life. But I have more of a sense of urgency now, like I need to get down to Olympia and as least try to find Amy Allen. That's all

I've been thinking about. That and you. Amy, if it's possible to help me in this, please try. I really need to figure things out..." While the wind kept the world outside in motion, he closed his eyes and gave himself up to the seduction of sleep. His dreams were again of a sun-washed beach with light breakers the color of the sky. And Amy.

*****

Robert watched from the pilothouse windows as he passed Doffelmeyer Point Lighthouse. Back to the east, sailboats and power cruisers bobbed at their moorings in Boston Harbor Marina. It was early afternoon and the last six miles of Puget Sound spread a blue carpet before the gently treading *NoraLynn*.

Robert powered back the engine to just keep ahead of the ebbing tide. He took a deep breath to clear his head. Whatever lay before him, the most important thing was that this was the beginning of his life without Amy. From the day she died until today he had been caught in a place of uncertainty. He needed to find a balance between what had been and the possibilities for the rest of his life. "I hope you were right, Amy," he said aloud, "I hope God does have something else for me."

*****

Within two hours *NoraLynn* was tied to the dock of South Sound Boatworks. One of the yard hands came down the gangway to where he waited.

"I've got a diesel motor from Jackson's boatyard for you guys."

"You Mr. Dawes?"

"Yup, sounds like Lonnie Brooks must have already talked to you."

"We been expecting ya, thought maybe you'd be here yesterday."

Welcome to Olympia, Robert thought to himself. "Well, I'm here now. Where do you want me so we can get this thing lifted off?"

"Pull her around to the side dock. There's a small crane; you'll see it. I'll meet you there and we'll get her pulled up."

"You got it," said Robert.

After the motor was hoisted up into the yard, a forklift carried the pallet away. Robert politely went through the formalities of getting a signature for receipt of the engine as Lonnie had asked him to. The yard hand helping him seemed to thaw a little by the time it was over, so Robert said, "Maybe you could help me out. I'm planning to spend some time in Olympia and wondered if you knew of a marina that might have an open slip for rent. I'd like to stay close in if possible." From where he stood at the boatworks dock Robert could look in three directions and see sailboats masts lolling on the tide.

The man thought for a moment. "Tell you the truth, I don't even own a boat, but I have a buddy who has a sailboat down at Capital Marina. It's the last marina at the south end of the bay. I *guess* he likes it and you can't get any closer in toward downtown than that."

"That sounds like just what I'm looking for. Capital Marina. You say it's the last one at the end of the bay?"

"Yep. You can't miss it. There's a big, old wooden schooner tied up on the outside breakwater."

*****

Robert cut the throttle back as far as he could but still make way. He peered through a forest of masts trying to see if there was a sign for the marina office. He didn't look forward to tying up and then limping up a steep gangway at low tide to look for an office. It may be that all he would find was a signboard with the marina phone number on it. It might be in another part of town, or worse, in another city. He had decided to go back out and to the north where he had passed the office of a huge marina run by the Port of Olympia. When he stepped out of the pilothouse to take a last look, a voice hailed him from the deck of the schooner the yard worker had mentioned.

"You looking for someone?"

Robert looked back but couldn't see anyone. "I'm trying to find the marina office. I want to find out if they have an open slip to rent."

"In that case, you've found it; and the answer is yes, we have open slips. Tie up aft of me and come aboard."

Robert slid *NoraLynn* up to the dock behind the schooner. He made his way to the steps outside the schooner's rail and hauled himself up. From the shadows above, eyes the color of gunmetal watched him. When he was on the top step a hand reached out to him.

"Give me one of your crutches. You can swing your good leg over first and I'll help you get to your feet."

Robert glanced at the hand and then did as he was told. "Thanks," he said, "I'm not getting around so well these days."

"I understand."

Aboard the boat, Robert had a chance to see his new

acquaintance up close. Framing dark gray eyes was a mottled complexion of pink flesh and the waxy texture of scar tissue. A shock of black hair surrounded his head and hung down over his collar. The top of his head was completely bald. The rest of his face was badly scarred and his left hand was missing three fingers.

"I'm Tony Cruz." He held out his hand again. Thin lips, taut from scarring, formed a smile. His teeth were perfect.

"Robert Dawes."

"So how long were you thinking of staying? We have a different rate for year-round moorage than month-to-month."

"I'm not sure," said Robert, "I'd probably just be month-to-month."

"It's $6.50 a foot month-to-month, and a flat $25 a month for power." Tony Cruz flashed his perfect smile. "You're not planning to live aboard, are you?"

"I guess I am. I mean I don't have anywhere else to live down here."

"Do you know anyone with a permanent address?"

"I do have a brother in town; that's one of the reasons I came down to visit."

"That's good enough. For the records I'll need a land address, and beyond that, who's to say how much time you spend on your boat. You can just pay me in person."

"I appreciate it. I want to stay as close to town as possible."

"So where's home?"

"Whidbey. I came down to deliver a motor for a boatyard up in the North Sound. Since I'm here, though, I thought I'd spend some time with my brother."

"Okay, what I need then is for you fill out an application. We'll prorate the rest of January and I'll need the last month in advance." Cold rain began to fall. "Let's go below and get out of the weather. We can do this at the galley table."

Robert followed Tony Cruz through a hatchway with double doors and down four steps to the salon. Robert paused. If *NoraLynn* was roomy and comfortable, the schooner was palatial and luxurious. Every detail of the oiled teak was spotless. Turned hardwood posts rose up to support the coachhouse roof. Tony Cruz had a living area set up with overstuffed leather furniture and an Oriental rug. Centered on the port wall of the salon was a bay stove across from the sofa. Every wall was covered with bookshelves or paintings.

"Wow, this is really impressive. Has this been a project or did you buy her like this?"

He laughed. "You should have seen this old girl eight years ago. She wasn't derelict, but she looked like it. What you see here represents about seven-thousand man hours and forty-five thousand dollars. I'm just about finished below deck, but there's still a lot to do up top."

"She's beautiful. Really. Beautiful doesn't cover it – this is spectacular."

"I bought her as a project. The old guy who sold her to me had done everything necessary below the waterline, but the decks were soft and the below decks area was a disaster. It took me two years working nights and weekends to get the deck back in shape. Then I started on the coach house and companionway. The skylights forward and above the salon leaked. She was a mess."

Robert continued to look around. "Well, it sure looks like you've accomplished a lot since then."

"I've still got to refinish all her spars and completely paint the topsides. There's still a lot of work to do. Although it helps to have a life-altering accident. After I spent a year in and out of the hospital I was ready to do something productive again. Since then that's about all I've been doing. Weird how disfiguring, third-degree burns cut way down on your social life."

Robert didn't know how to respond. "I'll fill out that application now if you want."

*****

After he had filled out the necessary paperwork and paid in advance, Robert got his slip assignment. Unfortunately because *NoraLynn* was thirty-six feet long, she had to tie up on the outer docks where the water stayed deep even during minus tides. That meant a longer walk to get up to the street. He wasn't sure how he would get around. Olympians had to rely on the bus or a taxi if they needed public transportation. The bus was out of the question, with all the fuss his crutches would cause, not to mention having to walk an unknown distance from the bus stop to his destination. A taxi wasn't a bad option, but meant having to phone ahead and then wait. Olympia weather in January was just as problematic as on Whidbey Island, so waiting for a cab to arrive could leave one needing a towel as much as a ride. Transportation would take some thought.

Robert shivered with the afternoon chill. He started a fire in the woodstove and sat down in the salon. He was finally in Olympia. For nearly ten days he had been driven by the notion of finding Amy Allen and finally he was here.

Now that he was moored and had a base from which to mount his search, he needed to call Mark. He wasn't sure if Mark would be home from work yet, but thought that Laura would probably be there. He dialed and got a busy signal. He'd wait until after six, by then Mark should be home from work. He lay back on the settee in front of the fire.

*****

Robert half-awakened to the sound of someone pounding on the side of the boat. The fire had died to embers, leaving the room dark, and a chill settling over the salon. He forced his consciousness up through layers of sleepiness that clung like cobwebs. Someone really was knocking on the pilothouse door. Getting to his crutches he limped to the pilothouse companionway. From where he stood he could see a figure standing onboard, silhouetted against the glow of the dock lights outside.

He called out, "Who's there?"

"Oh hey, you are here. It's me, Tony Cruz."

"Tony, can you come around to the salon door? I'll let you in there."

The shadow moved away and past the side windows, stopping in front of the salon door. Tony Cruz was specter-like in the shadows outside when Robert unlocked the door and opened it wide. "Hey Tony, come on in. What did I forget?"

"You didn't forget anything. Tell ya the truth I got to thinking about what I said about 'third degree burns' and all that. I apologize. Sometimes I say things before I think. I know that I made you uncomfortable. Anyway, I came by to say that I've got a couple of steaks that I need to grill, and if you don't have plans to go to your brother's for dinner, you're welcome to come on over. It doesn't look like you're probably up to walking to any of the local eateries."

Robert hadn't been able to get a hold of Mark yet. Anyway he was hungry and a grilled steak sounded good. If Tony Cruz was as good a cook as he was a carpenter, this should be outstanding.

"As a matter of fact, I haven't been able to get a hold of him yet. So sure, I'd definitely be up for a steak. What time were you thinking about eating?"

"I'm headed back to the boat right now to get started. You can come back with me now or things should be just about ready to go in an hour or so."

"I need to get a fire going again and make sure the diesel heater is set up to use. I'll walk over in a few minutes. Anything I can bring?" Robert offered although he really didn't have much in the pantry.

"Nope, I'm all set. When you get to the steps, give me a yell and I'll come up and help you with your crutches."

"Okay, see you shortly then." Tony Cruz left the same way he had come.

Robert set about stoking the fire again. A chill had settled over the bay. He went to the woodbox just outside the aft wall of the salon. With the door standing open he could toss three or four chunks inside without having to walk and hold anything simultaneously.

Before he went back in he checked the evening sky. A cold breeze was blowing in from the north. In the splash of light that traced out the Olympia skyline he could see the low overhang of clouds. 'It's going to snow', he thought to himself.

*****

"Tony!" Robert called out from the top step outside the schooner. From an area aft of the mainmast a tarp slung over the boom made a canopy over a charcoal grill. The smell of roasting meat met him even before he made it to the top step. A moment later Tony stepped through the companionway. He helped Robert aboard and led the way back down to the salon. A galley that could have been used for the set of a cable television cooking show opened up just to starboard. The countertop was strewn with salad fixings and spice bottles. A bottle of wine was open on the counter.

"Smells good up there." He made his way to the sofa. "Hope you don't mind if I sit down, but stairs always take it out of me."

"Make yourself comfortable. I need to run topside and check the steaks."

Robert sat in the glow of the bay stove studying the paneled walls and shelves lined with books. Tony Cruz was a mystery. His marred outward appearance gave no clue of the person inside. His boat was the same. The old schooner was deceptively ordinary, almost unattractive, on the outside but inside she was a work of beauty. Maybe that was the catch. Maybe that was the way Tony tested a new acquaintance. Do you see me or do you *see me*? One had to look deeper to appreciate what was inside.

"I think they need about five more minutes," said Tony, shuffling down the companionway steps. "That is unless you like your steak rare."

"Nope. I like mine medium-well. Although my wife used to say 'Just shave it and sear it on either side.' That's never appealed to me." Robert got to his feet. "Is there anything I can do to help? I'm not much of a cook but I'm good at cleanup."

"It's all done. I put a couple of baked potatoes in the oven first thing. They should be ready when the steaks are. I've got salads made and there's a bottle of wine, if that's your thing."

"I might drink a short glass since I don't have far to go. Although with the way it feels outside, there may be some ice and snow on the docks later tonight. Could be treacherous for a guy on crutches."

"When you leave I'll listen for a splash. I'll alert the Coast Guard if I hear anything." Tony smiled. "You mentioned your wife. Are you divorced?"

"She died last summer." Robert moved over to inspect a painting on the salon wall. "I see you like Andrew Wyeth. Amy, my wife, was a huge fan of his. We had four or five prints in the house."

"He paints life as it really is. Nothing is overly adorned. I've really only been aware of his work for the last few years." Tony came back to the topic of Amy. "Was your wife sick or did she die in an accident?"

"Cancer."

"I'm sorry to hear that." He handed Robert a glass of wine. "I think those steaks are probably ready to come off the grill. I'll be right back. Why don't you have a seat at the table?"

Tony returned with sizzling steaks and plopped one on each of the plates. He retrieved baked potatoes from the oven and did the same. Salad bowls were already filled, and a basket of warm rolls rounded out the meal. Robert was right, Tony's cooking prowess matched his woodworking skills.

Tony sat down. "So you came down to deliver a motor to South

Sound Boatworks? Are you a mechanic? Or a shipwright?"

"I wish. No, I had my boat up in a yard on Noble Island. Some things happened that made a trip to Olympia necessary, so I brought the motor down as a favor to the yard owner. It's an overhaul and the guy who owned the boat it came from got transferred to Olympia. Capital Boatworks is going to install it for him."

"So this is more of a pleasure trip then. Came to see your brother and delivering the motor was an added bonus."

"Sort of. I've kind of been distant since my wife died. My brother has called several times and I've never called him back. I even had the phone disconnected. Then I took a leave of absence from my job and rented out the house. Right after that I moved aboard my boat. I didn't even talk to him on Christmas."

"I guess I'd call that distant."

"Yeah. I don't know. I guess I just kind of withdrew when Amy died. I don't know exactly what happened. Since then I've been like an old dog, just sitting around licking my wounds. I never planned to exclude anyone. It's hard to explain. I didn't feel like I had much to say." Robert sipped his wine. The tart merlot rolled over his tongue and mingled with the smoky flavor of the beef. Maybe it was the wine, or maybe it was Tony Cruz, but for the first time in months he wanted to talk about Amy. He'd heard about processing grief through talking about it. Maybe that's what he was doing.

"I'm from Seattle," said Tony. "When I was injured eight years ago, I thought I'd never speak to anyone again. I'd look at my face in the mirror and think, 'You're a monster, like the Phantom of the Opera, you can't ever face anyone again'. In fact, I used to moor this boat up in Ballard, but moved it down here to try and escape seeing people I knew." He swirled the wine in his glass. "I think I understand why you didn't want to talk to anyone – even your own brother."

"So what was it that brought you out of it? I mean, you couldn't change your appearance. How were you able to come to terms with what happened to you?"

"I haven't. And even though I'm trying, I can't really pretend that much has changed. I'm still pretty reclusive. But you seem to be getting on with your life. Here you are wanting to hook-up with your brother and all. Noble Island to Oly is a long way to come just to deliver a motor."

For a moment Robert wrestled with whether or not to mention the letter. He hadn't intended to bring it up, but felt he could trust the insight of Tony Cruz. They had both been washed out to sea by the capriciousness of life, but for both, it appeared land was in sight. "You're right. Actually something happened about ten days ago that kind of started to get things turned around for me." He poured a little more wine.

Tony Cruz stopped eating. "What was that?"

"Well first, I should tell you how I was feeling. I already told you that after my wife died I took a leave at work, rented out the house and moved aboard my boat. All I wanted to do was hide. It wasn't that I wanted to hide from anyone in particular, it's that I didn't feel like I had a reason to get up in the morning. I don't know if that's bad, to have your life so intertwined with someone else's that when that person dies it's like half of you went with them. Honestly, I don't know if maybe I'm weak or what, but I didn't have any purpose. For months. Anyway, so my boat develops a leak – like close to a foot of water in the bilge kind of a leak. It was right about the time I discovered the leak that I slipped while getting off the boat and fractured my ankle. I was *really* down then. The doctor gave me pills that eased the pain, but I think they also made me more depressed than I already was. So, I thought, Since I'm laid up anyway, I'll make an appointment with the boatyard. They can work on the leak, the boat'll be up on the hard. I can get some rest, and at the same time I figured I could tear out one of the bunks in the forward compartment and build in a chest of drawers for more stowage. Anyway, to make a much longer story not quite so long, I had a guy from the yard help me tear out the old bunk. My boat was built in the thirties and originally had wide, interwoven canvas straps that supported the mattresses. Somebody put plywood platforms on at some point, and just stapled the straps to the plywood. So when we were tearing out the lower bunk we find tucked into the canvas webbing a letter written in the early forties and never mailed. It had the stamp and the address and everything, except a return address." Robert stopped to take a drink of the merlot. "That in itself, would have been interesting enough. Although I doubt that it would have motivated me to come all the way down here, but the really bizarre thing about the letter is that it's addressed to Amy Allen of Olympia, Wash."

Tony had been following the entire monologue until Robert stopped at 'Amy Allen of Olympia, Wash.'

"Okay," his gray eyes narrowed. "So what's the significance? How did that help you to come out of the dark place you were in?"

"That's the weird part. What I didn't tell you is that the addressee's name, Amy Allen, was my wife's maiden name. And as strange as it seems, it was like I felt connected to her again. Even though it's a completely different Amy Allen, and frankly one who is more likely to meet my deceased wife than me. Still I just felt like I needed to give finding her and delivering that letter my best shot. And if she's no longer living, then I'll try to get it to her nearest relative."

Tony didn't say anything. He seemed to be considering the soundness of Robert's logic. Robert went back to eating the perfect rib-eye that occupied much of the plate in front of him. Tony could ask whatever questions he liked, but the next words Robert spoke would be with his mouth full.

Tony continued to think over what Robert had said, but evidently decided, as did his dinner guest, that the matter deserving immediate resolution concerned the steaks and baked potatoes. For a few minutes they ate in silence.

"So how do you plan to go about finding her?" Tony placed his napkin on the table. "I don't want to sound discouraging, but aside from looking in the phone book, there aren't a lot of obvious methods of tracking someone down who might have changed their name several times since the forties and who might be long since dead."

"That's something I've been considering. I really don't know how to even begin to search for her other than the phone book. But see, that's the really crazy part about this whole thing – I realize I may be setting myself up for more disappointment, and yet I still feel so convinced that there's an unseen hand moving the whole adventure that I almost can't accept even the possibility of failure."

"You mean like a sense of destiny? Or fate? Or do you mean like God?"

"I don't know what I mean. I'm not a real religious guy. I not even sure what's considered possible in the orthodox sense. I mean is it possible that Amy is somehow leading me through this? Setting me up to learn something so that I can get on with my life? Trying to release me from everything that's had me bound to the past? This isn't something that I can rationally explain."

Whatever Tony thought, he didn't give Robert a hint as to what it might be. Instead, he changed the subject. "I'm playing the devil's advocate here, so let me ask you a couple more questions. Have you considered how you might follow up any leads that you might generate? How are you planning to get around? It appears that transportation is an issue. Even if you borrow a vehicle, you don't look like you can drive so well at the moment."

"I haven't figured that out yet. But that's one reason I picked this marina. It's the closest one in to downtown. I guess I figured I'd work that out when I really had tracked down a contact."

"That makes sense. Until you actually need to get somewhere, that's one thing you don't have to completely figure out. This may seem like a dumb question, but have you thought about what you might say if you are able to find her? What if you find her and give her the letter and she says, 'Thanks. That was very kind of you. Bye now.'"

"I don't know. I suppose if that's the way it works out, I'll just have to deal with it. As I said earlier though, at this point I can't even imagine something like that happening."

"Alright. Okay. I think a positive attitude is important. I only ask these questions because I'm really intrigued. I love the idea of you being able to find this woman and return something that's been lost for sixty years. This would make a great Hollywood script."

Tony pushed his chair back. "Tell you what I'll do. When you're ready to get started on this, I will volunteer my time and vehicle to chauffeur you around- that is if you don't mind being seen with the Phantom of the Opera."

Robert couldn't believe the offer. "Are you serious? What about the work you're doing on the boat? Will hauling me around put you off your schedule?"

"It might if I actually had a schedule. Anyway, it's January, and working on this boat for the past eight years hasn't been scheduled, like I have to fit it in to all the other plans that occupy my too, too busy life. It's what I do because I don't go anywhere or see anyone. The only people who have sat where you're sitting are people who have filled out moorage applications like you did. You are the first person other than my father who has ever had dinner here. *And he owns the marina.* I don't even go to the grocery store until it's so late I'm certain almost nobody will still be shopping or so early that no one is out shopping yet. All the material you see used to make her so homey – all ordered by phone, trucked in and unloaded up on the dock, a little at a time. So driving you around to try and find your mystery lady will be as much for me as it is for you. I haven't had a good enough reason to expose myself to the various responses my appearance produces in people, until you told me your story. So if you're interested, my offer stands. Maybe we'll both get something out of this."

Robert hardly knew what to say. "Thank you. I accept – gladly."

"Then it's done." Tony Cruz stood up. He gathered up the plates and set them by the sink. "I've got some gourmet French vanilla ice cream my dad brought down a couple weeks ago. Got room?"

"Always," smiled Robert.

"I'll put on some coffee, too."

*****

Robert awoke early. A sharp chill filled the forward compartment reminding him of his weather prediction from the previous evening. When he had left Tony's boat and scuttled back down the dock, *NoraLynn* was straining at her lines. Steady rain was blowing in from the north. There had been ice crystals in the raindrops, but then it wasn't snowing.

He pulled himself into a kneeling position on the bunk and slid aside the curtain over the port light. The landscape beyond looked like a movie scene where the hero returns to the family plantation after years away and finds everything in the house draped with covers. Robert recognized the snow-covered mounds rising up from the water as boats of various size and description, and yet now they could have just as easily been antebellum chairs and tables covered with white sheets.

'Must have snowed six or seven inches,' he thought to himself. A quiet excitement stirred inside him. For the first time in years there was no schedule to keep, and with no traffic to brave in an attempt to get to work on time, he could make a pot of coffee, build a fire in the stove and just wait for the snow to melt.

When he had a fire going, he showered and got some water going for oatmeal. Everyday was coffee day, but snow days were steaming oatmeal days.

When he finished cleaning up from breakfast and sat down in front of the fire, he felt the boat rock as Tony slipped over the rail and walked down to the salon door.

"It's open," Robert called.

Tony stepped in onto the mat, trying to keep as much snow outside as possible. He had lost all but the index finger and thumb on one hand, and despite the heavy scarring, showed remarkable dexterity as he removed his boots. "Hmm. Smells good in here. Don't tell me you've already made coffee and eaten breakfast."

"A day like this is why they invented oatmeal."

"I'll have to take your word for it. I've always been a bacon-and-eggs guy myself."

"So what brings you out so early?"

"I was thinking about you trying to track down the lady with the letter and it occurred to me that you probably don't even have an Olympia phone book. I have the one the phone company puts out and then I have the other one from the wanna-be phone company, so I brought the newest one over. It came out in September so it should be the most current." Tony pulled a new phone book from his backpack. "Do you have a cell phone or are you planning to use a payphone?"

"Cell phone. I've sort of been like you. I've hardly talked to anybody in the last six months, so I've got a ton of rollover minutes." Robert picked up the phone book. "Have you taken a look at the list of Allens? Is it totally overwhelming?"

"I was going to let you read for yourself but since you ask, I did check it out. The good news is that there's an Amy Allen at the top of the list, the bad news is there's only one, but there's over a hundred other Allen entries."

"Whoa! That's a little overwhelming. But who knows, maybe the Amy at the top of the list *is* our gal." They looked at one another. "Naaaah!"

PART THREE

CHAPTER NINE

"Hello? Oh, hello! Sorry to trouble you on such a snowy morning, but I'm trying to reach a Miss Amy Allen. Oh no? Okay. Well, thanks anyway. But listen, while I've got you on the phone, you wouldn't by chance be familiar with an older woman, say a shirt-tale relative named Amy, would you? Maybe a great aunt? No? Actually she may not go by Amy Allen anymore, but she'd definitely be elderly, pushing eighty I imagine. No, it's okay. It was a long shot really. I'm not even sure she's lived in Olympia since the forties. Anyway, I appreciate your time."

Robert snapped his cell phone closed and put a black line through another entry in the phone book. It was almost two o'clock and he hadn't taken a break since he started. Getting down on his knees he scooted over to the wood stove, banked the coals into a pile and added more wood.

The weather forecast was for more snow. The Seattle station was saying another six to eight inches in central Puget Sound with as much as ten inches additional accumulation for the South Sound. That meant Olympia could really get hit hard when the next front blew through.

He got to his feet and swung his crutches over to the salon door. The sky outside was the color of wet concrete. As he looked over the other boats up and down the dock, it didn't appear that even a little of the snow had melted. In fact, since he had gotten up this morning, the only change had been increased wind. Now the gusts were visible as the blowing snow hung a white garment on the northerly. It looked like the whole world had taken the hint and decided to wait out the storm inside.

He went to the galley and turned on the coffee maker. He picked up the letter and traced out the dark letters on the front of the envelope with his finger. Running a fingertip over the stamp, he whispered the slogan written over the eagles chest, "Win the war."

He thought about Mr. Porter and Rusty and Lonnie and wondered if they were as snowbound on Noble Island as the world seemed to be in Olympia. He especially thought of Rusty on a day like today. Work was his last real hiding place. Otherwise he'd have to be at home alone. Robert knew the loneliness of a house made full by two, suddenly reduced to a prison for one. He hoped the snow was lighter up north so that Rusty didn't have too much time in solitary.

He was still musing over the envelope when Tony hopped aboard and headed straight to the salon door. Turning his back to the north, he waited until a gust had blown through, then opened the door.

"Whew! It's nasty out there and supposed to get nastier." He closed the door and shook off the snow. "But it feels downright toasty in here."

"You must have smelled the coffee all the way down the dock."

"Not really, but now that you're inviting me, don't mind if I do." He took off his boots and jacket. "Actually I got curious about whether you've had any luck solving the grand mystery."

"I'm afraid sleuthing is not my strength. I've been batting zero since I started this morning. I just now stopped to build up the fire and make a pot of coffee."

"I was afraid that might be the case. I don't want to sound negative, but where do you go if the phone book strategy is a bust?"

"I haven't considered that. I've still got about half of the Allen entries to go, so I'm still hopeful that one of them will produce a lead."

"That's probably the right approach. No sense not staying positive. Still a contingency plan might be worth considering."

"You sound like you may have given this more thought than I have." Robert filled a second cup and set it on the counter. "Cream or sugar?"

"Just black, thanks. You know, I *have* been thinking about what I would do if I were in your place. I think if you can't find her by calling all the Allens in the phone book, you should open the letter."

"Why? How do you suppose opening the letter might help find her? Do you think there might be an address inside?"

"I guess that's one possibility, but knowing the contents of the letter might also help to put the whole adventure in perspective."

"I don't get what you mean." Robert grappled with his cup and moved to the sofa where Tony had plopped himself.

"My point is that if the information in the letter is just mundane jabbering written to fulfill someone's obligation to stay in touch, knowing that might take the pressure off...you know, to find Amy Allen *at all costs*."

"I get what you're saying. I suppose that if it comes right down to it, I may be forced to do that. I don't know. I really think that finding her and giving her the letter unopened would make it extra special."

"Okay, bro. I just don't want to see you get your hopes up and then have the whole thing turn out to be for nothing." Tony smiled. "Speaking of bro, did you ever get ahold of your brother? With all this snow, and what they're expecting later today, it may be a few days before Olympia digs out. Think he'll be worried?"

"I think I'll call and let him know that I'm okay, but I'll tell him I'm just sitting tight until the whole mess clears up. I don't think I'll even mention that I've already made it to Olympia."

"No sense having him come out if he doesn't need to. So how are you fixed for food?"

"Honestly, the pantry's a little bare. I was hoping to get out to the store to do a little shopping."

"It's too nasty to get to the store. I've got lots of canned food and sandwich stuff. Right now I need to go back and shovel off the deck and make sure nothing is leaking. If the weather guy is anywhere near accurate, I may have a lot more to shovel by morning. But after that I'll bring some stuff over and we can make some sandwiches and soup."

"Sounds good. In the meantime, maybe I'll get lucky and find her."

Tony finished his coffee and got ready to go back out into the weather. Before he could close the door behind him a blast of cold air filled the salon. Robert looked out to the north. The snow that filled the air was no longer just picked up and scattered by the wind. The blizzard had begun again.

*****

Snow continued to fall throughout the afternoon and into the evening. By the time Robert finished eliminating all the Allens in the phone book, it was nearly nine o'clock. He had struck out.

Evidently the thread connecting Miss Amy Allen to Olympia had broken some time ago. For the first time since finding the letter, he was forced to admit that the adventure may be at an end.

He opened the salon door to get some air. Another eight or nine inches of snow had accumulated since early afternoon. Around dusk the wind relented, and even though snow continued to fall, the sense of a frenzied storm gave way to a postcard winter scene. Robert watched his breath shoot forward and then dissipate into the night air. Where did he go from here? Maybe his excitement had been premature. Tony had warned him to consider the possibility of a dead end. It just seemed like everything involving the letter had a purpose. *He had a purpose.* Now he was back where he had been the day he set out for Noble Island. His ankle didn't hurt as much but his heart was beginning to ache again.

Carefully placing the tips of his crutches into the snow just beyond the threshold, he stepped outside into the darkness. Frigid air assaulted his senses. He realized the salon had gotten so warm he wasn't aware of how groggy he felt. Overhead the sky was beginning to lighten as the rising moon pushed a faint yellow glow through the clouds. Without warning the weight of Amy's death hung like a yoke on his shoulders again. He took a deep breath. Sleep suddenly became the haven he craved.

Back inside he stoked the wood stove, wrapped himself in a blanket and stretched out on the settee.

*****

"Amy Allen? Is Amy Allen here? Miss Amy Allen?" The voice belonged to a tall man pacing down the beach holding an envelope. A long waistcoat hung smartly over white breeches and a ruffled shirt. Gray hair was gathered into a ponytail at his back. Robert watched from beneath a palm tree shaded by sawtooth leaves agitated by the breeze. From where he sat it was apparent that there was no one else around. The man walked past without acknowledging his presence, continuing down the beach still calling for Amy Allen.

At each end of the tiny sand crescent, steep bluffs rose up from the sea. As he approached the end, the gray-haired crier turned about and started back toward Robert. When he came near to where Robert sat, he stopped and looked down. Evidently it had dawned on him that there was no one else within earshot.

"I don't think she's here." Robert shaded his eyes with his hand as he looked up at the messenger. "I haven't seen anybody else all day."

"I'm afraid that will never do." The gray-haired man swept the area with his eyes. "I have a very important letter for her. It is imperative that I find Miss Allen as soon as possible."

"Okay. Well, like I said, I'm the only one besides you who's been on this beach all day." Robert switched hands shading his eyes. "What's the deal with the letter, anyway?"

"Sir, I'm just a messenger. I don't know the specific details. I only know that when I'm sent to deliver a letter, it's *always* important."

"I see. Well, I wish I could help you, but I don't know your Amy Allen. Actually, I *did* know an Amy Allen, but she died. It was a different Amy, though."

"Hmmm. You're sure this Amy Allen is not the same person you know?"

"Knew. And yes, I'm sure the Amy Allen I knew is an entirely different person."

The messenger gave Robert a quizzical look. "Tell me, sir, if you don't mind, how it is you come to be on this beach today."

Robert considered the question. He didn't recognize the small beach with cliffs at each end. He'd never been here before as far as he could remember. The jungle behind him didn't offer any clues either. No, he was sure he'd never been here before, and had no idea how or why he was here today.

"I don't know. I'm just here. Why do you ask?"

"I've seen these things before. People assume that coincidence is the driving force behind various events in their lives. The truth is that very little can legitimately be attributed to coincidence."

"What exactly are you saying?"

"Sir, I think it's obvious that *you* are the reason that I'm on this beach today. I'm looking for Miss Amy Allen and you seem to be the contact that I've been sent here to find."

"Me? Wait, I think you've made a mistake. The Amy Allen I knew is dead. I was there. I watched her die. You've got the wrong person."

"How do you explain being here today, then? How do you explain being familiar with Amy Allen? *Sir, there is no such thing as coincidence.*"

Robert wanted to protest, but couldn't find the words. The messenger stepped over and placed the envelope in his lap.

"But I wouldn't even know where to begin. If *you* can't find her, how should *I* know where to look for her?"

"I suggest you begin with the address on the envelope. It's in a place called Olympia, Wash. Odd, but I've never heard of it before today."

"It's the capital of Washington State. That's where I live."

"There, you see, you've already got a good start. Shouldn't be any problem at all."

"But what if I can't find her. What if she's not at this address anymore?"

"There is one bit of instruction I can leave you."

"*This I gotta hear.* Okay, what is it?"

"*If despite your best, you're at an end, unseal the letter and try again.*" His voice was monotone, the words recited like a nursery rhyme.

Robert picked up the letter. He ran a finger over the name. This made no sense, but knowing that didn't seem to matter.

"I'm sorry. I can't." Shading his eyes again, he handed the letter back. The messenger, however, was gone. He was alone on the beach again. All was quiet except for the sound of waves curling their lips to kiss the sand and the rustling palm leaves overhead.

*****

Robert awoke with a start. His right hand was outstretched, still proffering the imaginary letter. It was twenty minutes after two. The fire had died to just a few wheezing coals. For a moment, he didn't move. The conversation from the dream was so real the words still echoed in his mind. Was this the sign he had been waiting for? Or was it the last desperate hope fashioned into images and words by a subconscious mind unwilling to admit defeat. Whatever it was, or wherever it came from, it seemed so real.

He pulled the blanket around him and slid onto the floor. When he opened the door to the stove the remaining coals caught their breath and began to flicker in earnest. He tossed in three sticks of kindling and blew hard on the pile. There was still enough life left in them to ignite the kindling, painting his face with yellow light. He added two bigger chunks and shut the door.

Cocooned in his blanket, he lay in front of the fire. He was all alone in a floating world of fire and ice. Wherever Tony and Lonnie and Rusty and everyone else in the world were right now didn't matter. Robert Dawes was alone with his thoughts, alone with the words from his dream, and alone with the sixty-year-old letter to Miss Amy Allen. He was the only one who could determine where to go from here.

As he lay watching the flames build in the stove, the crackling fire took on the voice of the messenger: *"If despite your best, you're at an end, unseal the letter and try again."*

He struggled to his feet and went to the galley sink. Filling a skillet halfway with water, he set it on the stove to boil.

While the water heated, Robert opened the drawer where he kept the letter. He was nervous. Although it really didn't belong to anyone, he felt like what he was about to do was a violation of something sacred.

He repeated the words, *"If despite your best, you're at an end, unseal the letter and try again."*

His hands trembled as he held the envelope over the boiling water. He waited until he was sure that the hot moisture had penetrated the paper, then placed the envelope face down on the galley table. He slid the end of a table knife under one corner of the flap. Holding his breath he pushed against the seal. At first the glue resisted, but then yielded to the polished edge of the blade. Without ceremony the bond concealing words written more than six decades before gave way. Robert raised the flap so that it was completely separated from the envelope. It was done.

CHAPTER TEN

For several minutes he stared at the envelope on the table in front of him. He could see a letter neatly folded inside. Dread formed a lump in his throat. Should he take it out and read it? What if it was nothing more than a thank-you note? This is what he had wanted to avoid. Knowing what was written on the pages might be so ordinary as to completely trivialize the importance of finding Amy Allen.

He held the envelope up and inspected the triangle of white visible under the flap. Before allowing himself another moment to change his mind, he slid a finger inside and pulled the letter out into the light. It felt stiff and fragile. Carefully, he unfolded the paper and turned it up to catch the light of the galley lamp. The page was a wash of unruly indigo lines. Frigid night air penetrated the closed galley window. Robert shivered and focused on the words in the upper right corner:

June 6, 1943

Dear Amy,

Sorry if this letter looks like a first-grader wrote it. It's a little after two o'clock and I'm writing this while scrunched up under the chart table by the light of a tiny oil lamp. Tonight I'm sleeping on the pilothouse floor because with the other guys aboard, there isn't a bunk for me. I really don't mind. If I was down below with the others, I'd just have to lay there and think about all the things I want to tell you instead of being able to write them down.

I hadn't planned to write tonight, in fact, I went to sleep when we all settled down for the night. I slept real well, too, until a little while ago. But now I'm

164

wide awake. I know the Skipper will have us up in another couple of hours, and I'll probably be draggin' all day, but right now all I can think about is you. All I can ever think about is you.

Amy, I am so excited about us being together I'm just about to explode. I know the war still has to be won, and Hitler and the Japs put where they belong, but that won't take forever. I may have to be gone for a couple of years, but after that we can be together forever. Honey, I know you still have doubts about whether that can really happen or not. I know that our folks probably won't ever approve. I'm pretty sure they would do almost anything to keep us apart, but I don't care what they think anymore. For the past few days I've been working with the Skipper and the men. I've been doing my best and the men treat me like I'm one of them. As much as I want to respect our fathers' opinions, I can't anymore. Amy, they are wrong. You and I love each other and that's all that matters. Do you hear me through these words? Imagine you can hear my voice. You are all that matters to me. I'll do whatever it takes to be with you. Baby, I can't imagine my life without you in it. We can't let our parents or anybody else make our decisions for us.

I'm hoping the next ten days or so are going to fly by. I hate the fact that I won't be able to read your letters during that time. I miss you so much already. Your letters are my lifeline. I don't know what I'd do if I couldn't feel your love through the words you write to me. I've saved every one you've written, and I've *read them all a dozen times. I even brought them along just so that I could read them again when I get to missing you too much.*

I guess I should close for now. I don't really know much. I just wanted to tell you that you're always in my thoughts, and that I can't wait till the day when we can be together without having to worry about what anyone else thinks. You are my future.

I love you with all my heart,

Ford

He laid the letter on the table in front of him. Whatever he had expected, it certainly wasn't this. The voice of the writer came through as determined, almost desperate. What had become of him? How could a letter brimming with such emotion be left tucked under a bunk on a fishing boat? It didn't make sense.

The chill had returned to the salon. Robert went back to the stove and added more wood. The temperature outside must have dropped as the clouds gave way to clear skies. Maybe the snow storm was over. Right now it didn't really matter, since even after having read the letter he was no closer to finding Miss Amy Allen.

Like the cold air from outside, the earlier weariness settled over him again. He knew that the information in the letter had been important to at least two young people some sixty years before. According to the remarks made about disapproving parents, it may have been important to a host of others, too. But Robert was too tired to consider all those possibilities. Anyway, he was beginning to doubt whether Amy Allen was still alive to read it. He pulled the blanket over him where he lay on the floor in front of the stove. This time his sleep was uninterrupted.

*****

At seven o'clock sunlight flooded the salon. Robert pulled the blanket over his face and tried to remember why he felt so stiff. Oh yeah, he'd had that weird dream last night and in a moment of weakness had steamed the letter open. And then like a fool he'd allowed the fire to entice him into sleeping on the salon floor. Every cell in his body was complaining about the cold slab where he'd spent the last several hours. He needed coffee.

While the coffee brewed, he got cleaned up. The envelope still lay on the table. Next to it was the letter, exactly where he had left it. Outside the galley windows he could see blue sky in every direction. A foot of snow was piled on every surface, but the sun had the sky all to itself. The combination of brilliant sunlight bouncing off ultra-white snow was like staring into a flash bulb. He had to shade his eyes.

He limped over to the table and picked up the letter. As he read the words again, delicious pain rose like incense from each sentence. Whoever had written them was filled with such hope, while at the same time the pain of having to defer that hope. Robert wanted to meet him someday. First he would have to find Amy Allen.

He left the pages on the table and went down to the forward compartment to change his clothes. When he came back up to the galley he poured a cup of coffee and sat down. He folded the letter and put it back in the envelope. As he was about to tuck the flap inside, the explosion of reflected sunlight illuminated a smear of words at the inside crease of the flap. Robert squinted against the intensity. The words were faint, so subtle against the yellowed paper they were almost invisible. It was only because of the extreme brightness that he even saw them at all.

Something was written inside the flap, but without magnification he couldn't read it. Where had he put that magnifying glass? Forgetting about his crutches he hobbled through the pilot house down into the area between the head and hanging locker. He jerked open each drawer, dumping the contents onto the cabin sole. Finally, tossed in with hand tools and fishing gear, was a thick magnifying glass. He snatched at the handle and held it up to the light. It was caked with grime.

Leaving his mess where it had fallen, he hopped up the steps and back to the galley. He scrubbed the glass lens and hastily dried it. Still ignoring his crutches, Robert seated himself at the table and picked up the envelope. Here he was again. He hesitated. What if it was nothing? "Lord," he prayed silently, "show me in a way 1 know can only be from you."

He adjusted the focus and concentrated. Finally, the scribble took legible shape. It said: *I Love A. Albermarle*

"I Love A. Albermarle?" he said aloud. What in the world could that mean? Who was A. Albermarle? And what was a statement like that doing obscurely traced inside the flap of a love letter written to Amy Allen? Rather than clearing up the mystery, this only further muddied already black waters. Robert lay the envelope back on the table. He needed another cup of coffee. Now he was really confused. This time using his crutches, he took his coffee back into the salon. The fire needed tending again. He banked the coals and added more wood. Leaning back against the settee, he considered his next move. Where could he go from here?

The phone book, still open, lay where he had left it last night. When it caught his eye, the idea of looking for an Albermarle entry sprang to mind. Why not? There couldn't be as many entries as the Allens.

He pulled the phone book onto his lap and flipped back one page. He read down the list: Albee, Alberg, Albermarle... there it was, floating all alone in an ocean of 'A's' – *A. Albermarle.*

Robert looked at his watch. It was seven-forty. Whoever A. Albermarle was, he hoped they hadn't planned to sleep late. He opened his cell phone and dialed the number. After the third ring a woman's voice answered. "Hello?" Her voice was soft.

Robert could hear his voice tremble. "Hello. I mean, good-morning. I apologize if I'm calling too early, but I'm trying to locate someone and this name came up as a possible contact. Who am I speaking to?"

"This is Amelia Albermarle. Who is it you're trying to find?" She sounded pleasant and willing to help.

"Well actually, the person I'm trying to locate is Miss Amy Allen. That may not be her name now but that would have been her name back in the forties."

There was no response. As the pause continued, Robert tried to imagine what was going through her mind. Finally he said. "Are you still there?"

"Who's calling?" The voice had morphed from affable to suspicious.

"My name is Robert Dawes, ma'am. I'm down from Whidbey Island. I realize this might sound crazy, but I've got something that belongs to Miss Allen and I'm in Olympia trying to locate her so that I can return it." He hesitated, hoping for something positive. "Do you know her?"

Again there was silence, then the voice came back, this time smaller, "Yes. Yes, I've known Amy Allen for many years."

"So she still goes by Amy Allen, then? Wow, I'm surprised. I called every Allen in the phone book yesterday and got nothing but a sore ear. It's really just a stroke of luck that I came up with your name."

"What is it you have for her, Mr. Dawes?"

"Oh, I'm sorry. I didn't mention that, did I? It's a letter. It's kinda weird, but I own an old trawler, built in the thirties. For many years it was a fishing boat and then was converted to a pleasure craft. I was recently doing a little remodeling in the forward compartment and found a letter tucked underneath one of the original bunks. It's addressed to Miss Amy Allen at a post office box in Olympia. There's a three cent stamp on it, which I was able to trace back to the forties as the time of issue, but it was never postmarked. I guess it must have been left on the boat for some reason and it's stayed tucked away there for all these years."

"And now you're trying to return it to Amy Allen. Who is the letter from?"

"That's another thing, there is no return address. If I had known who intended to send it, I may have tried to find them instead. But all I had was: Miss Amy Allen at PO Box 524, Olympia, Wash."

"I see."

"Would it be possible to get Miss Allen's phone number? I'm anxious to meet her. This has been quite an adventure – I mean trying to find her and all."

"That won't be possible. She doesn't have a phone. I may talk to her later today, if the weather permits. Why don't you call me back around, say, two-o'clock this afternoon. If I'm able to get out and visit her I'll let you know and we can arrange a meeting."

"That sounds great. I'll call you back at two sharp."

"Do you have transportation, Mr. Dawes?"

"Yes, ma'am."

"Very well, then. Call me at two and I'll let you know if I've been able to talk to her."

"Thank you so much for your help, Mrs. Albermarle."

"It's Miss Albermarle. And you're welcome, Mr. Dawes. I'll talk to you soon."

*****

Robert closed his cell phone, but continued to stare at it in disbelief. He had just talked to a real person who knew Amy Allen. The most incredible thing was that Amy Allen was still alive. And she was still Amy Allen. This was the best outcome he could have hoped for. Wait till he told Tony that they may have to dig his car out so they could deliver the letter later this afternoon.

CHAPTER ELEVEN

It was shortly after ten o'clock when Tony came aboard and headed to the salon door. He knocked on the glass and opened the door just enough to stick his head in. "Permission to come inside, captain?"

Robert had decided he wasn't going to let on immediately that he had found her.

"Hey Tony, come on in. Looks like the snow is gone and the sun's out."

"Yep. Now the weather guy says it's going to warm up later this afternoon and the snow is gonna start melting – fast. I've been up on deck with my shovel since the sun came up. How about this old girl? Are you concerned?"

"I probably should be. Since I've owned her she's never seen this much snow. I guess I'll just keep an eye on things, and hope she's caulked tight."

Tony smiled. "Okay, what's up? You seem different. Did you have any luck with the Allen clan?" He studied Robert's expression. It was hard to get anything past Tony Cruz.

Finally, Robert couldn't contain a smirk. "Aaaagghh! I wanted to string you along for awhile. I've always been a terrible poker player." The smirk became a broad grin. "*I found her.* Can you believe that? I found the long lost Amy Allen. But check this out, she still goes by Amy Allen, and she still lives here in Olympia."

"Wow! Well done! I honestly didn't believe you'd find her. Alive, at least. So, what happened? Did you finally connect with a relative?"

"You won't believe what happened. It's too weird and too long to tell you the whole thing, but let's just say I took your advice and opened the letter."

"Yeah? And what? You found another name that you were able to follow up on?"

"Something like that."

"What's that supposed to mean? What was in the letter?"

Robert held up the envelope. "I think you should read it for yourself. I guess now that I've opened it there won't be any more harm done. Somehow, I don't think Amy Allen will care, especially when she finds out I had to open it in order to find her."

Tony sat down at the dinette and spread the pages out in front of him.

"Wow, that's a letter that merits all the effort you're putting into delivering it. It sounds like those two had their share of troubles. I wonder if they were able to make it work."

"That's exactly what I thought. I'd really like to meet the guy that wrote it. Can't you feel how desperately he loves this girl? But knowing that she still goes by Amy Allen almost guarantees that they never got together."

"I still don't get how that helped you find her though. I'm impressed with how much the guy loved his girlfriend and all, but ..."

"Look inside the flap, right at the crease. See anything?"

Tony squinted. "Ummm, looks like there *might be* something written right above the crease. Why? What is it?"

Robert handed him the magnifying glass. "Have a look for yourself."

"What's that say? I love A. Alber...?"

"Albermarle. Amelia Albermarle. I got her number out of the phone book and gave her a call about two hours ago. I'm calling her back later to see if she was able to get out to visit Miss Allen, who doesn't have a phone. She said she's known her for a long time."

Tony Cruz kept looking at the penciled message through the magnifying glass. "I can't believe you were able to see that in the first place."

"Neither can I. It was because of the sun reflecting off the snow. The angle of the sun was just right earlier so that the whole salon was filled with this amazing light. I just happened to glance at the envelope on the table and that smudge stood out."

"So you got out your trusty magnifying glass and the rest is history."

"Pretty hard to believe, isn't it?"

"That raises the question as to what 'I love A. Albermarle' is doing covertly written in a love letter to Amy Allen. Think the guy was two-timing her?"

Robert shook his head. "I can't believe that's the case. He seems so out-of-it for Amy Allen. She's his 'future' and all that other stuff about their parents not wanting them together, but him not caring what they thought. I just don't see how he could have been involved with Amelia Albermarle on the side. I don't know what it means, but *that* doesn't fit."

"So, if the question of how you tied the two of them together comes up, what are you going to say? You'll have to tell the truth. It probably doesn't matter becaue he, whoever he is, may not be alive anymore. Women always outlive their men."

"*Not always.*"

"Sorry, Robert. You're right, not always."

"But I guess we'll find out. Right now though, the question is whether you'll be able to get your car out if we get the chance to go see her today."

"I think I can probably get my car out, but I don't think the streets will be open today. Depends on where she lives, I guess. Before I worry about the car though, I'd better get back and finish shoveling off the deck."

*****

At one fifty-five Robert sat watching the clock. The weatherman had been right. The wind had shifted from the north to a much warmer south wind. Outside the world was in flux as clear skies grinned from horizon to horizon, sending the snow back into the bay in tiny rivers.

At two o'clock he flipped his cell phone open and dialed the number. His heart raced as he counted the rings. As before, Amelia Albermarle answered after the third ring.

"Hello?"

"Miss Albermarle? This is Robert Dawes calling again."

"Oh yes, Mr. Dawes, how are you?"

"I'm well, thank-you. I was checking back to see if maybe you'd gotten out to see Miss Allen."

"I'm sorry, Mr. Dawes, it's just too messy out today. The snowplow hasn't come down my street yet and none of the sidewalks are shoveled, so I haven't ventured out. I'd hate to fall and break a hip."

"I understand, ma'am. It looks like it's a real mess out there. Would it be alright if I called again tomorrow? I don't want to make a nuisance of myself, but I'm very excited about seeing that this letter gets to Miss Allen."

"Of course. Yes, you can call tomorrow, or if you want, perhaps you could leave it with me and I could see that she gets it."

"No offense, but I really want to meet her and give her the letter in person. It's nothing against you, it's just that this letter, and finding her, has come to mean something to me personally."

Robert quickly added, "I'm sure that sounds strange, but finding this letter has had an...an effect on my life."

"Perhaps you can tell me more about that and how you found the letter when this snow situation is resolved. I'm sure Amy would like to hear the story, too. We both love a mystery."

"I look forward to it, Miss Albermarle."

"Please call me Amelia. Why don't you call back tomorrow around noon. We'll just have to wait and see how the snow clearing efforts go."

"Noon it is, then. I appreciate your help, Miss... Amelia."

"You're welcome. I'll talk to you tomorrow."

Robert closed his phone. He had resisted the temptation to ask who might have written a love letter to Amy Allen, and at the same time declare his love for A. Albermarle. That question could wait until he talked to them face to face.

Overhead the sky pulsed neon blue, while a south wind exhaled its warm breath over the frosty landscape. Together sun and wind teamed up to set the whole world in motion.

CHAPTER TWELVE

It was two o'clock when Tony came by to get Robert. Nudged upward by the tide, the gangway from the parking lot down to the slips was nearly level. Mounds of snow lay piled around the base of every light pole in the parking lot. But already many of the parking spaces revealed striped boundaries through a coat of slush.

Robert looked around as they headed for Tony's car. "This was one strange snowstorm. It just blew in and now it's going out almost as fast."

"Can't go out too fast for me. If I want to see the stuff, I'll drive up to one of the ski areas. Otherwise, I like rain. At least it runs right off."

When they got to the car, Tony came around and took Roberts crutches. "So how's that ankle? I haven't heard you complain much about it," he said, as put the crutches behind the seats.

"I think it's healing up. If I put my weight directly on my foot it still hurts, but it's nothing like it did a couple of weeks ago. For awhile I thought I might go crazy from the pain."

"You have no idea."

"I'm sure you're right. As much as this broken ankle hurt in the beginning, I know it couldn't compare to what you went through."

"I really had to fight the physical and psychological freefall when they cut back my pain meds. I wasn't sure that I could live without something to numb the pain, and not just the physical pain, either."

"I only know a little of your story, but I'm amazed at the way you've battled back."

Tony started the car and let it warm up. "There are still times, though, when I see my reflection in the mirror and ask myself why I'm still here. Some days, if I dwell on it, I get tempted to take things into my own hands."

"Tony, I can't pretend to know what it's like to be you, and everything you've had to go through, but man, I'm sure glad you've never gone that way."

Tony smiled. "What did you say her address is?"

"She told me 2815 North Stone," Robert looked at his watch. "It's almost two fifteen. How long will it take to get there?"

"I'm not exactly sure where it is. I know where North Stone is, but I'm not exactly sure about the address. Anyway, it's not more than fifteen minutes from here."

"Good. She told me to come by at two thirty. I want to try and make a good impression."

"In that case I'm not so sure I should come along."

"Why do you say that?"

"If you're worried about making a good impression, I mean. Not everyone feels comfortable around me."

"Man, don't worry about that. These little old ladies can't help but love you. In no time you'll have 'em eating out of your hand."

"Hmm. Maybe what's left of it anyway." He pulled out onto the street. "Okay then, let's go meet the elusive Miss Amy Allen."

*****

At exactly two thirty they turned into the driveway at 2815 North Stone. Steam rose from dark shingles where the snow had melted, heated by the afternoon sun. Amelia Albermarle lived in a one story bungalow. Visible from the driveway, a huge maple tree still partially covered with snow, thrust naked branches into the sky. A path had been shoveled from the driveway to a concrete stoop. Wood-framed storm windows, painted white, stood out against dirty clapboard siding. Every detail of the house and yard combined to say one word – *neglect*.

Robert unfastened his seatbelt and swung the door open. By the time Tony got around to the other side and pulled out his crutches, he was balancing on his good leg and holding onto the door handle.

"Whoa. Easy, soldier, you don't want to meet Miss Allen with a knot on your forehead and a soggy letter in your hand, do you? Here, take your crutches. I'm sure she can wait a few more minutes, since the letter's sixty years overdue anyway."

"You're right. I don't know why I'm so excited."

"Relax, bro. I just hope Miss Allen is half as excited to *get* the letter as you are to deliver it."

"I've been trying to imagine this moment ever since I found it."

"I hope she doesn't disappoint you."

"Me, too. Let's go meet the mystery woman."

Robert took the lead. He climbed the two steps to the stoop and teetered in front of the door. Above the doorbell was a wooden plaque in the shape of a Bible with black letters that spelled out

'This is the day that the LORD hath made, I will rejoice and be glad in it.' Robert smiled and pressed the doorbell. In the back of his mind he could see his Amy winking.

At first there was no sign of anyone home. Robert tried to peer through the storm door and beyond the sheer curtain that covered the window of the front door. There was a small anteroom at the front of the house, probably for coats and shoes to be removed on wet days.

He was about to ring the doorbell again when he heard footsteps approaching from the other side. The inside door opened. Finally Robert stood face to face with at least one person who actually knew Amy Allen.

'This must be Amelia Albermarle,' he thought to himself. She didn't look anything like he had expected. Through the wrinkles framing her eyes he could still see prominent cheekbones. Her hair was completely white and cut short. She swung the door open allowing the afternoon light to fall full on her face. As they looked at each other the corners of her mouth curled into a smile. Amelia Albermarle was still a good-looking woman. What Robert was unprepared for was that she was black.

"Mr. Dawes?" Her voice was soft.

"You must be Miss Albermarle." Robert held out his hand. "I'm sorry," he corrected himself, "Amelia."

"I am. Won't you come in?"

"We'd love to. By the way, this is my friend, Tony Cruz."

"How do you do Mr. Cruz?" Amelia looked at Tony and smiled. She shook his hand and said, "I'm so pleased to meet you both."

From inside a rush of warm air pushed past them, filling the entryway with the smell of something delicious.

"Mmmm. Something smells really good. You're not baking chocolate chip cookies, are you?" Robert sniffed the air.

"Actually, they're oatmeal and raisin. I hope you're not disappointed."

"Oh no, oatmeal and raisin is just fine with me. How about you, Tony?"

"Oatmeal and raisin is fine; no problem at all."

"Wonderful. I was just taking them out of the oven when you boys knocked. I'll put some on a plate and put another batch in to bake. That way there'll be some to take home with you."

"Really, you don't need to go to all that trouble for us. We don't want to be a bother."

"Nonsense, Mr. Dawes. I don't get many visitors, so this is a good excuse to do some baking. I love to bake *almost* as much as I love to eat. And Lord knows I don't need to get any fatter. So you fellas will be doin' me a favor."

"Okay, but you have to agree to call me Robert."

"Deal." Amelia Albermarle led the way into her living room and continued into the kitchen. "You fellas just make yourselves comfortable while I get the cookies. Are either of you tea or coffee drinkers?"

"Yes, ma'am. We both drink coffee, if it's not too much trouble." They went through the anteroom into the living room. Unlike the outside of the house, the inside was spotless. A tiled fireplace took up the center of the wall opposite the door. On the mantle a line of photographs punctuated highlights in the life of Amelia Albermarle. There was a picture of her as a young woman set against the backdrop of the Washington State Capitol. Amelia stood in front of a fountain, with jets of water frozen in space against the larger scene of the Capitol dome. She was smiling as though someone had just told a joke. Her hands rested on the shoulders of a young girl who wore braces on both legs. The little girl was smiling, too, like she'd been privy to the same joke. Her eyes were just as soft and deep as Amelia's.

That was the only photo of Amelia and the girl. One was of a much older woman, a grandmother perhaps. There were a couple of graduation pictures, each of a young black woman holding a diploma and smiling. Near the end of the mantle were a couple of group shots. These were more recent, with several women in each picture. Robert wondered if one of those women was Amy Allen.

"The coffee is on," said Amelia as she came back into the living room. "I hope you don't mind flavored coffee. All I have is some Irish Cream that my niece gave me for Christmas. It's been in the freezer, so it should be fresh."

Robert and Tony assured her that Irish Cream would be just fine. Robert couldn't contain his curiosity any longer. "Is Miss Allen going to join us?"

"I'm expecting her to. I told her niece that you boys would be here at two thirty and I hoped she wouldn't keep you waiting too long."

"No problem. We don't have anywhere we have to be. If it's alright with you, we'll just wait and chat for awhile." Robert smiled, "And enjoy some of those oatmeal raisin cookies, of course."

"Robert, what in the world did you do to your ankle? I'm afraid that cast gives the impression that whatever it was had to be very painful."

"I broke it getting off my boat. I wasn't paying attention and slipped, and before I knew it my ankle had rolled over and I came down on it with all my weight and broke some bones."

"Would you believe I'm eighty years old and have never broken a bone. I guess I should consider myself fortunate." She got up and went to the kitchen and returned with a tray of mugs filled with coffee.

"Well, you look great for your age."

"I don't feel much different than I did in my forties. All I have to do is avoid looking at myself in the mirror. That's always a disappointing reminder of my age."

"I can relate." Tony reached for a cookie and took a bite. "Outstanding. Amelia, you've got to share this recipe with me."

"I'd be happy to. I've been waiting to return the favor, Tony."

Robert looked at Tony. "Did she say 'Return the favor?'"

The old woman smiled. She was enjoying the game. "You don't remember me, do you, Tony?"

"Uh-oh. Now I feel stupid. I'm afraid you've got me. Have we met somewhere before and I don't remember?"

"It was two years ago in the summer. I hadn't been able to sleep one night, so I got up early and decided to walk over to Pender's Market to do my shopping. July was real hot, so I figured to go and get back before the traffic and heat got too bad. Do you remember now?"

"Keep going. If we met too early in the morning, it may take a lot of reminding."

"You were in line behind me, although at the time I wasn't aware of that. Of course, at that hour there was only one check stand open. When I left the house I put my wallet in my purse, but not my checkbook. So when I got through the checkout I discovered that I was about four dollars short. That's when I realized that I'd left my checkbook at home. The young man asked me what I wanted him to keep back from my groceries. And when I was just about pick out some items, a voice from behind me said, 'That won't be necessary. I'll cover the extra.' You put a five dollar bill on the counter. I remember how badly scarred your hand was, but that was all I saw."

"That's right, I vaguely recall that now."

"I was planning to thank you, but before I got turned around, Mr. Pender had called you down to another register to ring you up. So all I saw was your back. You were wearing a sweatshirt with the hood up. Evidently you must not have been buying much, because by the time the young man finished bagging up my things and putting them into my cart, you had vanished. I never even got the chance to thank you. But today, when you shook my hand, I realized it was the same generous hand that had blessed me on that early morning two years ago. So after all this time, please accept the thanks of a grateful old woman."

"Way to go, Tony." Robert said. "You know, Amelia, I haven't known this guy very long, but that story doesn't surprise me one bit."

"Mr. Pender always does that when he sees me. I guess he knows how uncomfortable it can be to have to stand in line. People don't always know how to handle being around me. That's why I try and shop when no one else is around."

"This may surprise you, but I have thought about you many times over the past two years. Every time I think about that morning I ask God to bless you in the same way you blessed me. I ask him to send someone into your life at just the moment you need them most."

"Thank you." Unconsciously, Tony touched the wrinkled scar tissue with his other hand.

"Okay. Now Robert, tell me about this letter. You say you found it on an old fishing boat? And it had never been mailed?"

"That's right. I was changing some things around up in the forward compartment of my boat and found the letter tucked into some canvas webbing under a bunk that goes back to when it was still a working fishing boat."

"So you own the boat now?"

"That's right. I've owned her for a couple of years. But she was converted to a pleasure craft quite awhile before I bought her. Since I live aboard now, I decided I needed some more storage. I was tearing out one of the original bunks when I discovered the letter."

"I see. So you live on this boat? Alone? Aren't either of you married?"

"Divorced," said Tony.

"I *was* married." Robert paused to take a sip of coffee. "My wife died last June. I rented out our house and moved on board the boat. That's why I was doing the work when I found the letter."

"Oh Robert, I'm so sorry. Was your wife ill?"

"She died of cancer. She'd been in and out of the hospital for most of the year before. She just kind of wasted away...but she hung in there as long as she could."

"So what made you decide to try and find Amy and return the letter? I think most people would have just thrown it away. After all, the chances of finding her after all these years is pretty slim. Didn't it seem that way?"

"Amelia, I am so glad to hear you say that." Tony looked from Amelia to Robert and back. "I've been telling this guy not to get his hopes up for that very reason. I still can't really believe that he was able to find her. I thought for sure this was going to be a dead end."

Robert said, "I admit that logically this *was* a long shot. What I haven't told you, Amelia, is that Amy Allen was my wife's maiden name. And at the time that I found the letter I was at probably my lowest point since my Amy died. I'd just broken my ankle, my boat had a nasty leak, I was totally aimless and for a few days nearly helpless, and I just didn't see much point in getting up in the morning." He sipped his coffee. "But finding the letter written to Miss Amy Allen kind of snapped me back to reality. At first it was a shock. Honestly, it kind of upset me. But then I got to thinking about what might happen if I could find this other Amy Allen, after sixty or more years, and finally place the letter in her hands."

"What did you think that might accomplish for you?" asked Amelia.

"I'm not sure what I expected. I guess the most important thing was that the letter got me moving again. I don't know if you've ever been stuck and it just doesn't seem like you'll ever break free, but that's how I was feeling. Stuck."

"I can't recall ever having been stuck, exactly. I know I've had some disappointments, even some painful losses over the last eighty years, but I really believe I've been blessed in my life." Amelia stood up. "Are you boys ready for some more coffee?"

"I'd love some more. Tony?"

"Sounds great."

Amelia came back with a carafe and a refilled plate of cookies. There was something familiar about her, Robert thought. In just a short time all three of them had become comfortable just chatting. He didn't want it to end.

"It looks like Miss Allen got delayed. If you've got other things you need to be doing, we could come back another time."

"Nonsense. I don't know what's happened to Amy. That woman's never been on time in her life. But *I* don't have anywhere to go." She paused. "You know, long life is a wonderful thing, but sometimes you outlive all your friends and loved ones. I guess that's what's happened to me. So don't you boys worry about taking up my time. This has been very enjoyable for me."

"You're very kind, Amelia."

"Robert, going back to the letter, I'm curious as to how you connected my name to Amy's. When you called you said my name had come up as a possible contact to Amy Allen. I'm curious who might have told you that."

Robert looked at Tony, who was smiling. The moment of truth had come, and the fact that Amy Allen wasn't in the room to hear the answer to Amelia's question came as a relief.

"I'll be happy to answer that question for you, but first, if you don't mind, may I ask how long you and Amy Allen have been friends?"

Again, the corners of Amelia's mouth curled slightly. "I guess I've known Amy most of my life. Since we were teenagers, anyway. Why do you ask?"

"I thought this might come up. I also thought that I would be better prepared. Oh well, here goes. Do you remember the other morning when I first called?"

"Yes."

"I told you that I had called every Allen listed in the phone book, but without any luck."

"I remember. Then you said my name came up as a possible contact to Amy Allen." Amelia sipped her tea never taking her eyes off Robert.

"I opened the letter."

"*My name* was mentioned in a letter to Amy Allen?"

"Yes, ma'am. That has been a little puzzling for us, too. I mean Tony and me."

"Tony read the letter, too?"

"He did, but that was only because I was so excited about finding you. Or finding Amy Allen. You have no idea how I've waited for the moment when I could deliver this letter to her." Robert reached inside his jacket pocket and brought out the envelope. "I'm not trying to be evasive, but the way your name came up is nothing short of miraculous. When I called you it had been snowing for the past couple of days. That's when I did all the calling to the Allens listed in the phone book. But then when I woke up yesterday morning, it had cleared up and the sun was out. My whole boat was covered with, like, a foot of snow. The reflection filled the salon with really intense light. Anyway, I had this dream the night before about ... oh, that doesn't matter. What's important is, in my dream I was told to open the letter. So when I woke up in the middle of the night I got up and steamed it open." Robert looked at Tony who looked as dumbfounded as Amelia. "*The point is,* I opened the letter and read it. It was then that I realized this wasn't just junk mail from a fisherman, but that this guy had something to say. After I read it, I laid the letter on the dinette table and went back to bed. But the next morning, after I got cleaned up, I looked at it again. This time though, the light reflecting in off the snow lit the whole place up. It was then that I saw something written at the crease inside the flap. So I got a magnifying glass and in that intense light was able to read the words written very lightly in pencil."

"And what did the words say?" Amelia hadn't moved since Robert started his monologue. "Robert?"

"They said, 'I love A. Albermarle.'"

Amelia seemed to lose her breath. Her eyes glistened in the hazy afternoon light. "Oh, my. I guess I wasn't expecting that."

"What *were* you expecting?"

"I don't know exactly. It could have been anything – just not *that.*

"Amelia, who do you think the writer was?"

"I'm not sure. You have to remember, that was a very long time ago."

"You must have known Amy Allen back then to have been mentioned in this letter to her. Did she have a steady boyfriend? Or was she engaged? I mean what's in this letter isn't the kind of stuff that casual friends would write."

"No? You know, as I recall, Amy did have a boyfriend back then, but I think he went off and joined the service. That was right during the worst years of the war. Most young men had to leave and go overseas." She stared out at the maple tree in the front yard. "Lots of them never came home. Lots of families were never the same again. The truth is I'm not really sure what became of that young man."

"Would you like to read the letter?" Robert held it out to her.

"Oh, I don't think I should. I don't think Amy would approve. I mean, it was one thing for you two boys to have read it, since that's how you found me and all, but I don't think she would want *me* to read it. Really. At least not before she does."

"Okay. If you change your mind just let me know." Robert looked at his watch. "I'm beginning to think that Miss Allen may not make it today. Is there any way you can call her niece?"

"I can try. I have her phone number in my address book in the bedroom. I'll go and see if I can find out what's taking them so long." Amelia stood up and brushed the wrinkles from her dress. "You boys have another cookie and some more coffee and I'll be right back."

When she'd left the room, Robert said, "What do you think the deal is with this letter? Was this guy maybe playing both sides?"

Tony shook his head. "I can't tell. Amelia seems so genuine, it's hard for me to believe she's not telling the truth. I guess only Miss Allen will be able to clear this whole mystery up." He chuckled. "That's assuming she *herself* can remember."

Amelia came back to the living room. "Well, I apologize. I don't have any idea what's happened to those two. I'm guessing that if she hasn't come by now, there's some reason she's not coming at all." She could see disappointment register on Robert's face. "I'll get a hold of her niece as soon as I can and see if we can set up another time. I hope that's alright."

"Sure. That's okay. We'll just do this another day." Robert looked at Tony and they both got to their feet.

Before they could get their jackets zipped Amelia said, "I feel terrible that you boys went to all this trouble and Amy doesn't show up. I have an idea. Why don't you two take off you coats and sit back down and I'll make some supper for the three of us. If by chance Amy is able to make it, then the time won't have been a total waste."

Tony looked at Robert and shrugged. "I don't have any commitments."

Robert grinned, "Amelia, you've got dinner guests. What can we do to help?"

"Wonderful! I have a pot roast in the refrigerator that I was going to make on Sunday."

"The deal is that you have to let us help."

"Robert, you and Tony are going to be my potato and carrot peelers. Take off your jackets and follow me to the kitchen."

CHAPTER THIRTEEN

"Amelia, I can't remember a better roast. I don't know what seasoning you used, but it was perfect." Tony pushed his chair back. "If I was to eat one more bite you'd have to roll me out to the car."

"Well, definitely don't eat one more bite, then," said Robert. "I don't want to have to try and drive back to the marina."

"*You* don't? Bud, you have no idea how that proposition frightens me."

Amelia smiled at the exchange. "Boys, now that will do. There'll be no arguing at the table."

"Sounds like you may have had to say that before, Amelia. Do you have children?"

"That's something I heard growing up. I had two older sisters. Seems Mama was always telling us to quit fighting at the table." She started to clear the table. "But to answer your question, Robert, I had a daughter. She died in the spring of 1953."

"I'm sorry. As unfair as Amy's death seemed, at least she had a life. The death of a child always really gets to me."

"Poor little thing, she got polio as an infant. After that it was a string of illnesses. Every winter we'd fight terrible bouts of bronchitis and pneumonia. She had whooping cough every winter for the last five years of her life. Finally her lungs couldn't do their job anymore. She died in April of '53."

"That must be her in the picture on the mantle. With the braces on her legs?"

"That's my Winnie. Her name was Winifred – after her great-grandmother."

"Did your husband die?" Tony got up and started to help clean up.

Amelia didn't answer. She set the dishes on the counter and started to fill the sink.

"I'm sorry. I didn't mean to pry."

"We were never married." Amelia spoke to the window above the sink. "I know that isn't considered a big deal today, but it was when I was young. I've never forgotten the shame and heartache I caused my Mama and Daddy." She turned to face Tony. "It's still something that's hard for me to talk about."

"I apologize. I had no right to ask something so personal."

"It's not that. And I don't regret having her – not one minute of it. I guess I still miss her, that's all. Sometimes it's hard to talk about her. I don't think a day has gone by since I told her not to worry about me, to just fly on home to Jesus's arms, that I don't think about her. You asked about her daddy. I don't know for sure what happened to him. One day he was in my life and we were in love, and the next day he was gone. I'm not real sure what ever became of him."

Tony shook his head. "That had to be rough. He just took off and left you two alone? Did he leave before the baby was born?"

"He didn't even know I was pregnant."

"Did something happen to him?"

"I'd like to think that, but, I don't know for sure. I got word through a family member that he had run off and joined the army. Almost every young man served in one way or another. Later I heard that he was killed in action."

"Amelia, how did you manage? All alone with a sick child? Did you live here then?" Both Robert and Tony stopped with their chores and focused on the old woman.

"I lived right here in this house. Grandma was alive then and she helped with the baby as best she could." She looked around the little kitchen and placed a hand on the wall. "This house belonged to my grandmother. She had been housekeeper for a wealthy sawmill owner in the twenties and thirties and was real close to the family. When he died, his wife moved back East to live with their oldest son. I think he was a lawyer in Cincinnati or someplace. Mrs. Wilson – that was the lady's name – gave this house to my grandmother free and clear. I came down from Seattle to look after her when I was seventeen and I've been here ever since."

"Wow, that's amazing. You don't have any family left in the area?"

Amelia shook her head. "Just one neice."

"How are you able to keep up with it all?"

"Lately I haven't. The place is in pretty sad shape. There's so much that needs to be done, but I just don't have the ambition anymore. And it's hard to find a handyman who doesn't figure his time is worth twenty-five or thirty dollars an hour."

"That may be something we can help with when the weather warms up." Robert looked at Tony, who nodded.

"That's very kind of you boys, but I don't want you two to feel sorry for me. I get along pretty well, even though things don't look perfect outside."

"Amelia, I didn't say we'd do it for free." Robert tried to act serious. "There would have to be some sort of agreement about cookies and the occasional pot roast written into the contract."

"And access to your recipe files," added Tony.

"I'm sure you both mean it, too, but let's just wait and see how the winter goes before we start planning our spring projects."

They finished washing and drying the dishes. When everything was put away, Amelia put on a pot of coffee and set out the rest of the cookies in the living room. "If you boys work real hard on these there probably won't be any left to send home with you."

"Speaking of work, what did you do all these years here in Olympia?"

"Back during the war I did some seasonal work around town. There were small farms that needed help in the summer. The rest of the year I worked as a cleaning woman. Grandma watched Winnie as best she could. Winnie was too sick to attend school so I taught her here at home. She was an excellent reader and a whiz at math. I think we were the only black family in Olympia for many years." She went to the kitchen and came back with cups and the carafe. "I applied for a job with the state many times, but it wasn't until 1960 that I finally got hired. I worked for the Department of Revenue for thirty-two years."

"What was that like in the early days?"

"Well, let's just say that my ability to do my job seemed much less important than the color of my skin. I think the only reason I got the job is because I wore the head of personnel down. He expected me to fail, but that made me even more determined to succeed."

Robert shook his head. "You are amazing. I feel privileged to have gotten to meet you. I really mean that."

"Amen," said Tony, "and that's not just the pot roast and cookies talking."

"Stop, you two, you don't want to see an old lady cry, do you?"

"You know what's weird about this whole letter mystery?" Robert looked at Tony but didn't wait for a response, "It's that we haven't even met Amy Allen yet. We've only met her friend, who is totally incredible and yet the letter was meant for someone else." He looked back at Amelia, "After reading the letter, Amy Allen must really be some kind of special, too."

Amelia smiled as though what he said reminded her of something. "Oh yes, the letter. You know I'd almost forgotten that's what brought you boys over to visit me. It feels like I've known you both for a much longer time." Her voice was quiet, "Robert, you asked me earlier if I would like to read the letter. Would you consider doing me a favor?"

"Sure, if it doesn't involve walking too far."

"Would you read the letter to me – out loud?"

"Now? You want me to read it right now?"

"Right now."

"Sure. I'd be happy to read it right now. What about what you said about Amy not liking it much? I don't want to cause a rift."

"I'll accept the responsibility."

"Done." He looked at Tony, "Toss me my jacket."

Robert situated himself under the lamp near his chair. He looked over at Amelia, who nestled down in her recliner with her head back and eyes closed. He began:

"June, 6, 1943

Dear Amy,

Tony silently observed the magic unfold as the resonance of Robert's voice brought images to life in the mind of a lonely old woman. At light speed the writer's voice bridged more than sixty years of silence.

"Sorry if this letter looks like a first-grader wrote it. It's a little after two o'clock and I'm writing this while scrunched up under the chart table by the light of a tiny oil lamp. Tonight I'm sleeping on the pilothouse floor because with the other guys aboard, there isn't a bunk for me. I really don't mind. If I was down below with the others, I'd just have lay there and think about all the things I want to tell you instead of being able to write them down."

Robert paused to look at Amelia, who sat with closed eyes, smiling.

"I hadn't planned to write tonight. In fact, I went to sleep when we all settled down for the night. I slept real well too, until a little while ago. But now I'm wide awake. I know the Skipper will have us up in another couple of hours, and I'll probably be draggin' all day, but right now all I can think about is you. All I can ever think about is you.

Amy, I am so excited about us being together, I'm just about to explode. I know the war still has to be won, and Hitler and 'The

Japs' put where they belong, but that won't take forever. I may have to be gone for a couple of years, but after that we can be together forever. Honey, I know you still have doubts about whether that can really happen or not. I know that our folks probably won't ever approve. I'm pretty sure they would do almost anything to keep us apart. I don't care what they think anymore."

Her smile vanished.

For the past few days I've been working with the Skipper and the men. I've been doing my best and the men treat me like I'm one of them. As much as I want to respect our fathers' opinions, I can't anymore. Honey, they are wrong. You and I love each other and that's all that matters. Do you hear me through these words I'm writing? Imagine you can hear my voice. You are all that matters to me. I'll do whatever it takes to be with you. Baby, I can't imagine my life without you in it. We can't let our parents or anybody else make our decisions for us.

I'm hoping the next ten days or so are going to fly by. I hate the fact that I won't be able to get your letters during that time. I miss you so much already. Your letters are my only lifeline. I don't know what I'd do if I couldn't feel your love through the words you write to me. I've saved every letter you've ever written. I've read them all a dozen times. I even brought them along just so that I could read them again when I get to missing you too much."

Amelia opened her eyes and stared straight ahead.

I guess I should close for now. I don't really know much. I just wanted to tell you that you're always in my thoughts, and that I can't wait till the day when we can be together without having to worry about what anyone else thinks. You are my future. I love you with all my heart.   *Ford*

Robert folded the letter and laid it in his lap. Amelia hadn't moved or spoken since the first words. Even before she opened her eyes, lines of tears ran down her cheeks. Without a word, she got up and went into her bedroom.

Robert looked at Tony whose eyes were glistening, too. "I don't get it. Something about this letter has to involve her. She seems really moved, but I can't figure how it all ties together."

Tony' voice was quiet. "I don't know either, bro, but something in that letter really touched her. I couldn't take my eyes off her as you were reading. At first she was smiling and then…"

Amelia came back into the living room carrying two envelopes bound with a ribbon.

"Amelia," Robert tried to get to his feet, "are you alright? Did the letter upset you?"

"Upset me? Yes, I guess the letter did upset me. Most of all, though, I'm upset with myself."

"Why? The letter wasn't even written to you." He sat back down in the chair.

"Because I'm just a stupid old woman. And worst of all I've been stupid for a very long time. In my heart I've always wanted to believe he felt that way, but I allowed myself to believe a lie instead."

"Amelia, I'm sorry, but none of this makes any sense."

"I'm sorry about *that*, too." She slumped into the recliner. "You boys have been so sweet to me. I had no right to take advantage of your kindness."

"You haven't taken advantage of us. Seriously, I haven't felt this at home since *my* Amy died."

"You boys are *so* kind."

"Amelia, what is the truth about the letter? Who is Amy Allen? How do you fit into this?"

Her lips trembled. As hard as she tried to control it, the flow of tears returned. She wiped her eyes and smiled. "That's just it. I'm so sorry for not telling you earlier. There *is* no Amy Allen. There never was. It was just a made-up name we used to fool our folks. That letter was written to me by the only man I've ever loved. And after all these years, I can almost dare to believe loved me, too – and would have loved our Winnie."

Nothing could restrain the emotion now. Decades of disappointment and loneliness found voice in deep sobs. Hunched over with her face buried in wrinkled hands, she still held the envelopes she'd brought from the bedroom. Robert reached over and eased the packet from her hand. She made no effort to resist. Tony moved from his place on the sofa and knelt down next to Robert's chair.

Robert turned them over in his hands. Two envelopes were bundled together and tied with a ribbon. He slid the top one out and read the front.

"It's addressed to Miss Amy Allen, PO Box 524, Olympia, Wash., just like the letter I found."

The flap was unsealed. Robert glanced at Amelia, and then pulled the letter out and quietly began to read.

July 1, 1943
*To Amy Allen or whatever your name is, I don't really care
how this letter finds you. I don't even care if you really*

exist. No, I take that back, I wish you didn't. But since you seem to have put some kind of spell on my son, I thought you should know that it's finally broken. And no, it's not for the reason you think, either. I know what the newspaper said about a 'young fisherman apparently lost at sea.' The truth is I sent someone out to get him and bring him back. We found out about his 'love affair' with some little nigger bitch he met on a city bus. That was all it took. It cost me three hundred dollars to have somebody go get him off that boat. But it was worth every penny. You'll never see him again. NEVER! Wes enlisted in the army on June 20th and right now is in basic training. I would rather see him go to war and get his guts blown out than let him take up with a no good tramp like you! I just thought you might like to know. Don't believe everything you read in the newspapers.

Al Johnson

He folded the letter and put it back in the envelope. Sliding the ribbon off of the second envelope, he read the address. It was identical to the first, written in the same frenzied scrawl.

July 21, 1944
Do you remember what I told you the last time I wrote? Did you understand that I didn't raise my son to have him run off with a nigger? I told you that I'd rather he died than to ever think he could betray his family by taking up with the likes of you! Just so you know, my son is dead! He was killed in the invasion of Normandy on June 6. My only consolation is that before he made the most terrible mistake of his life he finally came to his senses. When I put him on the bus for basic training he told me that he didn't know what got into him - that it was because you were different and easy. He apologized to me for betraying his family. The only good thing that has come of this is that he

realized he never cared about you before it was too late. So don't fool yourself into thinking you could have ever really had him. As far as I'm concerned you can go to hell!

Al Johnson

Robert put the letter back. What could possibly fill a man's heart with such hatred? Why would anyone go to such lengths to thrust a dagger into the heart of a young woman he'd never even met? And not once, but twice? Robert looked at Amelia. She seemed smaller and more frail than she had when she answered the door earlier in the afternoon.

Just then she got up and went into the bathroom. In a few minutes she returned. The tears were at last kept at bay, but her voice still trembled.

"Do you see now how foolish I've been all these years?"

Robert held up the letters. "All I understand for sure is that the man who wrote these letters was a really sick person. Beyond that, I'm still not sure what any of this means."

Amelia sighed. "In June of 1943, Wes – that was his real name – left to go fishing aboard the *Jean White*. He had just graduated from high school and was waiting for his call up notice. He decided to try fishing in the meantime to see if he liked the water." She smiled, recalling his comments about the army. "He always said he'd get fed better in the navy."

"So that's how the letter got aboard my boat. But why would he have left it there?"

"The local newspaper carried a brief article on June 15th, 1943, saying that the captain of the fishing boat, *Jean White,* had made an early morning discovery of a young deckhand who was missing and presumed drowned. But no body was ever recovered." She sighed again. "I think my Wes fell overboard and drowned. I've always wanted to believe that he really loved me, but those ugly letters from his father were so convincing."

"That's for sure," said Tony.

"I'd always wondered how his father could have gotten my address unless what he said about Wes was true. We never used return addresses, for that very reason, so that if either of our parents somehow found one of our letters, there'd be no trail to follow up. But in this letter Wes said he took all my old letters with him on the boat. When you read that, I remembered that it wasn't until after our first couple of exchanges that we decided to not use a return address."

"So Wes's father could have gotten your address off one of the first letters," guessed Robert.

"Which he would have found in Wes's personal belongings after the boat got back in," said Tony, as he and Robert alternately filled in the blanks.

"That's what I *choose* to believe. For the last sixty years I've lived with the horrible image of my beautiful Wes apologizing to his hateful, racist daddy for having betrayed the family just by falling in love with me 'cause I'm black. Or worse not really falling in love with me at all, but just using me like my mama said he would."

"So your parents knew about him, too?"

"Mama did. I don't think she ever told Daddy. Didn't matter though, he was so upset when he found out I was pregnant that he didn't speak to me for a long time."

"Would your father have approved of Wes?" asked Robert.

"Oh, no. My daddy was sort of like a black version of Wes's daddy. He'd had a whole lifetime of bitterness with white people. I don't think he would have done it, but if the roles had been reversed he might have signed his name to those letters."

"Amelia, I don't know if I've brought you a blessing or a curse. Please forgive me if I've upset things up by being so determined to return this letter."

"Robert. Dear boy. Don't you believe for a moment that I regret any of what's happened tonight – except maybe that I deceived two of the nicest young people I've ever met. For the first time in sixty long years I feel like some of my questions have been answered. I've spent so many hours lying alone in the dark wondering what could have been so…so ugly in me to make Wes abandon me like his father claimed. I don't have any evidence other than this letter, but the fact that it was written just days before he disappeared…after so many years of doubt, this is like a fresh start for me." She smiled at Robert. "So don't you think for a moment that this has been anything but a blessing to my old soul. For the first time in many, many years I feel like I can see this in a new light. Maybe, finally, I can chase away those demons that come in the middle of the night to accuse me of being unworthy of his love."

"Amelia, I've only known you a short time, but I think you're one of the most amazing people I've ever met," Robert told her.

"I second that. That you remembered me, and that you remembered me with anything other than a sympathetic shiver means more than you'll ever know," added Tony.

Robert looked at his watch. It was nearly ten o'clock. "We should probably think about getting back to the marina." Tony nodded.

"Oh, boys, I'm so glad you went to all this trouble to find me. I can't begin to thank you."

"Well, actually, maybe you can. How about letting us take you to breakfast tomorrow? Say around nine? Tony would you be up for that?"

"Sure. As long as we can do it on my boat. Amelia, do you like boats?"

"I don't know, I've been on land all my life. But I *would* like to see the place where Weston spent his last days. I'd love to come, if you both want me to."

"Absolutely. We'll be by around nine." Robert got his crutches under him.

"I'll make my special French toast with scrambled eggs and sausage. I don't make it for just everybody," said Tony.

"I'll be ready by *eight o'clock* then. Again, thank you both for this day. I can't think of one that's meant more to me since when my Winnie was still alive."

Amelia Albermarle hugged each one and kissed them gently on the cheek before closing the door behind them.

CHAPTER FOURTEEN

Robert lay in the starboard bunk with his eyes open. The clock showed 1:42 in crimson digits. He wanted to sleep. He needed to sleep. No matter how he tried to shut off the movie in his brain, a renegade projectionist kept the film rolling. Over and over he watched a young Amelia Albermarle with sculpted cheekbones and obsidian eyes fall in love with handsome Wes Johnson. They would hold each other and tenderly kiss, until Wes's evil father came and dragged him away, forcing him off to war. In another scenario he'd see Wes fighting for his life in oilskins and sou'wester as he tried to keep his head above the waves. In each scene he went down for the last time screaming, " I LOVE YOU, AMELIA!"

He rolled over and stared at the bureau. It was strange that he had laid awake so many nights after Amy died, never guessing what was hidden just a few feet away. It was there all along, waiting to change his life – and Amelia's – and even Tony's – without him knowing. That had to be a sort of sign, didn't it? It was too important to be simple coincidence. He had needed something to give him purpose again. Tony needed to find a reason greater than his fear of people, and Amelia needed to be paroled from a sixty-year sentence in a cell built of lies and bigotry. No, Providence had to have a hand in this. Even so, Robert had to admit that if this was everything, it wasn't enough. Of course, that is exactly what Tony had warned him about. "What will you do if the letter means more to you than Miss Amy Allen? What if she says 'Thank you very much. Bye now?'" Even though that hadn't happened, Robert lay in the darkness feeling empty. Right now what he wanted most was to escape to that sunny beach where he could meet *his* Amy, and then, if only for a little while, the world would be right again.

*****

Robert awoke to voices on the dock outside. A moment later he felt the boat rock, and heard someone pounding on the pilothouse door. He looked at the clock. 9:17. He was late.

"Robert. Yo, Robert, are you in there? Wake up, bro, it's after nine."

He pulled aside the curtain over his bunk. Dressed in a flowered red dress with a raincoat and white sneakers, was Amelia Albermarle. He smiled. Tony must have convinced her to put on the sneakers for climbing up and down the gangways. Robert lay back for a moment. "Okay, Tony. I'm awake. I must have overslept. Why don't you take Amelia down to your boat and I'll be there as soon as I get ready," he yelled.

"Okay. I hope this isn't your way of getting out of helping, though. There's always the dishes." He hopped onto the dock leaving *NoraLynn* rocking gently.

Robert got out of bed and cleaned up. When he got to the top step outside Tony's boat he called down through the open companionway. Tony met him with a smile. "So, did we sleep well?"

"Not really. That's why I overslept. I couldn't get last night's conversations out of my head. It was after two and I was still looking at the clock."

"That's okay. I slept like a baby, but woke up at six and couldn't close my eyes again. I don't know what you two did to me last night, but I feel like a new man."

"Outstanding. How's our guest feeling?"

"She said she stayed up going through old pictures and remembering those years in a whole different way. She went to bed at two, and hasn't slept so well since she could remember."

"Well, that's two out of three. Maybe it'll go better tonight."

Tony motioned for Robert to go ahead. "I'll be right behind you in case you fall. That way I won't have to try and get out of the way."

"Yeah. Thanks." Before he got to the bottom of the companionway steps Robert could smell coffee and cooking sausage. Something was baking, too. Tony was working his magic in the galley.

When Amelia saw him she came over and hugged him. "There's another one of my heroes," she said, "I hope we didn't drag you from a particularly special dream."

"Not that I recall. Sorry I'm late. For some reason I just couldn't go to sleep. Then when I finally did, I couldn't wake up." He looked at Tony. "I see one of us kept our promise."

"He was early, too, and reminded me I'd said I'd be ready at eight. We went over to Pender's Market to shop for breakfast. We had so much fun...I can't remember a nicer time at the grocery store."

"You two really have been ambitious this morning."

"I just took some scones out of the oven. Why don't you two sit down and eat one while they're hot. I made up some whipped honey-butter to go on them. It's going to be a few more minutes before breakfast is ready," Tony said.

"You don't have to ask me twice." Robert handed his crutches to Tony and plopped down at the table.

"Me either, no sir." Amelia sat down next to Robert. "So tell me what the problem was that kept you from sleeping last night."

"I don't know. It wasn't just one thing. I guess it was everything. Finding you - finding Amy Allen and then hearing your story." Robert sipped his coffee. "I kept imagining you and Wes as young kids, full of hope, and the way it all ended before it really got started. I kept seeing his father, blind with hatred, more interested in hurting you than grieving the loss of his son...maybe his only child." He met Amelia's eyes. "I honestly don't know how you've turned out to be such a positive person. Really, I lost my wife after twenty-three years of marriage and for the past few months I've been ready to write the world off."

"Robert, I've done my share of complaining to God about the hard times in my life. But there are always people who have had to go through something much worse that we have. I've come to realize that a grateful heart focuses on what it has received and not what it hasn't. Otherwise most of us could find some reason to be eaten up with bitterness."

"I guess."

"And by the way, Wes wasn't an only child. He had a little brother. I think his name was Ferdinand, or Fernando. I can't remember. It started with an F." She took a bite of scone. Steam escaped through melting butter. "Tony, this is too good to describe. You have a gift. I mean it, you should sell these."

"Wait till you taste my French toast. Those things will taste like they're made of sawdust."

Robert was thinking. "Sounds like the Johnsons were into strange names. I mean Weston isn't exactly common, but 'Fernando Johnson?' That's really pushing it." He couldn't help but chuckle.

"Now that you say it, I know that's not right. Ferd? No, Fergie! That's it. He had a little brother named Fergie. His real name was Fergus, but Wes always called him Fergie. I'm surprised that came back to me. Sometimes I can't remember where I put my reading glasses from two minutes before."

"Fergus Johnson. I guess that sounds more conventional. British or maybe Scottish. It definitely fits better than Fernando." Robert sampled the scone. "Wow! Amelia is right, Tony, I think you've got a winner here. You need to open a bakery or an espresso shop that features your homemade scones."

"Amen," said Amelia, "That reminds me. Last night after you left, I made myself a cup of tea and thought over everything that we talked about. I read the letter again and had myself another cry. Then I went and dug out some pictures that I had put away years ago. I brought a few along if you boys would like see them." She pulled some black and whites from her purse. "There's one of my grandma and Winnie together out under the maple tree. There's another of Winnie and me sitting on the floor folding laundry." She laid the pictures out on the table.

"These are great, Amelia, who took them?" Tony stood over her wiping his hands on a dish towel.

"Old Mr. Granger. He lived right next door to us when I first came to Olympia. I'll never forget him. He treated Grandma and Winnie and me like we were special friends. He always said he was 'color blind' when he'd come over wearing different colors of socks. But I knew what he meant. He was a real good friend to us in those days. He died not long before Winnie. I'm glad he didn't outlive her. It would have broken his heart."

"Who are these two?" Tony point at the last photograph she'd laid out.

"That's my Weston. And that's his younger brother with him. He wanted me to have a picture of him, but the only one he had was a shot taken of the two of them at the fair. I ran across it last night, too."

Robert picked up the picture of the Johnson brothers. Wes seemed to be seven or eight years older. He was tall and thin, with a shock of light hair and an infectious smile. He was grinning and resting his hand on the shoulder of his younger brother who appeared less enthusiastic about being photographed. After hearing the stories about Weston Allen Johnson the night before, it seemed like there was something familiar about him. It was like Robert knew so much about him that to finally see his picture only made him look more familiar. Even the pensive look on his little brother's face seemed to register.

"He was a good looking young man." Robert slid the photo back over to Amelia. "I think you two would have made a great couple."

"Thanks to you, today even *I* can believe that."

"No idea what ever became of the family?"

"After those hateful letters I gave up. Since I knew Wes was dead, there was no point in any more contact and thankfully his daddy never wrote again."

"That makes sense," said Tony as he brought plates piled with scrambled eggs and French toast with crisp sausage patties. "Let's forget about the bigots for now and enjoy breakfast?"

"Good idea," said Amelia.

*****

After the dishes were done they sat in the salon talking. Tony made another pot of coffee and refilled the cups while Amelia hummed softly between bursts of conversation.

"Honestly, I am amazed that I'm sitting on a big old boat with two young men who only a day ago were complete strangers. And I can't believe how my perception of the world has changed in just the last twenty-four hours. I feel like I've been given a pardon from a crime I didn't commit."

"Amelia, it's so good to hear you say that. When I decided to try and find Amy Allen I was afraid that the letter wouldn't mean anything to her. I was thinking last night, *instead of sleeping*, that this whole thing has been Providential."

"You mean like divinely ordained?"

"I suppose. I don't know how else to describe it."

"Robert, would it surprise you to know that I've been praying for over sixty years to know the truth about Weston? Either that or to know what it was in me that made him stop loving me."

"I guess that does surprise me. I can't imagine doing anything for sixty years. Especially with no result."

Amelia laughed. "That's the bargain, though, don't you see ? If everything we prayed for was instantaneous, there'd be no need for faith."

"So what do you think that means for me? Now? I mean, where do I go from here? Now that the letter's been delivered, I'm kind of back at square one. What I'm saying is that what I was hoping for was something to jumpstart my life again. Now I'm back where I was before I came down here. The only difference is that I'm here and not up on Whidbey Island."

"Maybe that's where you should start, then. Maybe that's the point."

"I don't get what you mean."

"Dear boy, don't overlook the obvious. Especially when nothing else is in sight."

"So, you're saying that you think I should stay here? In Olympia?"

"I'm saying that until something more obvious presents itself, this may be a good place to wait for further clarification."

"I guess I'll have to think about that."

"That's the good part about living on a boat," said Tony, "anyplace where the water's deep enough to tie her up becomes home."

"Well, the least I can do is give it some consideration. And I still want to see my brother while I'm down here."

"That reminds me, Robert, you said that I could see your boat. I don't know why I feel like that's important, but I do."

"Because you were in love with him and it's probably the last thing he saw before he died." Tony stood up and gathered up the cups. "That doesn't seem odd to me."

"Me either. Let me get my coat and crutches."

CHAPTER FIFTEEN

Outside the dock was washed in sunlight. The wind kept flags and pennants snapping to the rhythm of clanging halyards. Amelia stopped midway down the dock and looked up at the sky. She closed her eyes and let the sun warm her face. "I see why you boys like this place so much."

"Days like this certainly add to the magic." Robert stopped next to her and rocked on his crutches.

"Strange how different today is from a few days ago. It seemed like it was going to be cold and snowy until April. Sure is strange weather." She looked at the sky before continuing on.

"Here she is." Robert turned to face Amelia, "Of course in the forties she would have looked completely different."

"Different how?" She raised a hand to shade her eyes.

"Well, remember in the letter Wes said he had to sleep on the pilothouse floor the first night while they were still in port?"

"Yes."

"That's because none of this was here, then." He motioned to the salon, aft of the pilothouse. "This whole area you see here was originally just open deck with big hatches to access the area underneath where they stored the catch." He pointed to the salon again. "This was all added after the boat was no longer used for fishing. Right now you're looking at my kitchen, dining room and living room."

"Pretty small, isn't it?"

"For now it meets my needs. After Amy died I rattled around in our house. Every room reminded me of something. But since she never really liked the water, there wasn't much aboard to bring back painful memories."

"I understand."

"Would you like to come aboard and see what she was like in 1943?"

She paused and caught her breath. "I'd love to if these old legs of mine will carry me."

"You'll do just fine. We'll go nice and slow. Tony, come alongside please, and we'll help Miss Albermarle take a leap back in time."

"Aye, aye, Skipper."

Once aboard Amelia followed Robert to the salon door. Before they went inside she stopped and looked over the stern. "Do you suppose it was here that he went into the water? Or could it have been anywhere?"

"That's hard to say. I would think that if it was a wave that knocked him overboard it could have been anywhere along the rail. It doesn't really matter, does it?"

"No, not really. It's just that when I would allow myself to believe he might have fallen overboard, I used to lay awake and wonder what he yelled, or how terrified he was knowing that he was going to drown. I don't think about that much anymore."

Robert opened the door. "Let's go inside and you can look around. Until I removed the bunk where I found the letter, the forward compartment was left exactly the way it was when Wes was aboard. At least I'm pretty sure it's original."

Amelia and Tony followed him into the salon. "Robert, I love this little wood stove. And this area has such a homey feel to it. This is very comfortable."

"Not exactly the luxury of Tony's boat, but it's adequate for me."

Tony sat down. "You two go ahead, I've been slaving over a hot stove all morning, so I'm just going to sit here and close my eyes."

Robert motioned side to side. "Well, this is it. Galley over here to the right, dinette to the left." He pointed ahead. "Watch your step here Amelia and we'll go up into the pilothouse."

Holding the grab rail, she pulled herself up the steps ahead of Robert. When he hoisted himself up, Amelia was standing at the wheel. Her attention was focused on the oil lamp over the chart table.

"Is this original?" She pointed at the lamp.

"I'm pretty sure that would have been the same one Wes mentioned in his letter. I know for sure that this is the original chart table." He stepped back and pointed down. "This is where he would have slept that night before they set out for the coast. And down there is where he said he was 'scrunched up beneath the chart table.'"

"This is strange. After so long, to think that I'm standing on exactly the same wooden planks that he stood on the very day he died." Tears welled up in her eyes. "I'm sorry, Robert, I didn't think it would affect me like this."

"Let me show you where I found the letter." He touched her shoulder.

This time Amelia followed him down the two steps, past the head and into the v-berth. Robert sat down on his bunk. "You see this top bunk?" She nodded. "Up until a short time ago there was another one identical to it down where the lower drawers of the bureau are now. In fact, the top of that bureau is made from the plywood platform someone used to cover the original canvas webbing. It was there, concealed between two canvas straps that I found the envelope."

"So you think that Weston would have tucked the letter under his mattress?"

"I know that sounds weird, doesn't it? But for some reason he must have stowed it there, maybe to reread what he'd written, and then went overboard and nobody ever discovered the letter."

"When did they cover the straps?"

"I don't know for sure. Probably when there was enough complaining about how uncomfortable the bunks were." Robert got to his feet. "I don't imagine any Skipper would want his crew complaining about the sleeping conditions when it could be easily fixed. They just covered them up with plywood."

Amelia looked up under the upper bunk. "I don't see any straps here."

"I think they probably removed them because they would have become a nuisance for the person in the lower bunk. But since the lower bunk was so close to the cabin sole there was no need to rip out the canvas. That's why the letter was never discovered."

"So this is where he would have spent his last night on earth. He may have been in this very room thinking thoughts of me and reading over the letter. I wonder if he thought about that. 'I hope somebody finds the letter. I hope Lia gets it'…before he died, I mean."

"*Lia?*" Robert looked at her curiously. "Is that what Wes called you?"

"Lia is what everybody called me. I still have a niece that calls me Auntie Lia. It's only since I've become a senior citizen that I've gone back to Amelia."

"I'm glad you're listed as A. Albermarle in the directory, or I might never have found you."

"There's that Providence thing again. I only changed back to a phone book listing this year. I haven't had a listed number for years and years."

"Tony brought me over a new phone book to use, too. So, if it had been an old book I wouldn't have found you?"

"I'm afraid not."

"I can't imagine how I'd have felt if I hadn't been able to find you. I think not knowing would have been terribly frustrating." He shook his head. "I'm not sure that I can still believe this – that you're standing here and I know what probably happened to Wes and all the rest of the details." He sat back down on the edge of the bunk and gently rested his cast on the cabin sole.

"Robert, you sound like you're trying to convince yourself of something. What is it? Were you hoping for more? Or something else?" Amelia sat down on the edge of the bunk next to him.

He knew she was on to him. "I'm sorry. I know I should be grateful that this has turned out the way it has, but I still feel empty...like I've missed something." He looked at the old woman. From that angle he could see a haze in the depth of her pupils.

Patches of wrinkles gathered at the corners of her eyes and he noticed a droopiness in the folds of skin at her neck. Even the curve of her cheekbones seemed less prominent in the half-light of the forward compartment. "Tell me honestly, Amelia, has this been enough for you? Are you convinced that Wes died off the Washington coast and not at Normandy like his father said? Absolutely convinced? Does the letter prove beyond any doubt that what his father said was just a twisted lie?"

"Oh Robert, I wish you hadn't asked me that. The last thing I want to do is appear ungrateful for all the time and trouble you've gone to to relieve this silly burden I've been carrying for the last sixty years. And last night I was sure that I was sure about what that letter proved. Today, though, I find myself letting tiny rays of doubt pierce holes in the shield around my heart." She took out a handkerchief and dabbed at her eyes. "More than anything I want to believe that Wes wouldn't have written those beautiful words to me, and just days later have told his daddy that his interest in me wasn't love but...*curiosity*. That's what I meant about faith. I'm grateful for an answer to all these years of wondering, I'm just confused about what the answer is."

"I wondered about that, too. I mean, the letter seems to suggest that he loved you up until the end. But you're right. Who knows for sure what really happened. I guess what bugs me is that this has opened up as many questions as it has provided answers. Instead of settling things so we can all move on, we're just as unsettled as when we didn't know anything- and all because *I* decided to tear out that stupid bunk."

"There is one part of this whole story that I know has been a blessing. I've met two of the nicest young men I've ever had the privilege to know. So if nothing else comes of this for sure, that in itself will be enough for me." She reached out and touched Robert's hand. "You know that you're welcome at my house whenever you want to stop by. You too, Tony," she said, as she looked up at Tony who had come from the salon and been quietly listening. In the dimness of the passageway between the pilothouse and forward compartment Tony Cruz's smile shone white and perfect.

CHAPTER SIXTEEN

Gray clouds returned when the wind changed to its normal southwesterly flow. Rain was falling, tapping out a beat somewhere between rhythm and randomness. Robert listened from his bunk, unable to sleep for a second night.

He rolled over and threw off the covers, knowing that in a few minutes he'd feel the chill and cover up again. Not being able to get comfortable and not being able to arrest vagrant thoughts were all part of the torture of insomnia. Like last night, he found himself unable to escape the conversations from earlier in the day. Amelia had all but admitted that her initial confidence wasn't bulletproof. Robert, himself, was dissatisfied with what the letter left unanswered. He knew there was no reason to have such high expectations, and yet telling himself to be glad that he had even found Amy Allen didn't fill the void. He was restless. He was restless *and* rudderless, like a kite without a tail, with no more direction than when he'd set out to deliver the letter.

He looked at the clock for the thousandth time and forced himself to close his eyes. There was nothing that could be solved at this hour that couldn't be solved after the sun came up.

But it was no use, the picture of a young Wes Johnson with his hand resting on the shoulder of his kid brother burned an image on his retina. No matter how he tried to banish the juvenile faces, they kept coming back. Wes's smile hung frozen in time, while Fergie wore a pout, bordering on a scowl. There was something about both of them that seemed so familiar that Robert felt like he recognized them. Like he'd met them. Like he'd seen that smile somewhere before. Like that look of frustration on little brother Fergie already had a drawer and file number in his memory bank. *Insomnia was a curse.*

*****

When he awoke the rain had slacked off, leaving a gray sky with intermittent darker smudges. He had finally fallen asleep sometime after four o'clock. So today was the first post-Amy-Allen-day and he had no idea what he was going to do with himself. He needed to get ahold of his brother and arrange a visit, even though he didn't feel like it.

Despite wanting to stay in his sweats all day, he ran some water in the basin in the head and stared at his reflection in the mirror. What now? he asked himself. "Amy, baby, I need some help figuring out where I'm supposed to go from here. Some sort of sign…anything," he mumbled aloud.

There were probably a dozen things he needed to do. He hadn't sent the receipt for the motor back to Lonnie yet. Although Lonnie's office looked like it had been hit by a hurricane, part of the agreement was that Robert would mail the signed receipt back to him.

Hobbling out to the bureau, he opened a drawer and got out a hand towel. The drawer slid back in without a whisper. Of course, Rusty had been right about taking the time to do the job right. He ran his hand over the stained top and admired the drawer fronts with satisfaction. The anchor pulls and oak fronts were a perfect compliment to the vintage look of the forward compartment. It occurred to him that he had never appropriately thanked Rusty for his help with the woodwork. *That* would be a worthwhile project for a day like today. Amelia had encouraged him to look for ways to demonstrate his gratitude; to focus on what he *had received*, not what he hadn't. That's what he would do today, he'd look for some thank you gifts for Rusty and Lonnie.

After he'd shaved and dressed, Robert got out the phone

directory Tony had brought over. He had an idea of what he wanted to buy, but needed to find a sporting goods store. In just a few moments he found what he was looking for. Just off I-5 there was a warehouse-type store that specialized in all kinds of hunting and camping gear. Both Lonnie and Rusty could really use a top quality pocket knife. He'd find something that could be engraved, and deliver them in person the next time he went up to the island. Right now he needed to call Tony.

*****

The store was quiet when the automatic door whisked aside, inviting them to walk in. Neon signboards shouted ski and snowboard specials. After inquiring, they were directed to the back of the store where the guns, ammunition and knives were sold. Robert carefully picked his way through aisles of tents and racks of sleeping bags draped like quilts to show off their interiors. In the center of the store an area had been left open to set up a simulated campsite, complete with giant dome tent, folding picnic table and four life size mannequins: a happy couple and their two smiling kids. The only thing missing, thought Robert, was the smell of sizzling bacon. And the swarm of ants.

At the knife counter a young man greeted them. "May I help you gentlemen?" Although the salesman tried not to show surprise, Tony's scarred face startled him when he looked in his direction.

"We're looking for pocket knives. Something nice but functional and engraveable. Got anything that fills the bill?"

"We do. We got these in for Christmas and only have a few left." He pointed to a case with one hand while unlocking it with the other. "They're a new brand for us. Creighton is the name of the manufacturer. They're made right up in Nanaimo, British Columbia. We sold a ton of them at Christmas and I haven't seen a single one returned." The clerk took out the display model and laid it in Roberts hand. "Feel how solid that is? One other nice feature is that there's an engraving plate inlaid in the handle. They're all made with hardwood handles, a nice oiled cherry, and they have locking blades. The engraving plate is bronz, and the blades are high quality four-forty stainless."

Robert looked at the knife closely. He opened the blade and ran his fingertip over the edge. Handing it to Tony, he said to the clerk, "How much are they?"

"Originally they were sixty dollars. Like I said, we've only got a few left so they're on sale for forty-five." He looked from Robert to Tony. "That's a really good deal. They're great knives."

"Sold. I'll take two of them." Robert reached for his wallet. "Make that three."

"Yessir, good choice. I've got them in gift boxes down here beneath the display." He looked at Tony who handed back the display sample. "Will that be all? Or can I show you gentlemen something else?"

"That's all for me. Tony? Were you in the market for an assault rifle or bear skinning knife? Some bazooka shells, maybe?"

"Not today."

"I guess that's it, then. Where do I pay?"

*****

Outside in the car Tony was quiet. As they got on the freeway Robert asked, "Did that kid bother you?"

"You noticed. Yeah, well, that's the kind of response I

generally get. People look at me and something between horror and sympathy registers on their faces. Now you know why I don't go out much."

"Am I making things worse by dragging you around?"

"Nah. I've known for a long time that I'm going to have to get used to going out in public and dealing with the response- or get used to being a hermit."

"How can I help?"

"Just having somebody to go out in public with *is* a big help."

"Cool. I'm just the guy. Gimpy, but outgoing."

"So where to now?"

"I need to get these knives engraved. I suppose a jewelry store or maybe a trophy shop. Do you know of any place?"

"There's a trophy shop not too far from the marina. It's right downtown. We can swing by on the way home." Tony took the Plum Street exit and headed for downtown.

"Great. Let's see Lonnie's initials are 'L.B.', yours are 'T.C.' and Rusty's…"

"Mine? You didn't buy one of those for me did you? You didn't need to do that."

"I bought one for you because I *wanted* to, not because I *needed* to. You've been a real help through this whole thing, not to mention a friend. This is just a small way of saying thank you. But, you know what? Now that I think about it, I don't know what Rusty's initials are. I'm going to have to call Lonnie and ask him."

Tony stopped at a traffic light. "Do you want to wait, then? Or what? Do you want to try and call him now?"

"I'll have to look up the phone number of the yard. It's on the receipt I was supposed to mail back when I delivered the motor." Robert thought for a moment. "Lets go back to the marina and I'll see if I can get a hold of him. It's not quite lunch time. I bet he'll be at the boatyard."

*****

Robert punched in the phone number of the boatyard and looked out the salon windows. The gray horizon away to the north was interrupted only by legions of evergreens thrusting spiked tops into the clouds. Clusters of houses dotting the hillsides offered the only other hint of color against a gunmetal sky.

On the fourth ring Lonnie answered, "Jackson's Boatyard, Lonnie speaking."

"Lonnie, this is Robert Dawes."

"Well, howdy, Mr. Dawes. Rusty and I were just talking about you the other day. We were wondering if you'd found your way to Olympia before all the snow started falling."

"Yup, I delivered the motor and got tied up in a marina just before it started. We got socked in here for several days. I mean, lots of snow. And then it warmed up and it melted almost as fast as it fell. How about you guys?"

"We only had one real bad day. After that things were back to normal. I saw that most of the accumulation was in Olympia area. You say it's all melted now?"

"The only place that still has snow is the occasional parking lot where it was piled up real high. Otherwise, there's hardly a trace left. It's overcast and rainy today."

"Same up here. The Chinook that blew in melted everything in a hurry. So now it's just rain as usual. By the way, how's the boat? Bilge still dry?"

"Well, you know it's never completely dry, but she isn't leaking like she was. The reason I called is to tell you that I'm putting the receipt for the motor in the mail. I should have done it sooner, but with all the snow, travel has been a little crazy."

"I understand. Don't worry, it's really just a formality. Send it whenever you can. I hope you haven't been worried about that. Is that why you called?"

"Among other things. The truth is I wanted to send you two a little token of my appreciation for all your help when I was up there. Rusty, especially, was helpful with my woodworking project. The bureau is perfect. But what I need is each of your initials. I'm having a little something engraved, and I want to make sure they're right. Yours are L B, right?"

"Mr. Dawes, don't go to any trouble for a couple of old birds like us."

"L B right? Lonnie Brooks? I know Rusty's name isn't really Rusty, and come to think of it I don't even know his last name. It seems to me his first name is Gus. Is that right? But what's his last name?"

"Actually, his first name isn't even Gus, it's really Fergus, I bet you'd never have guessed that would you? It's Fergus Johnson. So that would be F J.

Robert closed his eyes. His breath came in violent puffs. Inside his chest his heart felt like someone had reached in and pulled it out and then put it back in upside down. He swallowed and managed to say, "F J, okay I got that. Lonnie, I'm on my cell phone and you're starting to break up. I'll call back later, okay. Don't say anything to Rusty, I want this to be a surprise."

"Mum's the word, Mr. Dawes. I'll talk to you later."

Robert's hand trembled as he closed his phone. This was the final piece of the puzzle and it had been dropped into his lap. He had asked for a sign, and here it was, not two hours later. So Rusty, *his friend Rusty*, was Weston Johnson's kid brother. He scanned the image from Amelia's photograph again in his brain. Of course that was Rusty. Robert had seen that same look when the old man sat staring into space while sitting at the dinette aboard *NoraLynn*. He had made a joke about Rusty contemplating whether the coffee was Folger's Crystals™ or not.

Now it was clear that finding the letter to Amy Allen was not a coincidence at all. The truth had to be that Rusty hid the letter in the canvas straps the afternoon that he removed the bunk. While Robert was up in the galley making coffee, Rusty had plenty of time to hide the envelope. In fact, he began removing the old webbing while Robert stood by watching. That's when Robert noticed the envelope sticking out. The sequence of events was easy to put together, it was the reason behind the deception that confused him.

CHAPTER SEVENTEEN

"So, what makes you so fired up for a road trip?" Tony looked at Robert after he had turned into Amelia's driveway.

"I don't know. I guess I'm a little antsy. Besides, I want to deliver these knives we bought the other day." He smiled at Tony. "Anyway, I think Amelia is looking forward to a Sunday drive. I don't think she's been out of Olympia in years."

Tony nodded. "You're probably right."

"I'm going to take everybody out to breakfast and then when we get up to Whidbey this afternoon, Lonnie and Rusty are going to meet us at Louie's Ristorante and we're going to eat the best Italian food you've ever tasted. You do like Italian, don't you?"

"I like Italian." Robert knew that Tony was on to him. Maybe he hadn't figured it out completely, but he knew there was more to the story than a road trip.

"Great. You won't be disappointed then. Let's go get our guest."

Amelia had been waiting at the door, peeking through the curtain. When she saw Tony get out she opened the door open and came out onto the stoop.

"Don't get out; I'm coming right now." She shut the storm door and hurried down the walk to the car.

Robert got out and left the door open. "Here Amelia, you sit up front next to Tony."

"Oh no, I don't want you to have to move, Robert. I can sit in back."

"I insist. You can see much better from the front seat and I've seen enough Seattle traffic to last me a lifetime."

"I don't think there'll be much traffic today. It's Sunday." Tony smiled at Amelia. "I trust you slept well."

"Truth be told, I hardly slept a wink. I was so excited after you two called the other day to invite me – last night I could barely close my eyes."

"I hope you're not disappointed. I'm trying to follow your advice and show some gratitude to a couple of people who helped with the boat. In fact, they're the same people who were helping me when I found the letter. I got them each a little gift, so they're going to meet us for an early dinner at my favorite Italian restaurant. It was always Amy's and my favorite place for special occasions."

"That sounds delightful, Robert."

"So Amelia, when was the last time you were out of Olympia?" Robert leaned forward to ask the question.

"Just last summer my niece Margaret came and took me up to her place in Tacoma. She had a few friends over to celebrate Memorial Day. We had a barbecue. It was very nice."

"Have you been in Seattle lately?"

"I honestly can't remember the last time. After I left home and had Winnie, and had to look after the house and Grandma, I didn't get up to Seattle much. I think I told you that my daddy was very upset with me."

"Did he ever see Winnie?"

"Never. That always bothered me. He was so upset that I'd gotten pregnant, Mama said he didn't hardly say a word for a month. She'd take the bus down from time to time, but he never came along. I've never understood how a man can hang onto bitterness for so long. They'll miss the most important moments in life, just 'cause they gotta keep their pride well-fed. And then blame somebody else for their misery. That was how my daddy ended up."

"Whatever became of him?"

"He died of a heart attack in '59. Grandma was real sick that winter, so I didn't go to the funeral. Mama and my sisters were there." Amelia looked straight ahead.

*****

"Robert, that was delicious. But now I'm so stuffed I don't know if I can eat again this afternoon." Amelia pulled a plastic rain hat from her purse and covered her white curls. She walked with Tony to the car while Robert brought up the rear. By the time he caught up, Amelia was seated and fastening her seatbelt.

In a few moments they were back on the freeway. "Amelia, does this look anything like it did when you lived here?"

"Not at all. Seattle was pretty sleepy back then. I think most of the folks we knew had come recently. Most of them were from places like Detroit and St. Louis, Chicago and even some from the South. People came up here 'cause there was more work. Especially after the war started."

"Not so sleepy anymore," said Robert.

"Tony, would you mind if we took a short detour?" asked Amelia.

"Not at all. Where would you like to go."

"Could we drive down to First and Pike? There used to be a bus stop at the corner. That's where Weston first saw me waiting back in 1942. He said he had to get on that bus just so he could meet me."

"Really? So it was love at first sight?"

"Not on my part. Oh, of course I was flattered that he'd gone to the trouble, but boys have always been boys. I just assumed he was out to prove how manly he was."

"And? What made you change your mind?"

"He just kept coming back. He'd get on that old bus and ride around for hours waiting for me to get on. Then he'd wave and call out my name from the back. That boy looked like a grain of white rice in a bag of black beans sittin' way at the back of the bus like that." She laughed. "My Weston was determined."

"Amelia, it's stories like this that make me think his father's letters were just bitter lies, made up to hurt you."

"If that was his plan, it sure worked. Uncertainty is an awful load to have to carry around."

Robert reached forward and put his hand on her shoulder. "If it was in my power to set the record straight, once and for all, that is something I'd do for you in an instant."

"Maybe it'll all come out someday. I guess in the meantime we have to get on with our lives, right?" She sighed. "I'm so glad you boys invited me today. This was a wonderful idea."

"Yes, it was," said Tony as he caught Robert's eye in the rearview mirror. He glanced at the clock. "I think we'll have just enough time to drive downtown and then make it up to Mukilteo to get in line for the Whidbey ferry." He looked back at Robert again. "What time did you say we were meeting your friends?"

"Three o'clock."

"It's about a twenty minute ferry ride over to Clinton, which should leave us plenty of time to get to Oak Harbor. We'll even have some time to do some sightseeing if we want."

"And shopping," said Amelia. "I collect coffee mugs. I want one that says *Whidbey Island, WA*."

"And shopping," echoed Tony. "Anyplace you want to go, Robert?"

He looked out the window and considered the question. "Not really. I was just thinking how pleased Amy would be that I've made two new friends."

"Okay, we're off then." Tony moved over into the left lane and caught the Seneca St. exit. He drove down to First Ave. and turned right. After a few minutes of silence he said to Amelia, "This is the intersection of First and Pike. There's the market over there. Does this still look familiar? Or has it all changed? I see a bus bench over there across the street. Is that it?"

The old woman squinted, trying to force her memory back across the years. "You know, I just can't say for sure. None of these tall buildings were here in the forties." She looked up at the glass sentinels. "Downtown sure has changed from when I used to come down here. I'm not sure I remember what was here back then other than the market. It doesn't matter. It was right here somewhere. That's good enough." She smiled at Tony. "Thank you for humoring an old lady

They got back on the freeway and headed north. "Next stop Mukilteo," said Tony.

"How long is the ferry ride?"

"It's only about twenty minutes. We can stay in the car if you want."

"Oh no, Robert. I want to get out and see the water all around me. I've never been out on the water. For me this will be an adventure."

*****

The westerly breeze was cold. Shafts of light squeezed through breaks in the clouds, so for a few seconds a distant hill would suddenly be illuminated and then just as suddenly swallowed in shadow as the sky boiled overhead.

Amelia stood at the rail facing into the wind as the ferry crawled through Puget Sound.

"This is unbelievable." She grinned and shouted into the wind. "The whole world's in motion. There's so much air out here I'm almost dizzy."

Tony stood next to her. "Pretty spectacular, isn't it?"

"Is this what it's like on your boat?"

"Not usually. The difference on a smaller boat is you're almost down at water level. Up here it hardly even feels like we're on the water. On a boat like Robert's you could almost reach over and put your hand in the bay."

"It must be exhilarating."

"I suppose if you've never been there before it might seem that way."

"Robert," she turned to where he stood behind them, "will you take me out on your boat someday?"

"Sure, Amelia, if you like. Could we wait for nicer weather, though?"

The ferry's whistle signaled its approach to the Clinton dock. The three of them hurried back to the car deck and got ready to disembark. They had been in the first few in line waiting to board, so now they were near the front of the line to leave the boat.

Tony got them off the ferry and onto Highway 525 headed north. "How long will it take us to get to the restaurant?"

"I told Lonnie and Rusty we'd meet them at three o'clock." Robert looked at his watch. "It's one fifteen. It shouldn't take more than an hour to get to Oak Harbor. That way we can stop downtown and you can see if you can find a coffee mug."

"Oh, good. I definitely want to take a mug back home."

The three remained quiet on the trip to Oak Harbor. Occasional squalls pelted the windshield, while the westerly buffeted the car as it followed the highway.

Robert stared out the window. The memories of a lifetime flashed by like the stripes on the road.

*****

It was exactly three o'clock when Tony pulled into the parking lot alongside the old brick building that was home to Louie's Ristorante. Plate glass windows framed either side of the entry.

Checkered curtains covered the lower half of the windows, while overhead ceiling fans rotated in slow motion. Even from outside the smell of Parmesan cheese and baking dough met them.

All three crowded through the door and waited. A small woman whose face shone from beneath dyed black hair came through swinging doors at the back. She walked directly up to Robert.

"Robert, you're right on time. I'm impressed."

"Hi Mama. What are you talking about? I'm always on time."

"Of course you are, dear," she said. "Your friends aren't here yet, but we're going to seat you in the back."

Robert looked around. There was only one occupied table, where two elderly women sat eating.

Reading his confusion, she said, "You haven't been in since we opened up the banquet room. Louie said to seat you and your friends back there so you can have some privacy."

"I guess you're right, it has been a while. I'm not sure how long. Since before Amy…"

She nodded. "Follow me. I think you'll like what we've done."

They walked to the back where a hallway opened up into a T. To the left, double doors led to the kitchen; to the right was a smaller dining room with half a dozen tables. At the far end of the room a stone fireplace took up nearly the entire wall. In the center was a hearth with pillows to sit on.

"Oh my," said Amelia, "*this is lovely.*"

"Very nice, Mama, very nice. Amy would have been

impressed."

"That makes me feel good. I miss seeing the two of you." She motioned toward the fireplace. "I'll bring your friends back when they arrive."

"*This is so lovely*," Amelia repeated. She slung her coat over the back of a chair. Letting her hands touch the chair backs as she went by, she walked to the fireplace and sat down on the hearth. "Robert and Tony, this was such a good idea. I don't know any more than I did when I got up this morning and yet I am filled with such hope. I just know that something good is going to happen...something good *already has happened*."

"What makes you think that?" asked Robert. He and Tony followed her to where she was seated in front of the fire. "I mean, what's happened today that makes you think this is any different than every other day this week? Or the last sixty years for that matter?"

She smiled at him, but didn't answer.

"I'm not trying to be negative, but I really don't understand your optimism. We've had a nice time today. We saw the corner where you and Wes met. We had a great breakfast, and even a nice ferry ride, but none of that was out of the ordinary. *It was what it was*. So what has you so sure something good is going to happen."

"You and Amy never had children, did you, Robert?"

"No."

"Well, I know you're too young to remember, but I'm sure your mother would."

"Remember what?"

"Oh, it's like when a mother has her child and knows it so well, she can hear its cry in the midst of a whole room full of wailing babies…and when she comes alongside and comforts her child, that little one knows that it'll be all right. You see, Robert, I've been like that crying child for so many years, and right now it's like I hear my mother, or maybe it's my *Father*, callin' to me and tellin' me it's all right. And then I know something good is going to happen and I don't have to be afraid anymore, 'cause He's nearby."

"So, is that the same as faith?"

"To me faith isn't believing He's there, nearby, it's believing that when He hears me cry, it's *me* that He hears in the midst of all the others, and even though I can't explain how, it's *my* tears that He wipes away, and it's *me* that He reassures with that love that we can only understand in human terms…like the way a mother loves her baby…with a violent love." She touched his arm. "I'm not making much sense, am I?"

Before Robert could answer Mama came around the corner. Following close behind was Lonnie Brooks, wearing a leather coat with fleece lining poking out at the cuffs. He wore a baseball cap and his face was covered with the beginning of a white beard.

Robert held his breath for a moment. It appeared to be just the two of them. When he got to his feet, he started toward Lonnie. "Rusty didn't make it?"

Lonnie was delighted by the surroundings and Mama's company. "Oh Rusty? Yeah, he came along. He just had to make a quick stop in the men's room. He'll be right out, Mr. Dawes."

"You folks make yourselves comfortable. Sit wherever you like and I'll come back in a few minutes to find out what everybody wants to drink." She looked from face to face. "I don't know if Robert has told you, but he had Louie make his special cannelloni for you folks today. So you're in for a real treat."

"Thanks, Mama," said Robert. "Lonnie, we were just sitting by the fire and chatting. Why don't you come join us."

Tony and Amelia sat down again. Robert stood in front of Amelia so that Rusty wouldn't be able to see her. "When Rusty comes in, I'll introduce everybody."

He had hardly gotten the words out when Lonnie said, "Speak of the devil."

Robert looked over as Rusty came toward the fireplace. He was wearing a jean-jacket and blue jeans. From beneath each pant leg polished cowboy boots jutted out. Rusty didn't need a cap. His hair was close cropped and neatly combed.

"Rusty!" Robert turned and extended his hand, still blocking the place where Amelia sat.

"Mr. Dawes! Nice to see you. I see you've still got those crutches."

"Not for much longer, I hope. Let me introduce you to some friends of mine." He stepped aside, giving Rusty a clear view of Amelia. "Lonnie and Rusty, these are my friends Amelia Albermarle and Tony Cruz – two really special people from Olympia."

For an instant Rusty stared at Robert, whose nod answered the question posed by his blue eyes. A pained smile formed on the old man's lips. Without hesitating he took a step toward Amelia, the invisible burden making him stagger until he sank to his knees in front of her. He raised his face to look at her, his eyes brimming with tears.

Amelia and Lonnie and Tony watched the scene unfold in slow motion.

"Lia," whispered Robert, "I'd like you to meet Fergus Johnson."

It took a moment for the words to register, but when their unadorned simplicity struck home, she reached out trembling hands and touched Rusty's face.

"We both loved him, didn't we, Fergus?"

"Yes, ma'am, we did."

Amelia pulled him close, wrapping her arms around him like a mother might a child. Rusty could hold it in no longer.

"I'm so, so sorry...I promised Wes...I would mail the letter... But when he drowned...Daddy was so mad...I was afraid...I was afraid and so I just hid it away..."

Robert stood beside them while Lonnie stared at his hands folded in his lap. Tony blinked back tears and smiled at Robert as if to say 'I knew you were up to something.'

Mama rounded the corner, order pad in hand. When she saw Rusty and Amelia she turned around and went back out.

Amelia cradled Rusty's head while decades of guilt and shame spilled out, until finally he fell silent. She looked up at Robert and smiled. Maybe it was his imagination, but there seemed to be a new light in her eyes. Now she knows for sure, he thought.

For several minutes no one spoke. The only sound was the crackling of alder logs being consumed by the fire.

CHAPTER EIGHTEEN

While Mama cleared away dishes, Lonnie patted his belly, saying he couldn't eat another bite.

"Does that mean nobody wants to try my homemade tiramisu?"

"Oh my, is that dessert? You know, I don't think I could…"

Mama put her hands on her hips. "I guarantee you won't find any half as good anywhere in Seattle."

"Better listen to her, Lonnie. It's the best."

"In that case, Robert, I will have some."

"Anyone else?" asked Mama.

"Bring some for everybody. What we don't finish tonight I'll eat tomorrow." Robert looked at Lonnie. "You called me Robert."

He shook his head. "No, I didn't."

"You did. You heard him, didn't you?" Tony and Amelia nodded.

Lonnie sighed. "I don't know. Maybe I did. I must be gettin' old."

Amelia opened her purse and took out the letter. "Fergus, now that we've gotten acquainted, and the past is behind us, will you please tell us the story of this letter?"

He held the envelope. "I was ten in the summer of 1943. Weston had just graduated from high school and had taken a job on a fishing boat, the *Jean White.* Those were real bad years during

World War II and Wes was anxious to get into the fight. Anyway, he left early on a Sunday morning. Mama got us up at some ridiculous hour to go down to Fisherman's Terminal and see him off. I remember I didn't want to go, but when we got down there and got to go on the boat, I got excited, bein' a little kid and all. So the Skipper tells Wes that he can take me below, down to where they sleep, and show me the boat. We looked at the pilothouse and then went down to the foc'sle…"

"What's the foc'sle?" asked Amelia.

"That's where I showed you the bureau that Rusty and I built," said Robert.

"Oh yes, of course. I'm sorry, go ahead, Fergus."

"So when it was just the two of us I started poking around. It was then that Wes says, 'Fergie, I need you to do me a favor.' I agreed and he says, 'I need you to mail this letter for me. It's already got a stamp and everything. All you have to do is tuck it under your shirt and later today when Mom and Dad aren't around go down and put it in the mailbox at the corner.' So I said, 'Sure.' And I had every intention of doing it, too. Then he says, 'It's *really* important. But Mom and Dad can't know anything about it. Promise?' Of course I promised.

So, he pulls up my shirt and stuffs that envelope halfway down in my jeans and covers it up again. That was it. We said our good-byes, got off the boat and went back to the car."

Rusty stopped to catch his breath and take a drink of water.

"I was sitting in the back on the way home, and all I could think about was how that envelope was scratchin' me and makin' me uncomfortable, so I slipped it out and hid it down between the seat cushions of my parents old Chevy. By the time we got home I had forgotten all about the letter *and* my promise to Wes."

"When did it occur to you that you'd left it in the car?"

"I didn't think about it again until the morning after my father got the phone call about Wes. I was already asleep when the Skipper called. The next morning when I got up Daddy hadn't gone to work. I asked where Mama was and he didn't answer. When I went up to their room she was still in bed. I thought she was sick. When I went in she pulled me up onto her lap. Then she said Wes was dead. That was all she said. But she wouldn't let go of me for a long time."

"Did you think about mailing the letter then?"

"At first I did, but then figured I'd better wait. I was going to tell my parents, but remembered that Wes had made me promise I wouldn't. I was scared and confused. Most of all I was ashamed that I hadn't kept my promise...but by then Wes was dead."

"So, how did your father find out about me?"

"Dennis Wilson, Wes's friend. I guess Wes had told him about you. When the Skipper of the *Jean White* told my folks about Wes acting...I don't know, goofy or distracted...he supposedly said it was because he was missing his girlfriend so much. They had Dennis come over to the house and he told them everything he knew."

"Including the fact that I was black."

"Yes, ma'am. That's what sent my daddy over the edge. He was terribly prejudiced against black people." Rusty blushed. "It was because of how upset Daddy got that I decided to hang on to the letter. I overheard him tell Mama that you'd come lookin' for Wes when you didn't hear from him and he was going to fix it so you'd never know the truth."

"He tried. And until today may have even succeeded. But, because of your courage, and Robert's persistence, I know for sure how Weston died. And that he was still in love with me. I can't put a price on that." She put a hand on his shoulder.

"Rusty, why did you go to all the trouble to hide the letter on my boat? And what made you so sure I'd really look for Amy Allen?"

"I wasn't sure. I was desperate. But I had known your father-in-law. I knew your wife's maiden name was Amy Allen, too. I'm sorry, Mr. Dawes, I didn't mean to cause you any trouble."

"No, I should thank you. I was so caught up in feeling sorry for myself I couldn't think straight. You know, if it hadn't been for the letter I might still be moping around up here on Whidbey. But *still*, it was such a long shot. What made you decide to chance it?"

"When I went down and checked the bilge on your boat that morning after you brought it in, the idea occurred to me. I've known that she'd originally been the *Jean White* since I was still working in Seattle. That got me to thinkin'. See, after Marie died and I was all by myself most of the time, I thought a lot about my promise to my brother and how I'd let him down. One night I was readin' my Bible and I ran across the letter, 'cause that's where I hid it. I was feelin' so bad about how I'd let Marie down, and how I'd let my brother down, so I decided to see what was in the letter. That night I steamed it open and read it. When I saw how in love Weston was with you," he looked at Amelia, "I determined that I was going to try and find you, one way or another." He blinked back tears. "I prayed that God would help me to find a way to deliver the letter and keep my promise."

"That's when I showed up," said Robert.

"It wasn't more than a couple weeks later and there I was, alone on the same boat that my brother had disappeared from. Then you asked me to help you with tearing out the bunk, and it all kind of fell in place. I hid the letter in the webbing just before you came down to the foc'sle the night we tore the bunk out."

"And I did the rest. I wanted to believe that it was a sign from Amy, so I ran with it." Robert looked at Lonnie. "Did you know what was going on when you made me the offer to deliver the motor?"

"No sir. I haven't heard a thing about this until this very moment. You taking the motor to Olympia just seemed like a good solution at the time."

"You know, that's how I found out about the marina where my boat is moored. From a guy that worked at that boatyard, I mean. Tony is the fella that runs the marina. But more than that, *he* was instrumental in helping me find Amelia. In fact, he brought me a brand new phone book that contained the listing 'A. Albermarle' after I had found her name written inside the envelope flap." He looked at Amelia. "What's strange is that up until this year she hasn't had a published listing in the phone book...for how many years did you say?"

"I can't even remember for sure."

"Sounds like more than coincidence to me," said Tony. "And what about the reflection off the snow that made it possible to see her name written there?"

"What?" said Rusty, "Where?"

"Take a look. See if you can see anything written at the crease of the flap in this light."

After careful inspection, Rusty passed it over to Lonnie. "I can't make out a thing. Are you sure there's something written there?"

"I don't see anything."

"It's there," said Robert.

Mama rounded the corner with a large tray. "Okay, here it is. Tiramisu for everybody. Enjoy! I'll be right back with a fresh pot of coffee."

Tony said, "I think you have a couple of presentations to make, don't you?"

"You're right! I almost forgot why we came up here in the first place." He reached into his coat and produced three small boxes.

"Lonnie, this one is for you. Rusty, this one is yours. And last, but not least, Tony, this belongs to you."

Rusty opened the box and squinted at the engraving. "F J. So that's how you figured it out. Lonnie told you my real name."

"That's another thing that came totally unexpectedly. Not long after we met Amelia, I got up one morning totally at a loss for what to do next. I decided to follow her advice and look for ways to focus on being grateful. That's when I called Tony and we went out to buy the knives. When I realized that I didn't know your initials I called Lonnie. I thought your name was Gus, so when he said F J because your real name is Fergus Johnson, I nearly swallowed my cell phone."

"So *that's* why you suddenly got so excited to take a road trip."

"I knew you were on to me, Tony, but I was afraid if I said

anything I might ruin the whole thing."

Rusty placed a hand on Amelia's arm. "I want you to know that meeting you and having the opportunity to set some things straight for my brother's sake, as well as my own, means more than I can tell you. I've made some awful mistakes in my life. Not mailing that letter is one I'm glad I don't have to live with anymore."

"Me too, Fergus." Amelia leaned over and gave him a long hug. "Will you promise me that this won't be the last time I see you? Will you come see me, *I mean us*, when the weather improves."

"Yes, ma'am, I will." He frowned. "Could we find a way to forget that name 'Fergus,' though. Just call me Rusty."

"Alright, Rusty."

"And I'm Robert."

They exchanged glances. "Alright then, Robert it is."

CHAPTER NINETEEN

On the Clinton to Mukilteo ferry Robert, Amelia and Tony sat quietly in the car. They could feel the boat shudder as the bow pushed through the ebbing tide. Beyond the car deck the world was black except for pinpoints of light in the distance. There was no need to talk; it had all been said, every stone had been turned, every pocket pulled inside out. Contentment settled over them.

On the freeway headed home Amelia asked, "What will you boys do now?"

Robert saw Tony glance back at him in the rearview mirror. "I'm not sure. What about you Tony?"

"For me, it's probably business as usual. I still a have a lot to do on my boat. I really couldn't even predict how soon she'll be finished."

"Robert? No idea at all?" she said.

"I don't know how to answer that. I'm going to see my brother, Mark, tomorrow night. I guess I'll see how that goes. There's really nothing to go back to on Whidbey."

"How about you, Amelia? Any changes coming for you?" Tony asked.

"That depends. With you two boys around Olympia, I'll probably start cooking more. It's a lot more fun to cook for a family than for yourself."

"Sounds good."

"I think you two should open up that espresso shop near the Capitol. You should make the scones your featured product. I bet all those state workers would beat a path to your door."

"That's not a bad idea, I could learn to be a barista, and Tony might even be able to teach me to bake."

"You'd probably eat all the profit, though."

"Seriously, I am pretty sure I'll stay around Olympia for a while. Amelia, you'll need some help with your house this spring, and I'm almost positive my brother will be starting a remodel project on his house. Maybe I can help him with that."

"I can always use an extra pair of hands on my boat, too."

"That sounds wonderful! I think I'll adopt both of you. You'll be the sons I never had. We'll have to set aside at least one night a week for family dinner at my house."

*****

It was 6:00 a.m. when Robert awoke. He'd had his island dream again. As before, he was standing in the surf. The breeze barely ruffled the palm trees on the beach. This could have been heaven, except for one thing: Amy wasn't there.

He turned around, hoping to find her sitting behind him. Instead he found an envelope. Inside was a single sheet.

Robert,
You'll be okay now. It's time to get on with your life.
                                                    Love, Amy
P.S. Amelia is right, appreciate what you have.

*****

Robert waited until five forty-five. Mark would be coming for him at six o'clock. He sat down at the dinette and tore out a check.

He signed it, filled in the date and wrote his brother's name on the bearer line. Looking out at nightfall on the bay he thought for a moment and then went back to what he was doing. He wrote 50, and then smiling, followed it with three zeros. Fifty thousand dollars should to be a good start. He liked the idea of sticking around long enough to help.

He checked his watch again and switched off the lamp over the table. The fire in the wood stove painted the room an abstract of shadows and umber light. 'Life could be a lot worse,' he thought, and pulled the door closed behind him.

William G. Hutchinson makes his home in Olympia, WA with his wife Nora. They have two children and three grandchildren.

CPSIA information can be obtained
at www.ICGtesting.com
Printed in the USA
FSHW021830010520
69833FS